THE CRIMSON DIARY

THE CRIMSON DIARY

C S C Shows

Dragonfly Hill Books, LLC

For more information, write to:

Dragonfly Hill Books, LLC, 996 Greensboro Rd., Eupora, MS 39744

Paperback ISBN-13: 978-1-952898-18-1

Library of Congress Control Number: 2024917816

Cover Design: Blackstone Book Cover Design

CONTENTS

"Home is behind, the world ahead,
    And there are many paths to tread
    Through shadows to the edge of night,
    Until the stars are all alight."
J. R. R. Tolkien, *The Lord of the Rings*

"And suddenly we see
that love costs all we are
and will ever be.
Yet it is only love
which sets us free."
Maya Angelou, "Touched by an Angel"

CHAPTER 1

KACEY

Kacey was an invisible woman. Instead of looking directly *at* her, people looked *through* her. She was nondescript. Average. Boring, even.

It wasn't nearly as interesting as H.G. Wells made it out to be.

Which is why when *he* walked through the door, she froze in panic, forgetting her position. Kacey's breath hitched in her chest as the dark, handsome stranger strode toward the library's front desk. He was that handsome—he actually took her breath away. She was glad the other librarian on duty, a middle-aged man named Paul, who snorted when he laughed and talked about his five kids constantly, was helping someone in the genealogy room. Now, she'd get to help this handsome man. Even a few minutes of conversation was better than nothing.

"Hi. Can I help you?" When her voice came out timid and breathy, she winced inwardly. Most of the time, she felt more like a mouse than a librarian. Kacey knew she was homely in her gray sweater and navy dress pants with her drab brown hair in a loose ponytail, but she gave the stranger her brightest smile.

"Yes," he replied.

Kacey squirmed under his gaze. His lashes were thick, and his square jaw gave him a superhero appearance. Her stomach flip-flopped. It'd been far too long since she'd been on a date.

He glanced around as if he didn't frequent the library often. "I'm looking for language books."

Wow, his voice is deep and soothing, she marveled. *I could listen to it all night long.* "Sure," she said, coming around the counter. "Let me show you where those are." She pulled at her sweater, which hugged her lumpy midsection a little too closely. Kacey needed to stop spending her nights eating cheese and crackers, drinking merlot, and watching horror movies until one in the morning. She'd let her gym membership lapse long ago. But why be fit when no one looked at her, anyway?

They headed toward the rear of the library. As she led him to the languages section, she turned back and looked up at him. "What language are you interested in?"

"French."

Kacey glanced at the curve of his lips, and she could imagine the way they felt. *Surely, you know French very well*, she thought and smiled at her indecent thoughts. Lost in them for a moment, she ran into a table and cursed under her breath as she turned forward again to lead him to the languages section, the pain in her leg a dull ache. She wished she was a woman who could flirt effortlessly instead of only thinking about the things she wanted to say aloud. Of course, it wouldn't be proper to say something like that to a patron, so she'd keep her thoughts to herself.

"Beautiful language. Going to France?" Kacey stopped in front of the section. She'd never been to France. She never went anywhere.

"No, I'm dating a French woman, and I want to impress her. I need to learn some quick phrases instead of going through those long language courses I found on my phone." He flashed a million-dollar smile, which made Kacey wonder what kind of woman needed to be *more* impressed with a man like this. His French woman must be a knockout.

Then, processing his words, Kacey's heart sank. Just another unavailable man in a city full of them. Of course, this beautiful man was dating a gorgeous French woman. *It's not like he was going to be interested in* you, *little mouse,* she chastised herself. Kacey pointed to the section of French language instruction books. "Here ya go. *Bonne chance.*"

He was already running his fingers across the book spines, looking for a title and ignoring her.

"*Connard,*" Kacey swore and smirked with satisfied contempt, knowing he didn't realize she'd just called him an asshole.

Kacey walked back toward the front desk, collecting discarded books on tables to shelve later. After placing them on her cart, she returned to the front desk and picked up the book she'd been reading, content to escape into someone else's life for a while. The book by Daphne du Maurier was interesting, but she couldn't get her mind off the handsome stranger with the deep voice.

Kacey was thirty-two and had no dating prospects. She hadn't been out on a date in over a year, and the last one had been abysmal. The guy had forgotten he'd taken her to a club and disappeared with friends soon after they arrived, and she had to pay for a ride home. It's not as if she'd been that into him, but still.

Most guys she knew around her age were already married, were the kind who refused to get married and only wanted a fling, or were lazy slobs who wanted someone to work while they sat on their rumps all day. She wasn't looking for casual sex, either. Kacey wanted the entire package—love, marriage, and maybe kids, too. She'd spent years in college and grad school, and she'd found a great position soon after she graduated. She loved working, but she also wanted the traditional family. Kacey longed to have the kind of family she'd been denied as a child.

Her prospects for a husband were dwindling faster than the patrons who actually walked into the library, which were fewer each year. She thought reading was a dying pastime, which made no sense. She easily consumed a couple of books a week. Sometimes more if they were on the shorter side. In fact, she considered it a depressing thought that so many books in the world were already written and so many more *being* written each day that she could never read them all. How many fantastic books would she miss out on? Kacey frowned as she smoothed her fingers over the black letters of the story in front of her. She loved books, and she loved being surrounded by them every day. If she had a superpower, it would be to read at lightning speed.

Maybe that's what men found dull about her. She spent more time in the world of books than in the world around her. The escape was often so much better than reality. She tapped her fingertips against the open pages of the novel and blew at a loose strand of hair tickling her nose.

Paul rolled the book cart to the front desk. "Why're you looking so glum, Kacey?"

"Oh, nothing. Just a little bored." She smiled thinly. "With life in general."

Paul gave her a faint smile. "Did I tell you about my eldest daughter Helen? She went on a hiking trip with her college friends over the weekend..."

Kacey tuned Paul out. She didn't care about hearing about the exciting life of his eldest daughter in college. Helen probably got plenty of dates. She probably had fantastic sex on her hiking trip with some hunky college boy who adored her. Kacey daydreamed as he droned on and on.

"...and her boyfriend proposed on top of the mountain."

"What?"

"Yeah, he proposed. Right at sunset, she said. In fact, one of their friends took some photos." He pulled out his phone to show her. "I can't believe my first baby is getting married. Lisa and I are so excited. Of course, paying for the wedding will be a challenge."

Paul handed her his phone. A magnificent sunset haloed Helen as if she were an ephemeral being, smiling down at a kneeling man with blond hair and muscular shoulders. The next image showed them embracing. The third picture displayed the guy smiling down at the diamond engagement ring Helen held out for the camera.

Great, one more female who's perfectly happy and getting married, with the pool of eligible men dwindling ever smaller.

Kacey gave Paul a weak smile, handed him the phone back, and shut her book with a snap.

The night drug on. She'd reshelved all the books and finished her paperwork while Paul helped check out books to patrons. At fifteen 'til seven o'clock, Kacey went back through the tables on the lower level to collect any books patrons had left. There were only two, so she quickly reshelved them and shut off the light in the genealogy room after checking to make sure no patrons were still in there. Then, she went to the second floor, where general fiction and children's fiction were located. Books were usually everywhere up here, so she would add them to the cart for reshelving in the morning.

Kacey started on the children's fiction side of the second floor, collecting books and adding them to her cart. She also picked up a few toys the little ones had scattered while playing. As she held a wooden block in her hand, she wondered if she would ever have little ones of her own to pick up after. Would she bring them here to play on rainy afternoons and read them stories and poetry? She finished putting the toys away as she tucked away questions about her future. *Que sera, sera,* her father had said more than once. Maybe this was all to her life that there would ever be. Maybe it would have to be enough.

She rolled the cart to the general fiction section, added a few more books to the stack, and left it by the tables as she walked down each aisle. People left unshelved books in the weirdest places sometimes.

Suddenly, the lights went out, plunging Kacey into darkness. "Damn it, Paul." She reached out a hand toward the shelf, trying to get her bearing until her eyes adjusted to the darkness. He had forgotten she was there again. He did that at least once a month, shutting off the lights and locking up with her still in the building.

Kacey's shoulders slumped. She hated being so forgettable. Of course, she didn't want to hear more about Paul's daughter's wedding plans, so at least she'd been able to achieve that. She shrugged her shoulders as she moved down the aisle.

Thankfully, light filtered into the large windows from street lights outside, casting a little light into the room. Still, she had to feel her way down the aisle, which was much darker.

Kacey spotted a red glow coming from a lower shelf, and she bent down, her brows knit together in confusion. At first, she thought something was plugged in—or maybe the reflection of the glow from an emergency exit sign. Upon closer inspection, she realized someone had laid a book on top of other books there, and she picked it up, wondering at its strange red iridescence. She smoothed her hand over the buttery soft cover. *It must be some kind of glow-in-the-dark print effect added to the cover.* Usually, those were yellow-tinted, though. Publishers were always coming up with new ways to attract buyers.

She tucked the book under her arm and made her way along the aisle and down to the first floor. She flipped on the emergency lights by the front door to grab her purse and phone before locking up, still shaking her head at Paul's disregard for her.

As Kacey went to the desk to get her purse, she remembered the book tucked under her arm, so she pulled it out and placed it on the counter. The book had no shelfmark number on the spine, which meant it wasn't one of theirs. It looked old but well-cared for. Someone must have left it in the library by mistake. But why had they brought their own book to the library?

Curious.

The cover was red and looked like smooth leather. No way had this thing been covered in some glow-in-the-dark material. It was much older than that. So what made it glow in the dark upstairs? Kacey frowned. She opened the book and noticed that someone had handwritten the print, but she couldn't read the words in the dim light. Kacey closed it and slipped it into her purse. She would check it out more closely at home and bring it back tomorrow, in case someone came back to retrieve it. She loved old books, so this would give her something interesting to do tonight instead of her customary movie fest.

CHAPTER 2

KACEY

When Kacey got home, she dropped her purse on the kitchen table and took out leftovers. She stood there eating a cold porkchop and eyeing her purse, wondering about the old tome she had run across. She washed her greasy fingers so she wouldn't ruin the book.

Kacey retrieved it from her purse and sat down on the couch to thumb through it. She opened it gently. The pages looked ancient, and they were rough to the touch. The Latin text on the first page was so faded that she could barely read it. Still, she recognized a few words from her studies at college. Kacey strained her eyes and tried to read the words, whispering aloud as she went over each line. After that, it seemed like different people had contributed to the book, as each page had a different handwriting. It was a journal of sorts. Sometimes, it progressed page after page in one hand, and at other times, it only recorded a brief entry or two before it changed to another's handwriting.

Kacey read through dozens of these entries, each one a frenzied scribble about love and lust and relationship details. A few detailed the conquests and successes of the writer. Kacey found some entries to be complete gibberish, while others were written in languages she couldn't read.

So strange.

Kacey closed the book, her eyes heavy with the effort of trying to decipher so many handwritings. She had never seen anything like this journal.

Kacey trudged to her bedroom, undressed, and pulled on her favorite nightshirt, an old oversized college t-shirt that had faded and softened with time. She laid the book down beside her in bed and turned on the TV. She started *Sleepy Hollow*, a favorite movie she'd seen many times before. Kacey was a creature of habit, and ending her night lost in the world of movies was one of her guilty pleasures.

As the flaming jack-o'-lantern flew through the night on the screen, Kacey drifted off to sleep. Her dreams were unnerving, but not defined enough for her to know the source of her anxiety. She only knew she was fighting with something exciting and terrifying at the same time.

Kacey woke up the next morning covered in sweat with the bedsheet wrapped around her legs. She sat up on the side of the bed, and her head pounded as if she drank too much wine, though she'd had none last night. She'd gotten more sleep than she normally did, but she was exhausted. Kacey noticed the book lying on the floor. She picked it up and put it on her nightstand.

In the shower, she let the cool water wash over her skin and hair. She used the bar of soap first, leaving the loofah hanging for the moment. As she smoothed the soap over her chest, she froze and looked down. Were her breasts bigger? Firmer? She gave them a little squeeze. She raised an eyebrow. Definitely firmer. She shook her head, grabbed her loofah, and washed up.

When she got out of the shower, Kacey used her towel to wipe the fog off the mirror. As she brushed her teeth and spit out the minty toothpaste, she looked at her reflection.

Something was different.

Kacey turned her head this way and that. Her teeth looked extra white. She glanced down at the tube of toothpaste, but it was the same old stuff she'd been using for years. She looked into the mirror again. Her lips looked a little swollen and pinker than normal. Her cheeks were flushed, but that was probably from the heat in the bathroom. Kacey's eyelashes seemed to be thicker and longer. Was she having hormonal issues? Growing extra hair? She pulled out her hairdryer and dried her hair, which usually felt thin while wet but seemed thicker today, as she combed through it. No tangles, either.

Once it was dry, she brushed through her hair. Yes, it definitely looked thicker. Her hair had volume and movement that it didn't normally have. It was shiny instead of frizzy. Her hair looked amazing, as if she'd just had a salon blowout, and Kacey smiled at her reflection. It was about time she had a good hair day.

11

She looked behind her at the bottle of shampoo she'd used. Same old shampoo she'd been using for years. She shrugged.

Kacey walked out of the bathroom and into her bedroom. She pulled out panties and a bra. She hopped on one foot while pulling the panties up one leg and then the other. Kacey grumbled, finding them too tight. She took them off and pulled on another pair that she knew should fit. They were tight, as well. Kacey blew out a huff of air in frustration.

Kacey grabbed a bra she had recently bought and worn a few times. At least it would fit great. It was her favorite at the moment. She pulled it over her breasts and tried to snap it in the back. She pulled as she twisted, trying to get the two sides together behind her. No use. She sighed with exasperation and the effort she'd just expended.

What was going on this morning? Was she retaining water? Kacey pulled out several bras and tossed them on the bed. Each one she tried on was too small. After finding one that was worn and stretched out, she managed to just snap it in the back. She hoped it wouldn't pop loose at work.

Kacey went to her closet and pulled out a pair of black slacks. If all her panties and bras were too tight, her pants were probably not going to fit, either. She bit her lip as she pulled the pants on. They were tight through the hips but too loose around her waist. Usually, her pants fit too snugly at her stomach. She ran her hand over her abdomen, which was flatter than usual. It was as though her measurements had changed overnight. She looked at her image in the mirror. Yes, there was a definite hourglass shape, where previously she'd looked more like an apple, holding much of her excess weight around the middle, with all of its associated health risks always in the back of her mind.

After trying on just about every pair of pants in her closet, Kacey sat down on the bed, nearly in tears, surrounded by

THE CRIMSON DIARY

ill-fitting clothes. None of them fit right. How was she supposed to go to work with no clothes to wear? She stood and went back to the closet. There was a black dress in the back that she'd had since college. She didn't know why she'd kept it. She hadn't fit into the dress in at least ten years. Kacey unzipped it, stepped into it, and pulled it up.

It fit her like a glove.

Kacey stared wide-eyed at the mirror. It hadn't even looked this good the last time she wore it. She turned this way and that as she smoothed her hands over the fabric. She looked amazing! Maybe she should lay off the wine and cheese more often. She didn't look a day over twenty-five.

It wasn't only her appearance, either. After the immediate headache dissipated, she felt energetic but focused. She felt more refreshed than she ever had, as if she'd been away on a long, relaxing vacation. Renewed. Ready to take on the world. Almost bubbly. She could get accustomed to this.

Kacey grabbed the book off the floor and slipped it into her purse before leaving for work. She walked the four blocks to the library, as she did every morning. Mr. Grady, the widower just down the street from her, stood in his robe, reading the headlines of his paper with a cigar in his mouth. He looked up as he did every morning to nod at Kacey, but this morning, he stared with his mouth open when she said, "Morning." His cigar fell out of his mouth onto his newspaper, and she almost laughed as he cursed at himself and swiped ashes from his paper.

Kacey arrived a little early for her shift, and she found she was working with Paul again. She walked up to the front desk, ready to give him crap about shutting off the lights on her the night before, when Paul glanced up and said, "May I help you, ma'am?"

"Help *me*?" Kacey raised her eyebrow.

Paul blinked. "Oh. Kacey. I didn't...You look different today."

"I know." She walked around the counter, and Paul followed her with his eyes. "I couldn't find anything that would fit right this morning except this old dress. I guess I'm going to have to go shopping after work."

"It's a good look on you, Kacey." Paul licked his lips.

"Well, anyway, what's with shutting off the lights on me again last night?"

"Oh, I did that?" Paul ran his hand through his thinning brown hair. "Sorry about that. Maybe I thought you'd left." He cleared his throat. "You going out on a date tonight?"

"Yeah, right. I haven't been out on a date in ages." She rolled her eyes, grabbed the cart, and rolled it toward the shelves to reshelve some books that had been returned.

"Uh, let me get those for you, huh?" Paul grabbed the cart from her and took off across the library, looking back at her as Kacey eyed him with concern. Paul never offered to help her reshelve books. He hated reshelving books. He would do anything else around the library so long as Kacey put all the books back.

Thinking that this day couldn't get any stranger, Kacey sat down on the stool at the front desk. She loaned out a few books to some regulars, and each patron looked at her the way Paul had, blinking as if they didn't quite understand what they were looking at. It made her uncomfortable. On a normal day, most of the patrons rarely glanced at her.

Kacey doodled on a piece of scrap paper to pass the time. It was supposed to be a butterfly, but it looked more like a fly. She scribbled circles around the doodle.

"Wow, that's amazing."

Paul's voice right behind her made Kacey jump. "Oh, no, it's just a doodle."

14

"No, this is art. Did you study art in college?"

Kacey narrowed her eyes, trying to note the sarcasm in his statement. Her drawing was crap. A four-year-old could have drawn something better. "Stop being weird, Paul." What was up with him today? "Are you feeling okay? Everything okay at home?"

"I'm great. And even better now that I'm here spending the morning with you." He grinned and stepped closer.

"Uh..." Kacey stepped back, making more space between them, and looked at Paul like he had grown a third ear. "Whoa, you're happily married, remember?" He had never hit on Kacey before.

"Ha, strangest thing." Kacey could see his Adam's apple jerk up and down with a swallow. "This morning, I don't care about that. Not one bit, not with you around." He came toward her again.

Kacey held up the pen like a sword. "Whoa, Casanova, you need to simmer down. I will *not* be destroying any marriages today." Kacey got around him and behind the counter. She gave him the stink-eye, hoping he would get her message and leave her alone.

Kacey went up to the second floor, and when she looked back, every eye was on her. Paul, the patrons, even the janitor. It was uncanny, and she felt off balance. She shook her head and entered general fiction. Only two people were there at the tables reading, and both stared at her as she walked around the room looking for books to reshelve. She tried to ignore their stares. She kept her head down and kept moving.

Kacey went down an aisle, more for privacy than to look for books. Maybe she could hide out here for a while. Perhaps she should fake a stomachache and go home early. The way Paul was acting made her stomach turn, so it wouldn't exactly be a lie. She took her time going down the aisle and then turned to go down the next one. A tall, handsome man about her age stood in the way. "Hi, there."

"Hi. May I help you find something?"

"I've already found it." He gave her a suggestive grin.

CHAPTER 3

KACEY

"Okay," she said, drawing out the vowel sound as she eyed him suspiciously. Was this guy going to be as strange as everyone else had been this morning? If so, she was going to play sick and leave work. She'd had enough of the strange vibes from people.

He held up a couple of books. "A new one in a series I'm reading, and one from Gillian Flynn that I haven't read yet. Just what I was looking for."

"Oh," Kacey said, her cheeks flushing. "Right. That's a good one."

"I'm Justin. I come here pretty often to read before going home." He reshelved a book he was holding in the other hand.

Kacey pressed her lips together to stop herself from grimacing and hoped he'd reshelved it correctly. She made a mental note to check it once he'd walked away. "Right, I remember you." Kacey recognized him like she recognized most of the regulars—by books. He liked thrillers and historical books. She had a knack for remembering which genres patrons normally gravitated toward.

"You're Kacey, right?"

Kacey's eyebrows shot up. She didn't think she'd ever introduced herself to him. "Yes, that's right. I'm sorry, but what'd you say your name was?"

"Justin." He moved the books to his left hand and held out his right hand for a shake.

"Nice to formally meet you, Justin."

"Likewise. I'm always happy to meet other book lovers," Justin said with a grin.

The way he said 'book lovers' made her chest flutter a bit, but she did her best to look serious. She mentally kicked herself for being so immature. She was in her 30s, for crying out loud. If a man said the word 'lovers,' it shouldn't make her act goofy. She'd had so little experience with men, though. So many missed opportunities.

"Anyway," he continued, "I'd love to get a coffee with you sometime."

"That might be—"

"Hey, is this guy giving you problems, Kacey?" Paul had appeared right behind her.

"What? No. Please man the front desk." Kacey held up a hand, hoping Paul would back off. "Everything is fine up here."

Paul eyed Justin as if he didn't trust him and then stalked off as Kacey shook her head.

"I'm sorry. I have no idea what is wrong with that guy today. Maybe he's having a mid-life crisis." She gave Justin a dismayed look. "It's been a strange day all around, actually."

"No problem." Justin looked down at the books in his hands and then back up at her. "So I was asking you out on a date, and you were saying?"

Wow, Kacey suddenly realized she liked this guy's forwardness. He seemed to know what he wanted, and he wasn't scared to ask for it. Basically, he was the opposite of her. "Um, sure, let me give you my number." Kacey still held the pen in her hand that she had wielded at Paul earlier. She wrote her number on Justin's palm.

"This isn't going to go to someone's great-aunt Bertha, is it?" he asked with a playful grin.

"If it does, give her my best," Kacey said.

"Thanks, Kacey. I'll call you soon." Justin left her standing in the aisle.

Kacey couldn't believe it. She sucked in a ragged, excited breath as she smiled from ear to ear. What a strange but wonderful day it was turning out to be.

Somehow, she successfully avoided Paul for most of the day. Kacey left quickly after Paul invited her over to his house for dinner and some fun, whatever that implied. Maybe he and his wife were swingers, but Kacey was *not* interested.

Kacey pulled her phone from her purse and found that Justin had left her a voicemail already. She was pulling it up to listen when she ran smack into someone on the sidewalk. It was like hitting a brick wall, and she fell back. Expecting to land hard on the concrete, she cried out. When she opened her eyes, she found herself in the arms of the handsome library patron who had come in for the French book the day before.

"I'm so sorry. Clumsy me. I was looking at my phone," he said. He stood her back up as though she weighed nothing and donned that amazing smile that made her squirm.

"I was, too," she confessed.

"Are you hurt?"

"No, thanks to you for grabbing me. I appreciate that. I just knew I was going to hit the sidewalk."

"Oh, no, I never would have let that happen." He gave Kacey a smile again. "I'm David. And you are?"

"Kacey Wiltson."

"Very nice to meet you, Kacey. May I buy you dinner for almost plowing you down? It's the least I can do."

Two men had asked her out on the same day. That had to be a record for her. She'd be insane not to go out to dinner with this handsome guy. Yet, she paused because he'd just said yesterday that he was dating a French woman. She frowned.

"Please, I'd be honored to share a meal with you."

Kacey shook her head. "I don't think that's a good idea." She slipped her phone into her purse.

"Why?"

"You told me about your girlfriend yesterday," Kacey said.

David's eyebrows furrowed. "I've never met you before."

"Yes, you have. I work in the library." She gestured behind her.

"I don't know what you're talking about, but I don't have a girlfriend." He gave her what appeared to be a sincere smile.

Maybe she had been wrong about what he'd said. Maybe he only said that he wanted to impress a French woman. She couldn't really remember if he said they were dating or not. Maybe she'd made an assumption. He was tall, dark, and handsome, so her attention may have wandered a bit while he was talking. Besides, Kacey wasn't exactly looking forward to the leftover Chinese food in her fridge. "Well...okay, if you insist."

"I do. Do you like Italian?" When she nodded, he said, "I know this little restaurant that you'll love."

This little restaurant ended up being the most expensive place in town to eat. She'd never eaten there because she knew she couldn't afford it. Even the appetizers were more expensive than what she'd typically paid for an entrée. She was glad she had on the little black dress because she would have been underdressed if she hadn't. Of course, if she hadn't worn this dress, she doubted David would have taken more than a glance her way.

Kacey paused and looked down at her dress as David took his seat across from her. Was this dress magic?

She thought back to her twenties when she'd last worn it. It had done nothing spectacular for her back then. She'd gone to a few clubs and a wedding in it, but she hadn't met Mr. Right in it. And men had *never* reacted to her like they had today.

Even their server was acting weird. With a bottle of wine, he stood over her, looking down at her cleavage, his mustache twitching. "Could I interest you in a glass of wine?" he asked.

Kacey shook her head and shifted in her seat. "Water is fine."

The man didn't move from her side, even after David told him he'd have water, too. David leaned toward him and said, "Look, buddy, if you don't move along, I'm going to smash your face."

Kacey noticed David's fist clenched atop the table, and she didn't doubt that he'd follow through with the threat. She looked up at the server wide-eyed, a little embarrassed for him but still annoyed with his unwanted attention. His face turned crimson, and he hurried away.

Kacey pulled out her napkin and laid it on her lap. She tore a piece of the rosemary bread from the loaf the server had left in a basket and dipped it into the olive oil and crushed pepper. She chewed as David watched her. "It's been such a bizarre day," Kacey murmured and sipped from her glass of water.

"I'm so sorry you're having a difficult day. Let me make it better for you. After a delicious meal, we'll go shopping. I'll buy you something beautiful. Something beautiful for someone beautiful."

Though his words were flattering, it felt wrong to allow a man she barely knew to buy her things. "No, the meal is enough. Thank you for bringing me here."

"I would do anything for you, Kacey."

She frowned at his declaration of devotion. That felt very wrong, too. He'd only known her for an hour or two.

David cleared his throat, noticing her unease. "What I mean is, you captivate me, Kacey. Whatever you need, I'm at your disposal."

The unease lifted a little, and Kacey smiled thinly. "Let's enjoy our meal together and get to know one another."

David leaned in and gave her a charming smile. His teeth were unbelievably white and perfectly straight. "Yes, I want to know all about you."

"Well, I've lived in San Diego all my life. I've—"

"Have you ever been to Paris?"

His interruption made her pause and frown again.

"I was going to go to Paris again tomorrow, but now, I can't remember why..." His brow furrowed.

Kacey bet she knew why. Probably for the woman he'd been trying to impress with his crash course in French. Kacey folded her hands on the table in front of her. She was getting a pretty clear view of what this guy was about, and she wasn't sure she wanted any part of that, no matter how handsome he was.

CHAPTER 4

KACEY

K acey woke up the next morning, her head throbbing, and she immediately touched the journal beside her in the bed, the smooth red cover a comfort to her. Thankfully, no one had claimed it yesterday, and she'd kept it hidden in her satchel, hoping that no one ever would. The book intrigued her, and she wanted to look at it some more.

The date with David the night before hadn't gone very well. After dinner, he'd gotten pretty gropey, and he didn't seem to be the type that was told 'no' very often. Kacey would not cheapen herself to a one-night stand with the Superman lookalike, however attractive he was. She'd gotten away from him successfully without too many protests from him at the end of the date, though he'd acted sullen. He'd driven her home, though, so he knew where she lived. She frowned. Kacey hoped she wouldn't end up regretting going to dinner with the guy. As handsome as he was, David was intense, and he scared her a little.

She sat up, pulled her pillows up behind her, and opened the old journal. She had had little time to delve into the entries, and she was curious about the stories hidden in its pages.

In college, she had studied Greek and Latin, and one of the earlier sets of journal entries appeared to be written in Greek. Kacey pulled her laptop from where it was charging on her nightstand and typed in some words to decipher them. It was tedious work because she had to use a Greek keyboard on her screen, and even then, the translations made little sense until she changed it from Modern Greek to Ancient Greek.

The first entry in this hand read:

"*I am a murderer. They would have had me killed, though, if I had not acted first. My influence and power are detestable to me for the stains they have left on my hands. Yet, it has kept me alive. What can be done?*

"*My sway over people is growing by the day, so much so that I can barely keep my suitors at bay. Julius comes to me nightly, begging for my company. For a while, I reveled in his attention, in the affections of the most powerful man on Earth. But it has changed.*

I am too much for him. He has become obsessed and smothers me. I stay because of our son.

"*I have fallen in love with another man. There, I have confessed it. I never meant to fall in love. Love is weakness, and I want to conquer the world.*

"*I am the one being conquered.*

"*Let it be done.*

"*I do not know how much longer I can handle this power over men. Though I have gotten riches untold, every extravagance known to mankind, and many memorable nights with the most accommodating of men, it has become too great a burden to bear.*"

Kacey rubbed her eyes. This seemed so familiar. Who was Julius? She pulled up a search engine and typed in "Julius, most powerful man on Earth." The first search result was for Julius Caesar. Her fingers paused over the keyboard. Julius Caesar? What did she know about Julius Caesar? She remembered the play from high school. He had epilepsy and was killed by his best friend, Brutus. She tapped her fingers against her jaw. *Shakespeare probably made up half the story*, she thought. She couldn't even remember who his wife was supposed to be in the play. She scanned the article. "Political and military genius... assassinated in 44 B.C."

Wait, that was over 2,000 years ago. No way was this journal 2,000 years old. Julius Caesar died before the birth of Christ. It wouldn't be in such good shape if it didn't completely crumble in her hands after that length of time. *So this entry has to be about some other influential Julius*, she thought.

Tired from working so hard at first translating and then trying to figure out the mystery, Kacey closed her laptop and rubbed the smooth crimson leather of the journal.

A knock at her front door pulled her from thoughts of sordid love triangles. She pulled her hair down from the messy bun she'd fashioned the night before and ran her fingers through it. *Not one tangle*, she mused as she went to the front door. When she looked through the peephole, she found a delivery man standing there with a dozen red roses.

Kacey pulled open the door. "Good morning."

"Uh," the delivery man stammered. He stood there looking her up and down. "Yes, uh, good morning to you. I have a delivery for Miss Kacey Wiltson."

"Okay, thank you. I'll take them."

"No, ma'am, there are a dozen bouquets here for you."

"Oh! A dozen dozen?" She looked at him incredulously. "Who would send me all these roses?" Her stomach turned a little when she thought again about how much David had pressured her the night before. If he thought this would be a better strategy, he was wrong.

"Uh," he said as he looked down at his clipboard. "It says here that these are from three different customers. Each one should have a card, so you'll know who sent 'em."

There were nine dozen red roses, one dozen white roses, and two dozen pink roses. The delivery man helped her bring them all inside, setting them on the bar and her coffee table, and he lingered for a moment at the door.

"I need to tip, don't I? I've never gotten a flower delivery before. Sorry," she mumbled as she searched through her wallet for some bills.

"Keep it, Miss Wiltson. A woman as lovely as you shouldn't have to pay when men fall at your feet." He went back to his truck, but he looked back over his shoulder at her as she watched him from the doorway.

"Okay," she said to no one in particular. How had her life gotten so strange so suddenly? The red roses were all bunched up on her bar, and she finally found the card in one of them. It read: *A dozen roses for each hour I have been away from you, my beautiful Kacey. Love, David.*

Well, it was sweet, though a little over the top for her liking. She found the pink roses and pulled the card from one of the dozen. It read: *I'll be missing you at work today. Yours, P.*

She cringed. Why would Paul send her two dozen roses? She didn't even like pink. Maybe that was Paul's wife's favorite color, which made her grimace. At least they smelled nice. Maybe she should take them to the library and drop them off to decorate the front desk. Would Paul get the hint? Or would he just assume she was trying to spend some time with him today? She shuddered and decided against going to the library.

Kacey pulled the card from the dozen white roses. It read, *Looking forward to getting coffee and talking books soon. Justin.*

Her eyes widened as she realized she'd forgotten to listen to the message he'd left on her phone. She'd taken the spill yesterday and landed in David's arms while she was trying to get to her voicemail. She went into her room and found her phone. Justin left a brief message letting her know he was looking forward to their coffee outing and that she could call or message him at that number. She decided to message him.

> Thank you for the roses. Are you free today?

> I'm glad you liked them. I work tonight, but I'm free until about 6.

> I'd love to get that coffee. Morning Grind? Do you know it?

> I do.

Meet you there in an hour?

Sounds good.

Kacey smiled as she touched the silky petals of one of the white roses he'd sent her. Then, she ran to her bathroom to shower. She was really looking forward to this date with Justin. Surely, it would turn out better than her date with David had.

CHAPTER 5

SIBYL

Sibyl ran her fingers through her wavy, long brown locks. She dabbed a pink lip tint onto her lips and pressed them together. It was all she needed. Her face was as fresh and beautiful as it always had been. She leaned toward the mirror, thinking she noticed a tiny wrinkle at the corner of her eye, but she realized it was only an eyelash. She breathed a sigh of relief. Her skin was smooth and flawless. She added a few bangle bracelets to her arm and adjusted the belt around the waist of her flowy chiffon skirt.

Sibyl looked down into the water in the sink. In its swirls and ripples, she saw a vision of the young woman she was searching for, surrounded by flowers. The woman was beautiful, but Sibyl felt a sense of her vulnerability and naivety, too. She could sense so much about the woman—her loneliness, her hope, her fear. Sibyl knew the woman was close. This one was not a worthy adversary. Sibyl pulled the stopper and let the water drain.

So many times, she had gotten close, but the owner of the book had always allowed themselves to become too entwined in its magic, too controlled by its influence, and too affected by its promises. This woman had just obtained the crimson book, so if Sibyl acted quickly, she'd be able to snatch it from her before the woman knew its powers.

Of course, she'd have to snatch it from the woman's cold, dead hands. Sibyl frowned. It wasn't fair that she couldn't just kill the twit herself. She was so tired of chasing after this book. It was hers. It belonged to her. She gripped the edges of the sink.

Sibyl left her hotel room and waited at the bus stop. *If only I can find the book faster this time*, she thought. A woman sat down beside her on the bench with a crying toddler. The little boy wouldn't be consoled, no matter what his mother did. Sibyl felt the anxiety radiating off the woman, so she turned to the child, caught his eye, smiled, and gave a wink. He looked into her blue eyes, hushed his crying, and returned her smile.

Though Sibyl hadn't touched the book in many, many years, she still held some of its power to entice and persuade. That's how strong the magic in the book was. Even away from it, she still held some of its power. And now, after so many women had imbued it with even more magical essence with each life it affected,

31

the crimson book was the most powerful magical artifact that she knew existed. It was like a parasite, giving power but taking more back in return.

Sibyl never anticipated that it would take her this long to get it back after it first disappeared. Elissa was the first woman to possess it. Sibyl saw great strength and intelligence in the young woman, and she had high hopes that Elissa would use the book well and grow its power. Elissa was passionate but volatile. When Sibyl confided that she'd made the book herself, Elissa had turned on Sibyl, refusing to give the book back once she'd gained the power she sought. Building up an entire city wasn't enough for her. Elissa fell, like so many other women would who gained the power of the crimson book—at the feet of the man she loved.

Elissa, who some called Dido, Queen of Carthage, committed suicide by Aeneas' sword. She let love conquer her and extinguish her light. Though it bothered Sibyl to see a great woman fall, it was the only way she could hope to get her book back. However, she found that whoever held possession of the book could not die by her hand.

Sibyl had tried time and again to kill Elissa. She'd poisoned the woman's wine, and Elissa had only suffered from an upset stomach. She tripped Elissa at the edge of a cliff, and Elissa somehow regained her balance and grabbed onto Sibyl for support, making Sibyl look like a hero instead. Sibyl even planted a dangerous snake in Elissa's bed, and Aeneus found and killed it before it bit her.

Sibyl had had to use other means. She learned to be cunning in getting rid of Elissa. The ambitious woman's love for Aeneus was the one thing that Sibyl knew she could use against Elissa. And Elissa would never know that it was Sibyl who persuaded Aeneus to leave, to sail away and leave her at the mercy of the lustful King Maxitani.

After Elissa's death, Sibyl thought Elissa's sister Anna had burned the book on the funeral pyre along with Elissa's body. Sibyl had seen Elissa take the crimson diary with her the night she killed herself, but when Sibyl searched her quarters, she could no longer find it.

Of course, it had already ended up in the hands of the next person who would use it. And on and on through time. So long.

The city bus pulled up, and Sibyl took her seat behind and to the left of the mother with her toddler. The little boy kept trying to catch her attention, but Sibyl ignored him. She looked out the windows of the bus, hoping to see the woman. She'd scour the city looking for the book's new owner. Sibyl was thankful she had the gift of seeing and knew what the new Keeper of the book looked like. She was also thankful that her visions showed her where the book would turn up this time.

Sibyl smiled.

This would be too easy.

CHAPTER 6

KACEY

When Kacey arrived at Morning Grind, she found Justin leaning against the building, waiting for her. He wore dark denim and a college football team t-shirt. She was glad she'd dressed casually. Though most of her clothes didn't fit, she found a pair of old shorts, and she'd chosen to dress them up with a pretty blue blouse and gold sandals.

Kacey gave a wave as she walked up, and Justin smiled. "You're a breath of fresh air this morning."

Kacey's cheeks flushed. "Why, thank you." He leaned in and gave her a hug, and she felt awkward as she embraced him with one arm. It was at once very casual and too affectionate. She tried to mask her apprehension with a smile as she tucked her hair behind her ear and hoped the rest of their coffee date wouldn't feel as awkward.

He held open the door for her as she entered the coffee shop. The chocolaty smell of coffee beans and the sugary scent of baked goods enveloped her like a warm, delicious hug. She'd worked in a coffee shop in college, and she missed the wonderful smells. It was amazing how smells could relax you so quickly. She shook off her apprehension almost immediately.

"What would you like?" Justin asked, looking up at the menu.

"I'll take a chai tea latte. I think coffee would make me too jittery this morning."

"Scone?"

"Absolutely. Blueberry, please."

Justin ordered his coffee and her tea, and they picked out some scones from the display case. As they waited for their order at the counter, Kacey glanced at the TV, where the news was covering a developing story. The female news anchor with a solemn face said, "Miss Galaxy Queen, Sena Shin, the first Korean-American to hold the title since 2001, was found dead in Toronto on Thursday. Her death is being investigated as a suicide. Shin, who was only twenty-four, fell from the thirty-third-story floor of this hotel where she was staying following a pageant-affiliated event in Toronto. A haunting message the night before left on her social media points to the possibility that she took her own life..."

Kacey didn't hear the rest because the picture they posted of the beautiful young woman from one of her social media accounts made Kacey's heart stop. The woman was posing by the ocean with a blazing orange sunset behind her and holding a red diary—*her* red diary. There was no doubt in Kacey's mind that it was the same book. It was the same size and the same crimson color. There was even the slight tinge of the glow she'd seen in the library when she first spied the book on the shelf.

She reached into her bag and felt for the journal. When her fingers met with the smooth cover, her heartbeat returned to normal. Why had this woman had her journal? How did Sena Shin have it only a few days ago in Toronto when it had ended up in her library the same day, over two thousand miles away?

Kacey frowned. She decided that there was no way it could be the same book. Yet, she could see the worn cover in the photo. It was uncanny how much the two books matched.

"You okay?" Justin asked, interrupting her thoughts. He handed her the chai tea latte she'd ordered. "You look upset."

"Um, yes, I'm fine. I was watching the news. You know how awful that can be." She gave him a tight-lipped smile.

"Tell me about it. I try to avoid it at all costs these days." He guided them toward a table by the windows and away from the noisy counter and the television. "Is this okay?"

"Perfect." She sat down and blew at her drink as steam rose into the air. "Mmm, I love the smell of chai."

"There's isn't much in here that doesn't smell heavenly."

The way he looked at her made her wonder if he was talking about her, too. She wasn't sure, though. She wasn't accustomed to anyone flirting with her.

Justin took a sip of his coffee and eyed the scones between them.

"If you're not going to dig in, I will." She broke off a corner of her blueberry scone and popped it into her mouth.

"Thank goodness. I was hoping you'd take the first bite because I didn't want to be a hog."

"I didn't have breakfast this morning," she said.

Justin chewed a bite of scone. "This is my breakfast. You actually woke me up with your text," he said.

"Oh, Justin, I'm sorry!"

"No, don't be. I'd rather be here than asleep anyway. I worked late last night."

Kacey could see shadows beneath his eyes now, and she felt bad all over again. She took a sip of her tea, savoring the flavor. "You know what I do for work. What do you do for a living?"

"Nothing very exciting. I work in the archaeology department as a research assistant and curator part-time, and I work nights bartending. I've been working on my Master's in archaeology, and I'm actually about to graduate. Then comes the awful job search part, and right now, I have no leads. I might pursue my doctorate eventually, but I'd like some more field experience first. Anyway, I'm fascinated by the ancient Romans, Greeks, and Celts, specifically."

"Hmm, that's interesting." She tucked a strand of hair behind her ear. An idea dawned on her. "Maybe you can help me with something history-related. I was reading this text that referenced a Julius, but I don't think it's two thousand years old. So, other than Julius Caesar, which other important historical figure was named Julius? Maybe someone more recent?"

"I don't know. There were many men throughout history named Julius, precisely because Caesar's influence was so great."

Kacey chewed on a bite of scone, savoring the buttery flavor as she thought about that. "Any that would be associated with a Greek woman?"

Justin shrugged. "Julius Caesar himself. Cleopatra was Greek, not Egyptian, as most people think. She was from the Ptolemy line. She would have spoken Kione Greek, her native language."

How had Kacey not known that? She tapped her fingers on the table. Should she show him the journal? She felt possessive of it, as though she expected someone might take it from her. Justin looked like someone she could trust, though. He had an honest face. What did she really have to lose? She obviously needed help, and fate had deposited a history expert practically right into her lap. She pulled the diary from her bag and set it on the table between them. "Care to guess how old this might be?"

Justin looked from the journal to her face and back at the journal. He picked it up, flipped through the pages, and turned it over to inspect the back and spine. "I don't know. Probably not very old. It actually looks fairly new. Why?"

Kacey frowned. It didn't look new to her at all. "Well, it's all the entries. Look at this," she said as she took the book from him and opened to some of the beginning passages. She stopped on a language she couldn't decipher, possibly Sanskrit. "Weird, huh? And here," she said as she flipped to the entry she'd translated the night before. "This is definitely ancient Greek."

Justin looked at her like she was crazy. "Are you joking?"

"No, I studied Greek in college. I know what Greek looks like," she said with an eyebrow raised.

"Kacey, there's *nothing* on these pages."

CHAPTER 7

SIBYL, 1266 B.C.

S ibyl hummed to herself as she made a special paper. She'd peeled papyrus reeds and cut the pith of the reeds into thin layers. For several days, she soaked them in water mixed with blood from the most beautiful woman in all of Greece—Helen, the daughter of Zeus. Sibyl had also mixed in dirt and ash from

Witheryn, a mystical Netherworld type of place, and she'd mashed a golden apple from Aphrodite to add to the mixture. She had big plans for the magic this book would produce.

Sibyl rolled out the excess water and pressed the concoction into sheets. Then she wove in strands of Helen's hair to strengthen them and give them the magical energy they needed. She then pressed, dried, and sanded the sheets down smoothly. She'd worked on this project for a few months now, and it was almost complete. These pages would be strong, influential, and eternal.

Sibyl was coming into her powers of prophecy, and she knew Apollo would be there hours before he arrived. As she looked in the water where more papyrus reed strips were soaking in the magical mixture, she saw his handsome face in the ripples. She put away the dried paper she was sanding down with a pumice stone and cleaned her hands. Then, she took some of Helen's strands of hair and plaited them into her own, speaking a prayer as she did so. She wanted Apollo's help, and even the hair of Helen's head held a more persuasive allure than anyone else's on Earth. Besides, the Mágos could be cruel sometimes, and if she said something that made Apollo angry, the magic in Helen's strands would temper his wrath.

Sibyl stepped out of the cave into the sunlight as ravens descended upon the field in front of her abode. They came down like a dark blanket, rose back up in a dark wave, and Apollo suddenly stood before her in all his golden glory. She wet her lips as she bowed to the ground. "Oh, great, Apollo! I'm so glad you have chosen to grace me with your powerful presence this day." His golden curls were as bright as the sun and surrounded his head in a warm glow.

"Rise, faithful prophetess."

Sibyl stood, and her eyes scanned his muscles visible beneath the folds of his blue cloak. His golden bow and shiver of silver arrows were casually draped across his back. She daydreamed for a moment about when she'd raked her fingernails across the muscles of his back, and she sighed with a renewed desire.

"I have a task for you. Pythia at Delphi tells me that she sees a giant horse that will be a gift from the Greeks to the Trojans. Now, Agamemnon has given back the innocent daughter Chryseis to my faithful priest Chryses, and I need to know if this horse is a sign that the Greeks will give up the war. I tire of this war between the Trojans and the Greeks, though I think my father, Zeus, delights in its divisiveness. I need to know how this war will end. So many deaths for mere entertainment," he scoffed.

"Come with me to the sea." Sibyl's grandfather was Poseidon, and much of her prophetic powers came from "reading the waters."

Her cave was but a short walk from the ocean. They stood along the shoreline only for a short time before a wave crested in the distance, and Sibyl saw the horse. It burst apart into the air in a dramatic spray.

"No, Apollo, this horse is an evil portent. You know that the horse is Poseidon's sacred animal. He has sided with the Greeks."

"Is it possible that my uncle will turn from the Greeks, then?"

"That I cannot know. I can only give you the impression the vision had on me, and it was not positive." Sibyl looked up at his face and saw the pensive frown he tried to hide from her. She did not understand why the Mágos cared so much about one war. Surely, future generations would bury this war in the annals of history and forget about it in several hundred years. Man had already fought and then forgotten how many wars?

Apollo wandered down the beach, and she let him go for the moment. She concentrated hard on the water, so hard that her head ached from the intense mental effort. She stepped into the water, looking down at the swirl of sand and shells as the tides pushed against them.

In the water that swirled around her legs, she saw Apollo covering Hector as Achilles charged. She walked further into the water. She saw an arrow pierce Achilles' foot, though she could not tell from where the arrow came. In his weakness, Achilles faltered. She fell into the water, seeking the vision, trying to see more, swimming down lower and lower, watching King Priam, who'd accepted Helen in because of Paris' love of her, retrieve Hector's body, his beloved eldest son, and then die by the hands of Achilles' son. She saw Helen in the arms of Menelaus. It was jumbled and confusing, and she fought against the current as she swam deeper to see more.

Strong hands pulled her up, and Sibyl found herself in the arms of Apollo, sputtering, coughing up briny sea water, and rambling about the things she'd seen. Apollo laid her on the beach and sat beside her. "You are made new. Water will never hurt you again," he promised her as he stroked her wet hair. He sat there a long time as he pondered her prophecy, so long that the sun and wind dried her hair. She feared he might be angry about her visions, and she stayed silent. "You did well, Sibyl," Apollo said quietly.

Sibyl touched the braid with Helen's hair plaited in it. "What do I get in return, my lord?"

"What do you desire, prophetess?" Apollo's eyelids dropped with wanton lust. He expected her to ask for another night with him, and she wanted to, but she had higher ambitions than that.

Sibyl looked at the waves rolling, at the steep cliffs, at the sun high in a hazy sky. The breeze from the ocean soothed her wet skin, and the sound of waves lulled her almost into a trance. She had to word her request carefully. "My desire is to serve you for many, many years." Sibyl picked up a handful of sand. "Grant me as many years of life as grains of sand that I hold in my palm that I may serve you throughout the ages." *And serve my own ambitions,* she thought.

Apollo laughed heartily, but she could see tenderness in his eyes. "As you wish, Sibyl. I will be glad to have you around longer." His lip curled. "However, you failed to ask for youth." He stood and looked down at her. "You will still grow old and wither before you die."

Sibyl grimaced but raised her chin. "No matter. It will be a very long time before that happens."

"Now, tell me, priestess, how many grains of sand do you hold in your hand? How long will you live on this Earth?"

"I suspect until the sun devours it, for I hold 28,267 grains of sand in this one hand; it will be a very long time before I grow old in the body that will last that long." She smiled triumphantly as the sand fell from her outstretched hand and blew away in the balmy wind.

Sibyl would be a slave to the whims of no man or Mágos, either. That gave her plenty of time to achieve her goal—to become empress over all mankind.

CHAPTER 8

KACEY

Kacey cut her coffee date short with Justin, not only because she looked insane, babbling about the writing that he couldn't see, but also because she had to shop before work tomorrow unless she planned on going into the library naked.

As she walked, she shook her head in confusion again as she replayed Justin looking at her like she'd lost her marbles. Apparently, he only saw blank pages in the journal, which meant one of two things: Kacey was losing her mind, or she'd stumbled across a magical book.

She turned her eyes skyward. Neither option made her feel better. Insanity or magic. Maybe they were one and the same. Regardless, her life was sure to never be the same, and that left her with a sour stomach. She'd liked her nice, quiet, boring life... hadn't she? Her shoulders slumped. No, she hadn't, if she was being honest with herself. But this book was a little more than what she had in mind. All she wanted was to be swept off her feet by some dark, handsome man who was also good to her. Was that too much to ask?

Justin would probably never ask her out again. She'd found him interesting and cute, and it would be a shame if she didn't get to know him better. She couldn't blame him, though, if he never called her again.

Kacey stepped into a used bookstore, scouring the racks for a book that fit her mood. Books always made her feel better when her day was going sideways. She settled on a pretty hardcover copy of Shakespeare's *A Midsummer Night's Dream*. She hadn't read it in a few years, and it was one of her favorites. Besides, what was more appropriate than a story of fairies, magic, love, and appearances?

As she always did, Kacey snapped a selfie with her new book purchase and posted it to her social media account, tagging the bookstore to make sure they got a little attention, whatever little reach her small account could afford them.

Coming out of the shop, Kacey noticed that the sky had darkened considerably, as though it would rain at any moment. The wind picked up, shaking the fronds of the palms overhead.

Just what she needed—to get drenched on top of the already sucky day she'd had.

Kacey wandered from store to store, trying on clothes in sizes she shouldn't even be wearing. It's like her body had suddenly turned into the classically desired hourglass shape overnight, and though she looked amazing in whatever she put on, she wasn't accustomed to how her body felt with new measurements or the kinds of stares she got from people these days. It was hard to shrug off. She'd gone from invisible to unforgettable in a matter of hours.

It wasn't just at work anymore, either. People everywhere stared at her, and she imagined this was how it felt to be a big movie star or singer. But she had no idea *why* people everywhere were taking notice of her. She hadn't really done anything notable her whole life. She was average. Average looks, average intelligence, an average career.

Kacey decided on some outfits that she wouldn't normally wear. Since she was feeling so physically different, she decided her frumpy old style didn't suit her anymore, so she picked up a black pantsuit, a cobalt blue wrap dress that would have never looked good around her midsection before, and a few tops that hugged her curves. She also found a couple of pairs of jeans that felt amazing. She'd never had so much confidence looking in a mirror.

After her mini-shopping spree, Kacey decided that her most important order of business was to get properly fitted for a bra. She went into a boutique where she knew someone knowledgeable would measure her and help her find the right size.

A thin blonde woman in a pinstripe dress rushed to her side before she'd gotten fully into the front entrance. "May I help you find something?" she asked in a high-pitched voice with a smile plastered to her face. "Negligee, perhaps?" She looked Kacey up and down like most people were doing these days.

Kacey almost snorted. It had been a long time since anyone had been interested enough in seeing her naked for her to even think about buying fancy lingerie. "I need some new bras, for starters."

Kacey followed the woman into a dressing room, and she removed her blouse and the too-tight bra she was wearing.

"Oh, dear, you were definitely wearing the wrong size. These marks mean this bra is way too small."

"Yeah, I've had a bit of a late-bloomer growth spurt, I guess."

The woman used a tape measure to measure Kacey. "Mmmhmm, just as I thought. You should be in a 36DD."

"A what?" Kacey had been a 36B all her adult life, and if she had to admit it, she'd barely filled up a B cup.

"Yep, I'll be right back with some in that size." The lady said over her shoulder, "They'll make your ta-tas feel amazing!"

Kacey stared at herself in the mirror. She could definitely tell the difference, but why had her body changed so much? Whoever heard of a woman in her thirties having a growth spurt? Kacey could hear the rain outside hitting the roof of the building. She wished she'd brought her umbrella. There had been no rain in the forecast.

The lady knocked lightly on the dressing room door, and Kacey wrapped her arms instinctively across her breasts. "Here you go. Give these a try. I've brought you a variety. Different outfits look better with different types of cups. For instance, this balconette goes great with a low-cut blouse. This full-cup bra with wider straps is great for wearing with t-shirts, sweaters, and such. And this convertible bra is really versatile for wearing with just about anything. If you could only buy one, this is the one I'd recommend. See what feels the best, and give me a call if you need some help."

Kacey found that the woman was right—36DD fit her perfectly now. She felt like she could breathe for a change as she tried on a sheer black lace bra, and her mouth dropped open when she turned around to look at herself in the mirror. This was sexier than any bra she'd ever owned. It was going home with her for sure. Next, she tried the convertible bra, and she also selected a lavender pushup bra, mostly because it felt so supportive. She pulled on a white and gold lace bralette that looked and felt like a second skin.

Kacey sighed and pulled out her phone to check her bank account app. She wasn't sure if she had enough money for all this lingerie. Each piece was pretty pricey, and she still needed to buy undies, too. She logged into the mobile app and pulled up her checking account. She nearly dropped her phone when she saw $7,458.92. Her paycheck should have hit, but she still shouldn't have more than about $2,500 in her account right now, especially with the purchases she'd already made. Where had $5,000 come from?

She shook her head in disbelief. It had to be a mistake. Should she call the bank? Yet, there was a deposit on her list of debits and credits. Her mind flitted to David trying to take her shopping last night. *Surely not*, she thought. How could he get her banking info?

It couldn't have been her parents gifting her money. Beyond college, they didn't pay for anything for her. They barely even spoke to her. They were currently living in Colorado Springs, where her father had gotten a teaching job, and Kacey hadn't seen them in a couple of years.

Kacey couldn't dwell on it long because a friend of hers, Amy, texted her with a screenshot. It was the post she'd made with the special edition book of the play she'd just bought that afternoon. In the image, the post already had over 65,000 likes.

In under two hours.

Chapter 9

Kacey

Kacey's mouth fell open. Nothing of hers had ever gone viral. She had a thousand followers on all of her social media accounts combined—if that.

> Check your Instagram. Ur famous!

No, that'd be the immortal Shakespeare.

Uh, since when does Shakespeare go viral these days?

Also, new filter? Your skin is practically glowing!

Nope, no filter.

Pregnant?

You have to be getting some to get knocked up.

Whatever ur hairdresser did to ur hair, I need done to mine.

Lunch soon?

Kacey tousled her hair with her hand as she peered at herself in the dressing room mirror. She hadn't been to the salon in half a year. She typed back 'yes,' but she knew it was a hollow promise. Kacey and Amy hadn't spent much time together at all since college. As the years went by, their friendship dissolved into an occasional text and an even rarer call. Amy was married and had a little boy who was now three years old. Kacey could count on one hand the times they'd been out together since her baby shower over three years ago.

Kacey pulled up the post Amy referred to and stared at it stupidly, as though the picture of her with the book would somehow reveal what made this post go viral. She scanned the comments, which were mostly adoring compliments, when she heard a light tap on her dressing room door.

"Come in."

The blonde lady popped her head in. Kacey still wore the bralette. "Ah, that's perfect! Do you like it?" she asked, nodding yes, as though she wanted to convince Kacey to buy it. She was probably working on commission. "You should wear it out instead of the bra you came in wearing."

"Thank you." Kacey snapped the tag off the bralette and handed it to her, along with the other ones she wanted to purchase. She pulled on her blouse.

"Can I get you the panties to match these that you've selected?"

"Yes," Kacey said with a smile. *Why not?* she thought. She had the money in her account, and she needed something that fit her new shapely bubble butt. Her old ones were giving her a wedgie.

She followed the saleswoman out of the dressing room. As the lady picked out the rest of her purchases, Kacey examined the delicate, sexy outfits in luxurious fabrics in every color imaginable, hanging from racks and mannequins throughout the store. She touched a simple satin chemise nightgown in a deep eggplant purple and wondered what it would be like to sleep in something like that instead of old t-shirts. On a whim, she pulled the hanger from the rack and placed it on the counter.

"Very nice selection. I have that one in cobalt blue," the saleswoman said.

While Kacey waited for her to ring up the purchases, a woman in a flowing skirt and tank top entered the boutique. She was obviously wearing no bra at all, and Kacey smirked, thinking this woman definitely needed to be there. She was envious of the woman's confidence, though, as she walked right up to Kacey, which caught her off-guard. Kacey fidgeted with her wallet.

"Don't I know you from somewhere?" the woman asked, her voice smooth and calming like a bubbling brook. Her features were fine and dainty, but her gaze was intense. It was as though the woman knew all the mysteries of the world in those eyes.

"Unless you have a current library card, I doubt it." Kacey turned away from her and paid the cashier for her lingerie. She picked up the bag, so light for hundreds of dollars' worth of garments. She decided she'd have to call David to see if the money was his doing. It unsettled her that someone she barely knew would give her money. She'd leave out the part about spending some of it on intimate apparel. Kacey didn't want David's mind to go there—or for her to give him false hope.

"No, I *do*," the woman said thoughtfully. "I saw you this morning while I was getting ready." The woman donned a blossoming grin that totally transformed her face and made Kacey smile right back.

"Oh?"

"Yes, you were on the news—you know, the Social Buzz, or whatever they call it. Something about a sighting with the movie director David Fiore and an unknown bombshell." She arched her brow and looked Kacey up and down, but unlike everyone else around her, this woman's gaze wasn't appreciative. It was...curious. Appraising.

"David?"

"Yes, do you know who I'm talking about? Impossibly handsome, dark hair, million-dollar smile, rich."

"Um, yes, I know David. Kind of." *I mean, he asked me to sleep with him last night,* Kacey thought. *And he possibly deposited a bunch of cash into my bank account, hoping he'd get that chance really soon. That was going to be an expensive lesson for him, though.*

Then, the thought occurred to her that maybe he'd paid her off for her discretion if he really was a movie producer. Maybe he was afraid she'd go to the media. How had she not known he was famous? Her mind whirled with more questions than answers. She bit her lip and shoved the receipt into her bag, suddenly not feeling as excited about her purchases as she had in the dressing room.

The woman's eyes were dark blue and stormy. She held out a slender, graceful hand. "I'm Sibyl. Nice to meet you." Something about Sibyl made it hard for Kacey not to like her. She barely noticed that Sibyl bought nothing, chatting easily beside Kacey as they both exited the store together. Though she heard torrents of rain when she was trying on clothes, those clouds had moved on quickly, as the day had turned back sunny. Not ten steps out of the boutique, camera flashes stopped her in her tracks.

A reporter elbowed her way through the photographers. "Ms. Wilson, do you have a moment?"

"Wiltson," Kacey corrected her.

The reporter continued without acknowledging her mistake. "You were spotted out with Mr. Fiore last night. Was it for pleasure or business? Rumor has it that he's working on a new film."

"I have no idea about that."

"So it was for pleasure." The reporter looked into the window of the boutique and gave her a knowing smile. "Any more plans with Mr. Fiore in the near future?" She said it more like a statement than a question, as if she had already assumed the answer. And if Kacey had to be honest, she would have thought the same thing in the reporter's shoes. The man was gorgeous and apparently famous, too. What had Kacey gotten herself into here?

"No comment." Sibyl grabbed Kacey's arm and led her around the paparazzi.

As they hurried down the sidewalk, Kacey said, "Thank you. I don't even know what that was."

"Don't mention it. I could see how nervous you were." Sibyl glanced over her shoulder behind them. "I told you I saw you mentioned on television this morning. You're on their radar now. It's only going to get worse, I'm afraid."

"Why?"

"They've seen you with someone interesting, and let's be honest here, Kacey—you've got that magical aura about you."

"I do?"

Sibyl nodded. "People are going to want to know you." She smiled at Kacey, but it didn't make Kacey feel any better. "Let's go get pizza."

"Pizza?" Kacey asked, still a little dazed from the confrontation on the street and the new information about the guy she'd gone on a date with the night before.

"Pizza is always the answer." Sibyl laughed and hooked her arm through Kacey's like they were old friends. "It's been my comfort food for *ages*."

CHAPTER 10

SIBYL, 41 B.C.

The "Inimitable Livers," they called themselves, were a rowdy crowd of friends of both Cleopatra and Antony, who had met nightly to drink, feast, and play games. It was only a distraction from the strained relationships of the triumvirate, of course. No three men could set aside their egos long enough to rule together. They should have known better.

It had taken Sibyl years to track down her book, and this time, it was in the hands of the Queen of the Nile, Temptress of Rome, the demure Greek who'd stolen hearts and killed her own brother for the throne. What most people didn't know was that Cleopatra's possession of the journal was the very reason she had been so successful.

First, she'd won the hearts of the Egyptians, and they'd proclaimed her daughter of Re, the sun god. Then, Cleopatra won the favor of Julius Caesar when he restored order in Egypt after Pompey's defeat. After spending weeks together, Caesar left her side to conquer Asia Minor, saying "*Veni, vidi, vici,*" as he departed. "I came, I saw, I conquered." It was he who had been conquered, though. Cleopatra soon had his son, Caesarion.

After conspirators in the Roman Senate house murdered Julius, something Cleopatra had a part in herself, which Sibyl found out later, Mark Antony summoned Cleopatra to Tarsus to answer charges brought against her by the Second Triumvirate. Sibyl was there waiting for her when Cleopatra arrived. She'd realized that this woman *had* to be the one currently with the crimson diary—a woman who had charmed the Egyptians—not an easy feat itself, who had conquered the heart of the stoic Julius, and who had killed her own brother to claim the Egyptian throne as hers and her son's. Sibyl's assumption proved true when Cleopatra came off the gold-bedecked river barge dressed as Venus, with the red book tucked safely under her arm. Sibyl, who had charmed her own way into Mark Antony's care as a seer, became the constant companion of Cleopatra from then on.

Sibyl settled down to watch the festivities from the fringes of the party. Some played a drinking game. Several were having an orgy in the corner, while others watched. Most everyone there was already drunk with wine. Sibyl was smarter than that. She popped a grape into her mouth and chewed as she considered her options. Cleopatra and Antony were in love, and it was a passionate affair. He was her one weakness. Cleopatra only ever made poor decisions where he was concerned, so Sibyl had to figure out how to use him to defeat Cleopatra. Cleopatra's death would release the book and allow Sibyl to harness its powers.

"Thank goodness for you, my friend. If not for your advice on all matters, both politically and personally, I don't know what I would have done over the past year. And this year has been the happiest of my life. My desire for Antony grew into real love, something I've never truly felt before." Tears glistened in Cleopatra's eyes. Did this woman know true love? Sibyl highly doubted it. Cleopatra knew ambition, and like a petulant child, she wanted what she wanted, and she wanted it now. Mark Antony was no different. He was a conquest. Eventually, she would tire of him, too.

"You, my dear Cleopatra, were destined to be Queen over both Egypt and Rome. I saw it in the dark waters of the Nile, once I'd traveled here." *A white lie, of course. One she'd told Cleopatra over and over to pacify her in moments when her frustrations were bubbling over.*

"Have you seen anything lately?" Cleopatra asked eagerly.

On Cleopatra's current course of action, Sibyl had seen the ruler's demise. Cleopatra's seduction of Antony had already made Octavian angry and distrustful of the Roman general. Sibyl just had to make sure that Cleopatra stayed on course. And Antony would lead Cleopatra right to her end.

Sibyl smiled. The book would be hers again. And with the powers of the book, Sibyl would overtake Egypt, Greece, Italy, Macedonia, and eventually all of Asia and make people bow at her feet for thousands of years. She would be a god to them.

Alexandria suited her. It was a beautiful city, and she didn't mind spending the winter here. Sibyl popped another sweet grape into her mouth, bit down, and let the juices flood her tastebuds as she chewed. She watched Antony drinking wine and laughing with his friends. She knew that the only way to get that book back was to use Antony against Cleopatra, and she needed to do it soon, while Cleopatra was so smitten with him.

Sibyl looked down at Cleopatra's kohl-rimmed eyes and touched Helen's magic-filled hair, still plaited into a little braid underneath her long mane. "I consulted the waters a few days ago, my beloved Queen. Antony will help you to victory. There will be setbacks, stormy seas, and foreign ships, but don't worry. In the end, you will be triumphant. You must be patient."

Cleopatra smiled and kissed Sibyl's hand. "Thank you, my dear friend. Back to merrymaking, I go." Cleopatra finished the wine in her goblet and sat down in Antony's lap.

Antony looked at Sibyl as Cleopatra whispered into his ear. She could already see his undoing of Cleopatra in the dark pools of his eyes.

CHAPTER 11

KACEY

At a place in Little Italy, Sibyl laughed as a string of melted cheese hung between her mouth and the slice of pizza in her hand. The restaurant was small, and instrumental music competed with the din of clattering pans as workers baked pizzas and patrons chatted in the dining area.

"I note a slight accent, though it's almost imperceptible. Where are you from?" Kacey asked.

"Everywhere. I was born in Greece, but my dad was a seaman. I've been all over the world." Sibyl sprinkled a little red pepper onto her slice.

"That must have been fascinating." Kacey sipped her soda.

"It definitely has been. I've lived a thousand lives, it feels like." Sibyl took another bite, placed her pizza on the plate, and blotted her lips with a napkin as she chewed. "How about you?"

"Oh, nothing exciting. I've lived here my whole life. I went to college here. Rosegate? Have you heard of it?" When Sibyl shook her head, Kacey continued. "It's a small but prestigious private college. My father was an alumnus. Anyway, it afforded me an excellent education. I decided to study Library Science, with a minor in languages. By the time I'd completed my Master of Science, I'd found a head librarian position in the city."

Sibyl sat back and crossed her arms. "A librarian?"

"As a kid, I spent some of my happiest moments in libraries in hidden corners, exploring someone else's life or another world entirely."

"Hmmm. How will you change the world as a librarian hidden away like that?"

Kacey frowned. "I never said I wanted to change the world." She took a bite of her own pizza, chewing as she thought about that. She'd never had lofty ideas of fame or fortune. Ambition wasn't a part of her personality. She wanted a happy, comfortable life. She was about as down-to-earth as they came, she guessed.

"Everyone has ambition, Kacey, even you." She narrowed her eyes. "If you could make one wish that would transform your life, what would it be? I mean, set aside ideas of world peace or curing cancer for a moment. What would *you* want out of life?"

Kacey sighed. She barely knew this woman, but Sibyl was so easy to talk to that the words tumbled out with little consideration. "I guess I'd want to be noticed. I've lived my whole life as average and boring. No one really knows who I am. And that was perfectly okay until here lately." She looked down at her bag, which held the crimson diary. She thought about the way David had suddenly noticed her and how good that had felt. Well, until she'd gotten to know him. It had felt good to succumb to poor judgment and go out with him, despite red flags. "That seems to be changing, though," Kacey mumbled.

"It *is* changing."

There was a twinkle in Sibyl's eyes, and Kacey wondered how they'd changed from dark blue to sea green over the past hour. It must be the light in the restaurant.

"And with my help, you can get the recognition you deserve, Kacey. You have a brilliant mind. I can tell. Let me be your personal assistant and take care of public relations. You'll need it now that your own fame is growing from your association with David Fiore.

"Besides, it's kind of my thing, and I know I can get you noticed," she continued, without letting Kacey interject. "I've worked with lots of women, many of them here in southern California. Plus, I know PR, and I do my job well. I'll even do it for free for a week to see if you like working with me. If I can impress you with my skills, we'll talk about a work contract. What do you say?" Sibyl fingered the little braid hanging down from underneath her flowing hair.

"Yes," Kacey said with a little shake of her head, as if she were trying to clear it of a cobweb. She didn't know why she needed a personal assistant, but she had the overwhelming urge to hire this woman. Suddenly, a bubbling happiness overcame her, along with a sense that hiring this woman was the best thing for her right now, especially considering the media swarming her today. Her confidence in the idea grew quickly, like an invasive vine reaching for sunlight. "Yes, let's try it. What do I have to lose?"

CHAPTER 12

KACEY

Kacey waved to Sibyl as the woman walked toward her hotel. After giving Sibyl her phone number and address, Sibyl promised to get to work and be in touch soon.

Sibyl said she was staying at the nearby Hotel Republic. Kacey felt the sudden urge to follow her, to make sure she wasn't lying. She had no idea why, but she listened to her intuition.

Kacey followed her down Kettner Boulevard, staying far enough behind her that Sibyl wouldn't notice her if she turned and look back. Kacey's heart hammered in her chest, nevertheless. She didn't want Sibyl to think she was a stalker, but she needed to make sure Sibyl was being sincere. There were so many weirdos and scammers out there nowadays.

Besides, a little research would have told Sibyl that Kacey's family was well off, not that her parent's fortune affected Kacey's life. She barely even saw her parents. But having money in the family could sometimes bring out the scam artists. Kacey felt a pang of guilt for suspecting the worst of this woman who'd offered to help her.

Weaving in and out of the people on the crowded sidewalk, Kacey felt like a detective or a secret agent, and she smiled to herself as she watched for the flowing blue skirt billowing behind her new friend. The golden glow of the Hotel Republic, with its triangular-shaped front that mimicked the flatiron buildings of bigger cities, came into view, and she watched as Sibyl swept into the front doors underneath the glowing neon sign.

Okay, thought Kacey, satisfied with Sibyl's honesty. *That was ten minutes of extra walking for nothing.* She stood in front of the building and looked up. The entire hotel swarmed with people.

A tall black woman near the entrance in a gold pantsuit, smoking a long cigarette, watched Kacey. Did this woman know that smoking was prohibited on the sidewalks in San Diego? She obviously wasn't from around here. Kacey turned, looking for a bus stop, when she felt a firm hand on her arm.

"You, come with me." The black woman stood beside her, still gripping Kacey's arm.

"What?" Kacey asked. Her heart thudded in her chest as she wondered if Sibyl had a female bodyguard. She was tall and muscular, and she looked like she didn't take crap off anyone.

"Where've you been? The show is about to start, and you haven't even been to makeup. Come on!" She had the look of someone with authority, and her intent gaze, coupled with the set of her full lips, gave Kacey the impression that she was a no-nonsense woman. The woman pulled Kacey by the wrist into the hotel. "I knew you were one of my models as soon as I laid eyes on you. Always gotta look for the lost ones." She let Kacey go and moved forward, her high heels clicking on the floor like an impatient finger snap every half second.

Model? Model for what? "Uh," Kacey said, but the woman wasn't listening. She turned as she walked, raising a long-fingered hand to beckon for Kacey to follow. Before she knew it, Kacey found herself in a stuffy room with at least forty other people, some getting naked right in front of everyone as others shrugged on clothes. The smell of hairspray lingered heavily in the air.

"What is—"

"I don't have time to talk. I've got to go out. This is a huge night for me, and I'm running around looking for my models because my assistants are incompetent." The woman towered over Kacey, but her eyes scanned the room, assessing the scene. "Get dressed and find some shoes. You're up in ten minutes." The woman left Kacey standing there with her mouth agape.

Kacey set down her shopping bags and looked around at the flurry of movement. She didn't know what she was supposed to do or what she was supposed to dress in. Everyone else moved purposefully around the room, ignoring her. For a moment, she considered grabbing her bags and walking out, but the woman had sounded desperate to have her there helping, and Kacey didn't want to abandon someone in need.

A man with a ring through his bottom lip touched her shoulder and began brushing her hair, right where she stood. "This'll have to do," he said as he pulled the front up and stuck bobby pins into her hair at the top of her head while a young woman with blue-streaked hair added blush to her cheeks and eyeshadow to her eyes. The man produced a can of hairspray and covered her in a cloud of sticky mist. She coughed.

The woman added a little lipstick to Kacey's lips. "She doesn't need much makeup, thank God," the woman said.

"None, to be honest. This hair is glorious," he cooed. "She looks terrified, though," the guy said, as if she wasn't standing there listening to them. He turned to a table and turned back to Kacey with a shot glass full of an amber liquid. "First time? Here, this will help." He shoved it into her hand. "Okay, over there is the rack. Pull your dress, grab some shoes, and line up!" the makeup artist commanded.

"What?" Kacey asked, but the two walked away from her without listening for further questions. That was becoming the norm around here. *Bottoms up*, she thought as she looked down at the drink. Kacey took the shot in one gulp, and it burned all the way down. She grimaced as she wiped the corner of her mouth with a finger. She set the shot glass on a table, went to the rack, and looked at the clothes that were left. Someone in only panties grabbed a silver dress off the rack, and Kacey tried to avert her eyes. Kacey touched a dress. These were all designer pieces. *This is a fashion show!* Terror struck her. *I'm not a model.* Her head reeled. *How can I—*

"Move over," a tall blonde told her. She grabbed a gold dress from the rack, her blonde locks slapping Kacey in the face as the model turned to get dressed.

Kacey looked at the rack. Was she really considering doing this? Why did these people think she was one of their models?

She chewed at a fingernail. Only two outfits were left—a black jumpsuit with a plunging neckline that would surely show her belly button or a tiny white dress with fringy silver strings that would barely cover her backside.

A redhead with impossibly long lashes and cherry-red lips stopped beside her. She wore a turquoise bustier under a short white jacket and white high-waisted pants that had metallic threads running down the sides. "The white dress. Trust me." She gave Kacey a quick look down and back up. "It'll make your legs look longer. Get it on. And find the highest heels you can walk in. You're kinda short for a model." The woman hurried away to line up.

Kacey pulled the dress from the rack, stepped around to the other side, and tried to hide behind the remaining black jumpsuit as she undressed. She stuffed her clothes and shoes into her bag, pressing them protectively over the crimson diary. Then, she stepped into the dress as quickly as she could. Luckily, no one was watching her since the women were moving out onto the runway and into the throbbing music. She looked through the shoes lining the wall and found a pair of silver heels that were high but not so high that she thought she'd take a tumble in them. They were tight, but Kacey stuffed her toes and heels into them. She took a few tentative steps before she shuffled toward the back of the line of women waiting to go onstage.

Only three women remained in front of her, and then it would be her turn to go out. Her heart fluttered, and she found it hard to breathe. The liquor had warmed her, and she felt flushed. *Maybe I should just walk right out of here,* she thought. *This is insane!*

The redhead directly in front of her headed out. The stagehand directing the models held onto Kacey's arm for eight beats, as if she thought Kacey might turn and run the other way.

She couldn't say she hadn't thought about it. "Now!" she said as she pushed Kacey forward.

Kacey stepped into the light, and for a moment, she couldn't see anything but flashes as cameras took pictures beyond the faceless forms of people. She took a ragged breath and did her best to put one foot in front of the other and keep her face expressionless as she'd seen models do on television. It wasn't hard to do because she was terrified and feeling a lot like a deer in headlights. *Step, step, step, step, stop, half-turn, turn.* She was already headed back toward the dressing room. *Almost there,* she thought, and relief bubbled up inside of her. She passed through the exit, and it was over. She sighed as she went backstage and broke into a huge grin.

Her new sense of confidence faltered as her stomach dropped. The women were lining up again. Her grin turned into a grimace as she realized they were heading back onto the runway.

"Get back in line," the redhead mouthed and pointed behind her. *Again?* Kacey wondered. She ran toward the women waiting to go back out onto the runway. "We all go back out together behind the designer in a parade," the redhead said when Kacey was back in line behind her. "Is this your first show?"

Kacey nodded. They went back out, with Kacey bringing up the rear, and the cameras continued to flash as people clapped. When they were all back behind the stage, the designer broke into a toothy smile. "Beautiful, ladies! Absolutely beautiful! You've just walked the Spring Showcase for Fashion Week San Diego. Stay for champagne."

Again, Kacey found her mouth hanging open. Someone handed her a plastic champagne flute. "What the hell," she said with a shrug.

CHAPTER 13

KACEY

Kacey hopped on a bus to head home. She was dead tired. It had been a long day, and her feet hurt. She wanted to soak in a hot bath.

Kacey caught several people on the bus watching her, and she had the uncanny feeling that all of them knew exactly who she was.

She tried to ignore the stares and scooted down in her seat. All her life, she'd thought she would enjoy more attention, but now that she had it, it was odd and disconcerting.

She pulled out her phone to check her social media, and someone had tagged her in the picture outside of the lingerie store. People were already commenting on how beautiful she was, how lucky David was to be dating her, and how she was destined to be a star in his upcoming film. *I'm not even an actress*, she thought, her eyes wide with amazement. She shook her head in disbelief and put her phone in her bag. Her hand grazed the diary, and she longed to read more of its words. Kacey decided that she'd feel better after curling up in bed with some wine and a charcuterie board full of her favorite things to eat. Then, she'd spend the rest of the evening reading.

At home, she fed Jareth a fresh can of kitty food and took a hot bubble bath. Then, she settled down in her bed and opened the red book. After rereading some of the Greek translations she deciphered the night before, she wondered how the words of Cleopatra and the book itself had survived for over two thousand years. Kacey sighed, flipped a few pages, and looked for something a little less taxing on her brain. She stopped when she came to a pretty cursive handwriting in blue ink. She adjusted her pillows and nibbled on a cracker as she read.

"I spent many years in the orphanage and in foster homes, and I kept myself small and quiet as a mouse. No one minds a mouse if they aren't seen or heard. I love books of any kind. I can lose myself in reading, and I like to consider others' points of view. When I came upon this book one day out of the blue, left on a park bench near the Van Nuys Drive-In, I picked it up to read it, and my life has been changed ever since."

Kacey nodded as she read. She could certainly relate to every bit of that, feeling like a timid little mouse, hiding within the pages of books, and then happening upon this extraordinary diary. She sat forward a little, her food and wine forgotten, as she read more of this new cursive in blue ink.

"It is as if a light bulb has come on over my head, and I clearly see the way the world works now. Women hold the real power and sway in this world, and men beat at their chests, demanding the power they'll never really have. They talk and hit and shoot and capture and yell, but what do they really ever achieve? Women can start or end wars, women can create life, and women can make a man do anything with the power between her legs. One long look, one curve of red lips, can make any man fall to his knees and beg."

Kacey paused. Well, she certainly hadn't come to that conclusion herself. Whoever wrote this must've had a lot more experience with men than Kacey had. She flipped the page and continued reading.

"This knowledge hasn't calmed my nerves or given me more confidence, though. And it's not as if I want to conquer men. I find men fascinating, especially intellectuals and writers. I have a poet's heart. Besides, I want to be loved and valued. I want to feel secure and important to someone. My own parents could not give me that.

"Since finding this journal, boys and men trip over themselves following me around or fall at my feet with sexual adoration. I can't say that I don't enjoy it. My bed is never cold. I've been offered modeling contracts left and right, little ol' me from nowhere in particular. Hmmm, it does make me wonder."

The first entry was signed N. J. Kacey searched the Van Nuys Drive-In on her laptop, but it gave her no clues. It had been closed down since 1996. She also tried "N.J. model," which only gave her a bunch of entries for models from New Jersey. Kacey set her computer aside and read another entry, this time in the same pretty cursive but written in black ink.

"*I've never believed in magic, but what else can it be? What do all these entries in strange languages mean? Are they magical incantations that have given this book some profound power? Have I stumbled upon witchcraft?*

"*I tried to leave it behind when I divorced my first husband, a man who could never understand the transformation into the woman from the sixteen-year-old girl he'd first married. Even my body transformed. What people said was surely cosmetic surgery was none of the sort. It's... magic, pure and simple.*

"*But all this adoration comes with a price.*"

With her throat dry, Kacey paused and sipped her wine. What kind of price? Would this book get Kacey into trouble?

"*Part of me felt like this book caused my marriage to fall apart. I wanted to rid myself of it. When I left him, I left it behind. Yet, the farther away from the book I drove, the more I ached, the more anxious and depressed I felt deep down in my soul, and the more chaotic my mind became. I actually mourned the book. So I returned and retrieved this red diary or spells or magical thoughts or whatever it is. I'll have to deal with whatever horribly fantastic magic it holds.*"

Kacey glanced at the cover of the book. She'd only had it a few days now, but she felt an intense protectiveness over it. She never left it too far away. It was always on or near her bed, and she took it with her in her bag wherever she went. Allowing Justin to touch it had given her so much anxiety. Maybe this book *was* covered in a strange magnetic magic.

"*Now, I'm being offered a film role, and I think it's time to take a stage name to separate myself from the mouse. I will create a whole new persona for my stage name, perhaps my middle name and my mother's maiden name. It has a nice ring to it. The actress will be the outrageous best friend and seductive lover to the public, and I'll keep the mouse hidden away for home.*"

Another entry from the same handwriting followed. The cursive was now more elongated and lighter on the page, as though time had passed and the writer felt weary.

"For the longest, I was afraid to write in this book, but I felt a strange pull to add to it over the years. When I finally did commit to adding to its pages, things really began to change in my life. My career accelerated at a breakneck pace. Powerful men left their wives to hang onto my every word and tremble at the slightest touch. Men in important positions bent over backward to attend to my every need.

"Infatuation became love. Love became obsession. Men cheated and died, and lovely, naïve women cried. Every man I count on for intimacy fails me. No one trusts me anymore. I'm adored everywhere I go—and hated for it, too, and I've never felt so lonely. I'm so incredibly lonely.

"One man is never enough. Maybe someday, I'll find a man with a big enough brain that anything he lacks won't bother me. I adore a sharp mind, but Arthur lacks affection, and I need loads of affection. I thought having his baby would make him love me more, but I am obviously condemned to be barren. The loss hurt us both, but I think it killed something vital within my psyche. I can't even write about that heartache; it hurts so badly."

Kacey came to another entry with the same cursive writing.

"I love lots of men—actors, musicians, politicians, mob bosses, princes—but I'm not in love with any of them. I think I'm incapable of falling in love with one man. Well, maybe Joe. But he was wildly possessive and jealous, and a marriage with him was a prison.

"With fame and glory, I got role after role, though I don't think anyone takes me seriously as an actress. I'm just the ditzy bombshell that spreads her legs easily. I fell right into that stereotype, not unlike so many of the beautiful actresses I've worked with in Hollywood. If you're beautiful, you can't have a brain, right? I'm

not so sure I take myself seriously anymore. Maybe I should try Shakespeare. No one takes classical literature lightly.

"I think I'll die young, though. I fear I won't have time to become a Shakespearean actress. Actually, I'm afraid I'll die by drowning. Once, a mob chased me into the ocean, and I thought I was a goner then. Thankfully, a boat came by and picked me up. Another time, I fell into the river with waders on while filming a movie, and they filled with water and pulled me under. Now, I dream about water overtaking me. I sink down under the water, I allow it to cover me, and I think, 'This is it. This is how the movie star and the mouse both cease to exist.'"

Kacey closed the book and rubbed her eyes. What had she gotten herself into picking up this book and reading its words? It was more intriguing than anything she'd read lately, reading someone's innermost thoughts, but a dark mood settled over after she read this woman's words.

Who was N.J.? And what happened to her?

Kacey fell asleep before she read N.J.'s last entry.

CHAPTER 14

KACEY

K acey awoke in the middle of the night. Her bedside lamp was still burning, and the diary lay open beside her. She wiped her eyes. There were six messages from her friend Amy—all about her modeling in the Spring Showcase at Hotel Republic. Amy was mad that Kacey hadn't invited her.

Apparently, Kacey had made the news, and her strange newfound fame had grown even more overnight. She sighed, put down her phone, and picked the book back up again, hoping to find some other clue about who N.J. might be.

"People seem to think I'm depressed because I drink and take sleeping pills. What actress in Hollywood doesn't? People don't understand anxiety at all. This is how I cope when I'm working on a film. So I forget my lines sometimes or feel too anxious to film for a day. If I'm such an asset to the company, then give me some love and understanding. That's all I've ever wanted from people. Though I never have the nerve to ask for what I want unless my clothes are off!

"Something's Got to Give is the movie I'm currently working on. I filmed a scene in the pool where I was swimming naked, and it took them a full day of shooting to convince me to get in. I've become terrified of water. But the cool water sliding over my skin felt wonderful. I felt so alive. And then I thought how silly I must have sounded being afraid I'd drown with all those people around me."

Kacey nearly dropped the book. She knew exactly who N.J. was now—Norma Jean, better known by her stage name, Marilyn Monroe. Her hands shook as she continued reading. She remembered seeing a documentary about Marilyn's death and the conspiracy theories surrounding it.

"Once the movie wraps, I'm making another trip down to Mexico, and I'm so excited to go. Joe says I shouldn't make such a trip, especially considering the eyes turned toward me back in the 50s, but he knows he can't stop me. What if they're watching? I don't care. The whole world is watching me.

"I once said that if you give a girl the right shoes, she can conquer the world. That's what Marilyn would say. Norma Jean would say, 'Give a girl the right book, and she can conquer the world.' At least for a while. Nothing lasts forever.

"I told my therapist recently all about why I thought my three marriages failed. I think we're getting somewhere with the psychoanalysis. He's using free association techniques to help me uncover some of my deep-seated unconscious fears and desires. Dr. Greenson is a gem; he really is. And when we talk, I don't feel like the stupid blonde bimbo that people make me out to be. He knows I'm intelligent and inquisitive. He's one of the few men in my life who doesn't only listen to me so he can get in my pants.

"President Kennedy and his brother both are so afraid that I can't keep my mouth shut about things that have gone on between us, probably because I called out Joan on our little sexual tryst. Or maybe it's because I'm seeing Joe again, and both of them are jealous. But look at everything I have kept under the lid—the FBI doesn't know half of what they think they know about me. I've dated more important men than anyone could imagine, and I've never gotten any man in trouble with his wife if he didn't want it found out, okay?

"I've connected them with the ones who can do their jobs. What do they need me for anymore? Men use me until they find something new to use. I really can't stand human beings sometimes.

"Something Bobby said the other day keeps haunting me. He's paranoid. I can't really speak candidly with anyone anymore, except maybe Dr. Greenson. With everyone else, I have to overthink every utterance until my head aches.

"Or maybe it's the champagne I've been drinking tonight just to calm my frazzled nerves. Maybe vodka would put me to sleep. I desperately need rest. I've asked my housekeeper to stay the night with me. Maybe with someone else here, I can get some peaceful rest.

"Peter wanted me to come out to a party at his house tonight, but I don't feel like clothing myself in the Marilyn persona right now. It's too heavy. I know what kind of party they want Marilyn for, and I can't stomach it tonight."

That was the last entry in the lovely handwriting. The next person's handwriting was entirely different.

During her research about the movie *Something's Got to Give*, Kacey discovered that production came to a halt when Marilyn died, and the movie never released. Marilyn's housekeeper found the actress' lifeless body, and the coroner ruled it as "probable suicide," though the autopsy revealed no sleeping pills in her stomach. Further, it was hours before authorities were called to the scene. What happened to Norma Jean that night?

Kacey's fingers paused over her keyboard, and then she typed, "Marilyn Monroe red diary" into the search bar. She scanned the resulting articles, and each one mentioned Marilyn's red diary that mysteriously disappeared the morning her body was found.

Kacey's eyes fell on the book that lay open beside her, and she sighed deeply. What had Kacey gotten herself into?

CHAPTER 15

KACEY

T he next morning, Kacey awoke to a knock at her door. She frowned as she glanced at her clock. It was only 7:32. Surely, she wasn't getting a delivery this early. She bit at the inside of her cheek as she headed to the door. She hoped it wasn't a delivery at all. The last thing she needed was more bouquets of flowers. She grabbed a robe on her way and covered the chemise she'd picked up at the lingerie shop the day before.

Kacey opened the front door to find a short, thin woman with a grim face standing there with her arms crossed over her torso as if it were cold, despite the sunny spring San Diego morning. She looked distraught. Kacey's first thought was that she was in trouble, and Kacey looked beyond her, wondering if her car had quit or if someone was harassing her.

"May I help you?"

The woman frowned, and Kacey's next thought was that this woman might be up to no good herself. Living in the city, she'd learned to be distrustful of people. Kacey took a step back, ready to shut the door in a hurry if need be.

"Are you Kacey Wiltson?"

"Yes. May I help you?" she repeated. The woman looked familiar, but Kacey couldn't place her.

"Yes," the woman said through clenched teeth. "You can stay away from my husband."

Who she was talking about. David? Justin? Were either of them *married*? She felt a little sick. "Excuse me?"

"Paul," she spat out, exasperated with Kacey. "You're all he's talking about these days, you, you, *Lolita*!"

Kacey's eyes widened. "Whoa, look, I don't have anything going on with Paul beyond a professional working relationship." Kacey glanced at the woman's hands to make sure this distraught woman wasn't hiding a gun or something. The woman clutched her own shirt as if she was fantasizing about wringing Kacey's neck. She didn't appear to have a weapon. Still, Kacey's heart pounded in her chest. No one had ever accused her of adultery, and her stomach roiled at the thought of *anyone* suspecting her of that. She didn't need to have a front yard brawl over *Paul*, of all people.

"Really? Because I keep a pretty sharp eye on our finances, and he bought flowers yesterday." Her hands lowered into fists at her side.

Kacey's stomach sank as she thought of the flowers that had indeed come from him the day before.

The woman's eyes narrowed, and her mouth set into a grim line. "He never buys me flowers, so imagine my surprise. I waited all day, actually, and they never came. He came home talking about *you* again, and that got me thinking. So I called the flower shop and did a little sleuthing. It turns out they were delivered here."

Kacey couldn't deny how that looked. "Um, that's true. He did send flowers here yesterday. I was off work." Kacey sighed. "Look, I don't know what's going on with Paul. He's been acting really weird this week, but I can assure you that I'm not messing around with your husband. I don't know why he's taken a sudden interest in me, but—"

"Well, look at you!" When the woman looked Kacey up and down, she pulled her robe closer. "You're a freaking goddess."

"No, I'm not. And I'm not, nor have I ever been, interested in Paul. I think Paul is going through a midlife crisis. Honestly. He's not well. He's not himself this week. Just give him time."

A tear rolled down the woman's cheek, and her fists relaxed. "I've given him my whole life. Now, he wants to throw all that away. I don't understand."

Kacey shifted and lowered her eyes to the ground. "Neither do I. Over the past couple of years that I've worked with him, he's always spoken so sweetly of you and your children. That's why I think this is just some weird midlife thing. But I promise you, it's not my doing."

Her mind flitted to the diary. *Had* she done this to him? Had finding that diary made Paul fall in love—no, in lust, in obsession—with her?

"I haven't encouraged him." That was certainly true. She could say that without guilt. She wasn't interested in Paul at all, and she truly hoped he'd stop this nonsense and not ruin his marriage over something that would never happen between them.

"Fine. I'll deal with him." The woman turned on her heel and left without waiting for a response. As ominous as that sounded, Kacey was just glad to have the jealous wife off her front stoop. Let Paul deal with the drama he'd created himself.

Kacey let out a sigh of relief and closed the door. Maybe she should call in sick and let this blow over. If the wife confronted him at work this morning, Kacey didn't want to be in the middle of it. She went back into her room and picked up her phone from the nightstand. She heard another knock at the door, and she threw her hands up in the air. What more could this woman want to talk about?

Kacey took a deep breath and pulled open the door as she said, "Look—"

David stood in the doorway, his back to her as if he were scanning the street. He turned, and his face lit up with a broad smile when he saw her. "You look absolutely ravishing first thing in the morning." He thrust a box of Godiva chocolates at her. "Sweets for the sweetest woman I know."

CHAPTER 16

KACEY

At a loss for words, Kacey took the box of chocolates from David, but her robe fell open, and she tried to ignore the look of wanton lust that crossed David's face as his eyes moved down her body in the satin nightie. She quickly pulled her robe closed with a huff of exasperation. "What are you doing here, David? I'm about to get ready for work."

He cleared his throat as his eyes returned to her face. "I wanted to catch you early this morning in hopes that I might ask you out to dinner tonight."

Kacey narrowed her eyes. "Will I get paid for this date, too? Because, to be honest, I'm feeling a little like a prostitute at the moment." She wasn't entirely sure he'd even given her that money, so she was going out on a limb, but it was the only thing that made sense.

He ran his hand through his thick, dark waves and cringed. "That was a gift. That's all. I'll deposit another gift, whether you go out with me or not. I want you to have nice things."

"Stop putting money in my account. Do you know what the media would do with that info if they somehow caught wind of it? You can't go throwing money at women and expecting them to fall at your feet—or maybe you can, but that won't work with me."

He held up his hands. "Okay, noted. We'll say our dinner last night was a business meeting. You should be paid for your valuable time. Where would you like me to make us reservations for tonight?"

"You are so presumptuous. That's your problem. I'm not going to dinner with you tonight."

He looked pained by her words. "But you will go to dinner with me some other night, then?"

Kacey half-laughed as her mouth fell open with incredulity. This guy wouldn't stop. "I'm sorry, but I don't think we're very compatible, David."

David looked hurt. "Everyone else thinks we are."

He was right about that. People all over social media and the news thought they were a great couple, but Kacey didn't think any of them knew the real David. Looks could only get him so far with her.

"Look. I had no idea that you're famous. It's too much. The paparazzi are following me around."

His dark eyes showed genuine concern. "I'm so sorry about that. Part of the reason I wanted to talk to you tonight is that I'm currently working on a project, and I hoped you'd help."

"What kind of project?"

"May I come in? I'm not a fan of extra media attention, either." He glanced over his shoulder again.

"I guess so." She didn't particularly want him in her house, but she didn't want to be rude. Against her better judgment, she opened the door wider.

David walked over to the bar, which was still covered in vases full of roses. "I see you got my flowers."

Kacey crossed her arms. "Yeah, I think you went a little overboard."

"Perhaps. I'm sorry. To be honest, I don't know what came over me. For some reason, I get a little overzealous when it comes to you."

"I'll say."

"Look, I apologize for the other night. I shouldn't have asked for sex. It was uncouth." He smoothed his hand through his hair again. "Like I said, I don't know what came over me. Regardless, if you forgive me for my *faux pas* or not, I want to offer you a job."

"I have a job."

"I know. You said you were a librarian, right? I bet that doesn't really pay anything. I've looked you up on social media, Kacey. People love you. Now, you're doing some modeling. Have you ever thought of going into the entertainment industry?"

Beyond her short-lived desire to be just like a young Selena Gomez when she was ten or twelve, Kacey had no entertainment-industry dreams. She couldn't sing, and she'd never even tried to act in high school or college. "No, not at all."

"You certainly have the look for it, and your online presence is huge and growing fast, too. Have you seen it?" He held up his phone. When she shrugged, he pulled up one of her accounts. "Look at this," he said as he handed her his phone.

It was the account where she'd posted a picture of herself with the book yesterday. It was already up to over a million likes, with several hundred thousand comments. Kacey shook her head in disbelief.

"That's star-level engagement, Kacey. You're blowing up. The public loves you."

Kacey handed him back the phone. "One viral photo is hardly fame. This is just a fluke."

"It doesn't have to be. I can make you a true star."

His comment made her think of Norma Jean's journal entries. Was fame the new way to conquer the world as Cleopatra had tried to do with sex, politics, and religion? Marilyn's story *was* rife with rumors of political conspiracies and sexual exploits. How much did she affect world matters during her brief life? And in both instances, their rise to fame became too much for them. That was a heavy price to pay for fame and influence.

Kacey didn't want that kind of burden on her shoulders.

Though she had no inclination to be a movie star, she said, "I'll think about it." It was more to get him out of her hair so she could get ready for work.

David seemed satisfied with her answer and beamed. "By the way, the lady who just left looked a little crazy. You may want to invest in a ring cam for some added security. This is a nice enough neighborhood, but with the extra attention on social media, you never know what kind of fruitcakes will show up at your door."

"Okay," she said, already guiding him to the door. "I'll look into it."

"I could have a really good security system installed here by the end of the day if you want me to."

"No, David," she said, practically pushing him out her front door. "I'm fine. I'll take care of it myself."

David turned to her as he stepped onto the front stoop. "I love an independent woman." He gave her a quick peck on the cheek, hopped down her stairs with a bounce in his step, and almost ran into Justin on the sidewalk, who looked from David to her and back to David with confusion.

Kacey knew exactly what this looked like to Justin, and her stomach filled with dread. Would she be able to convince Justin that before 8 a.m., David had come over only to talk about the movie business and had not just spent the night with her? She sighed. *Can this day get any worse?*

CHAPTER 17

SIBYL, 36 B.C.

Each year that passed, Sibyl conspired to end Cleopatra's life and regain control of the crimson book. Cleopatra's influence grew each time she wrote within its pages, intensifying Sibyl's envy. She hated someone else possessing her book. Still, she couldn't deny the book's mounting power from every mark on its pages and with each death that it caused. She could sense the magic, and when she had it again, the power would be all hers.

Several years earlier, in Rome, Sibyl's plans for the book had failed. True, she convinced Brutus and Cassius to murder Julius by planting seeds of doubt in their minds. They believed Julius was too ambitious and arrogant and that he would bring about the fall of Rome, which was easy to accomplish because they believed in her oracles. Sibyl even gave them the date—the Ides of March, the Roman day for settling debts. However, the men were supposed to execute their plan while Julius and Cleopatra lay together just outside the city.

Instead, the men murdered him at the Curia of Pompey, and unfortunately, Cleopatra was far away and safe from the bloodshed. Sibyl suspected Cleopatra had discovered their plans and changed the venue, but she had no proof—only a foreboding from when she'd consulted the waters before the assassination.

Cleopatra and Sybil met with Antony to give him more riches so that he might prove himself against the kingdom of Parthia. Afterward, they sailed back to Egypt, with Sibyl manipulating the winds and waves to aid their journey home. Sibyl had little faith that Antony would succeed. He wasn't a powerful ruler by himself, and he certainly was no conqueror.

"I'm so very tired, Sibyl," Cleopatra said. "This latest mess with Octavian has done me in. I cannot stand that Antony married Octavia, though I know he does not love her. He only did it to appease Octavian. And Octavian thinks that a marriage between his half-sister and Antony would really keep Antony out of *my* bed." Cleopatra smirked as she laid her hand protectively over her stomach. She sighed. "I wish he had more of a spine, though. It is his only weakness, other than his devotion to me."

"He loves you more than life itself," Sibyl agreed.

"He doesn't need Octavian to rule the empire. Octavian isn't even a legitimate heir of Caesar. My son Caesarion is." Cleopatra adjusted a bracelet on her arm—a golden piece adorned with sapphires and emeralds. Her stomach was already swelling with her fourth child—the third child by Antony.

"Queen, you and Antony will rule the empire together, bringing Egypt and Rome into a powerful union. Octavian cannot win against both of the fleets you're building. Stay the course." Sibyl ran her fingers through Cleopatra's long, brown hair. She wove gold strands through it as she plaited it. "Besides, Isis favors your rule, and Dionysus favors Mark Antony. You are divinely destined to be victors."

Though Sibyl's statement wasn't true, Cleopatra liked her ego stroked, and Sibyl knew that boosting her confidence would ultimately do the prideful queen in.

Years earlier, when Mark Antony summoned Cleopatra to Tarsus, Cleopatra identified herself as the goddess Isis. Sibyl knew the truth, though. Isis, or Hathor, as Sibyl knew her, was an Egyptian mother goddess, one of the Mágos, who ascended with Horus and Ra long ago. Sibyl knew Cleopatra used the Isis title to validate her rule over Egypt, but Cleopatra knew nothing of the true power of a real magical being. While it gave Cleopatra's rule a great measure of validity in the eyes of Egyptians and some Greeks and Romans, Octavian saw it for what it was—a strategic power move.

And it gave Sibyl a stronger desire to end this woman's life. No one with plans to conquer a world can abide another person with the same desire. And Cleopatra, with the power and influence of Sibyl's book, began to see herself as divine and untouchable.

Because Sibyl's plot to have Cleopatra killed with Julius Caesar failed, she now planned to use Octavian and his powerful army against the queen by way of Antony's devotion to Cleopatra. Octavian considered Antony loyal, but Sibyl also knew that he worried about Cleopatra's influence over Antony. And now that Antony had shown his weakness for her yet again by publicly rejecting his wife Octavia and returning to Cleopatra, Sibyl was certain she could put an even bigger wedge between the two male rulers—and create a war.

In her prophetic waters, Sibyl saw Cleopatra succumb to a terrible poison and die in her mausoleum, so she was confident in her plan. Her time was coming.

Until then, Sibyl would bide her time. What were a few years when she had millennia left to live and rule this world?

In the candlelight, Cleopatra's olive skin looked green, as she'd felt ill on the trip across the ocean. Sybil, herself, felt drained, too. Restraining the waves and storms over the long journey had taxed Sibyl's powers.

"Tell me, Sibyl. What will this child be? I want to begin calling him or her by the name I've chosen."

Sibyl stood and kneeled before Cleopatra. Placing her hands and her ear against Cleopatra's stomach, she felt the waters inside Cleopatra's womb sway. She closed her eyes and envisioned the tiny hands and the little toes. She saw its heart beating and the hairs on its head moving with the undulating amniotic fluid. This baby would be born in another month or so. "You'll have a boy, my Queen."

The baby gave her hand a strong kick, and Sibyl opened her eyes.

Cleopatra clapped her hands together. "Ptolemy, after my line, of course. Ptolemy Philadelphos, 'the loving brother.'"

"The perfect name," Sibil agreed. *Too bad he won't remember much of his mother*, Sibyl thought. *He'll need the love of his siblings once she's dead.*

CHAPTER 18

KACEY

"That wasn't what it looked like," Kacey insisted.

"Um," Justin said as he approached her door. He looked conflicted and turned halfway around as if he were going to leave instead. "I texted you, but I got a message to forward correspondence to your personal assistant. I was trying to find out where you were so I could talk to you in person, but I didn't know I was going to run into a guy coming out of your place. So, honestly, I'm a little embarrassed to have come by unannounced. By the way, why does a librarian need a personal assistant?" He shook his head, turned, and walked back down her steps.

"You're misreading this situation." Kacey took a few steps toward him.

Justin turned back to her. "Am I? It looks like this guy just left his girlfriend's house after spending the night with her."

"David did not spend the night here, nor has he *ever*." Kacey saw a flicker of hope in Justin's eyes. He *had* to believe her. She didn't want to mess things up with such a sweet guy.

Justin stuck his hands in the pockets of his jeans and looked down at his boots. When he looked up at her, distrust had returned to his eyes. "Last night, I couldn't believe it when I saw your face on TV at the bar. My sweet, shy librarian caught with David Fiore by the paparazzi. But here, this guy is coming out of your house, so I'm sorry if I can't really believe that."

"It's not the way it seems. The media is spinning it how they want to." She frowned. He sure seemed possessive for having only gone on one coffee date with her. Was he affected by the book's influence, too?

"So you haven't gone on a date with that guy? You're not dating the famous director? I saw photos of you with him on TV."

"Yes, we went out, but—"

"Okay." Justin turned and quickly descended her front steps.

"Justin, let me explain, please."

"I can't compete with that, Kacey. And I'm not a third-party kinda guy. You don't have to explain yourself to me. We only went out for coffee," he murmured as he walked away. "I'm not even angry about it. Disappointed, I guess. I got here too late. It was good to meet you, Kacey."

"One date is *not* dating."

"You're right," he called over his shoulder. "I'm no one. It's none of my business."

She huffed in exasperation. She'd meant her one date with David. Why was Justin being so frustrating? Why wouldn't he listen to reason? "Justin, I'm not interested in him like that."

Justin was already too far down the street to hear her. She wanted to go after him, to make him understand, but she was still in her nightgown and robe. Kacey's shoulders sagged. *Yep, this day is definitely getting worse.*

She'd call him later. She wasn't going to let a little misunderstanding like that ruin her chances with a good guy like Justin. He was just reading the situation wrong.

Kacey went back inside and closed the door. She shook her head at all the craziness that had transpired before she could even have a cup of coffee. She rested her head against the door, closed her eyes, and took a deep breath. If anyone else knocked, she resolved not to answer it.

Kacey opened her eyes and looked at the clock on the wall. *And now I don't have time for coffee!* She tore off her robe and chemise as she ran to the bathroom, where she showered in record time and put on one of her new outfits. Glancing in the mirror, she marveled at how great she looked, but she didn't have time to wonder about it. She needed to get to the library. She pulled her hair from the clip, ran her fingers through her bouncy waves, and grabbed her bag before heading out the door. Maybe she could talk some sense into Paul before his new attraction to her ruined his marriage.

As Kacey powerwalked toward the library, the cloudy sky threatened rain. Up ahead, she spotted a coffee shop, and she glanced at her phone to see if she had time to stop. Just as she neared the shop, Sibyl strode out with two large cups in her hands.

Sybil's face lit up with a smile. "Good morning! I was headed your way with your coffee," she announced, falling into step with Kacey. She wore a flowing teal dress that swished around her legs like water as she walked.

"How'd you know I'd need a coffee this morning?"

"I'm good at my job," Sibyl said with a wink. "By the way, I've typed up an agenda for this week, and I created some graphics for your social media accounts, which are already scheduled to post. *And* I have one of the best talent agents in the business ready to negotiate a contract for you."

Kacey, who was looking at Sibyl wide-eyed, frowned. "What for?"

"Did David Fiore not meet with you this morning? He contacted me about you working on his next film. He said you'd agreed. I just spoke with him again a few minutes ago, which is when I got on the phone with the agent. And apparently, this runway show you did the other night garnered a lot more attention. How in the world did you score a spot in Spring Fashion Week?"

"Oh, yeah, that."

"You continue to surprise me, Kacey. Anyway, you did agree to work with Fiore, right?" Sibyl asked with an expression that said she'd be a moron not to take the offer.

"Uh, maybe I agreed to it." Kacey shrugged. "I was trying to get him out of my house, honestly. He's a little intense." She took a sip of her coffee.

"*Intensely* handsome, you mean." Sibyl grinned.

"Eh, not my type, though. Mmm, this tastes good. What is it? I taste hazelnut."

"It's a latte with two shots of espresso, caramel, butterscotch, and hazelnut."

"Yes, that's exactly what I needed this morning. Something to sweeten the sour mood I'm in— and to give me some energy. I'm already drained, and the day just started."

"We'll look at the contract he's sending over in the next few days. Don't worry. I won't let him cheat you. In the meantime, I'm going to work on your platform and brand."

Kacey sighed. She didn't even know what that entailed or why she needed it. Maybe she should stop all this before it got out of hand. Just as she opened her mouth to voice her concerns, an ambulance and three police cars blaring sirens sped down the avenue. "I wonder what's going on."

Trying to steady their hot coffees, both women picked up their pace. When they rounded the corner, Kacey saw where the police and ambulance had stopped. "It's the library." Her face crumpled with worry as officers tentatively entered the building. "Something terrible has happened. I can sense it."

Sibyl shot her a quizzical look.

"I mean, not really, but you know... Come on." Kacey took off toward the sirens, but police were already holding a group of people back. Kacey stood on her tiptoes, but she couldn't see anything. "I work there. What happened?" she asked the other bystanders.

A guy in a suit said, "Good thing you didn't come to work early today. It's a shooting."

Kacey clamped her hand over her mouth to muffle her cry. Who got shot? How could someone do this? Why would they come into the library with a gun? The library shouldn't even be open yet. She felt dizzy and sick to her stomach.

Still more than a half block from the entrance to the library, Kacey saw the police emerge with a woman in handcuffs. Then, the EMS rolled in a gurney. Shuffling left and right to see around the heads of the other onlookers, Kacey's eyes widened. Her stomach lurched.

Paul's wife was the woman in handcuffs. She wore the same grim frown at Kacey's door that morning, but now, her shoulders sagged in defeat.

"Hey, you look white as a ghost. Want to sit down?" Sibyl took Kacey's coffee and ushered her to the curb. Feeling lightheaded, Kacey nodded and complied. Sibyl sat down beside her.

"I've ruined someone's life," Kacey whispered. Paul's wife was probably going to jail—all because men were falling at Kacey's feet. She replayed her conversation with Paul's wife less than an hour ago. Kacey gulped, realizing the woman could've just as easily pulled a gun on her this morning. She felt hot, but her hands were icy cold, and she wondered if she might be going into shock. Tears streamed down her face. A crack of thunder made her jump, and people scattered, whether from the threat of rain or fear of another shooting.

Kacey looked toward the library and wondered what carnage lay inside. Had she gotten Paul killed?

CHAPTER 19

SIBYL, NOW

S ibyl watched as Kacey's face transformed from curiosity to horror, realizing that the shooter was the very woman Sibyl had sent to her house that morning. Sybil suppressed a smile. Before dawn, she had peered into a fountain's shimmering water and seen the jealous wife grab a gun and leave her house. Sibyl had been certain that Paul's wife would kill Kacey over his interest in the young librarian, but it hadn't turned out that way.

That was fine. Sibyl had lots of other ideas about how to get her book back. If all else failed, she'd cover Kacey's house in black mold. After all, it worked on a young Hollywood starlet not long ago. Britt had been impressionable, so Sibyl introduced her to an older man who was reclusive and paranoid about the government. After they married, he convinced the actress that she was being watched and was in mortal danger. She changed from a confident, bubbly starlet to a frail, frightened shell of her former self. Britt fell out of the Hollywood scene and became as reclusive as her husband before she succumbed to the mold and resulting pneumonia that wrecked her lungs. It killed him, too, because even after his death, he stayed holed up in her house, where the mold spores multiplied and thrived. Totally clueless.

Though she didn't snatch her book in time, Sibyl's friendship and working relationship with the rising star had given her a firm foothold in Hollywood, which would come in handy when dealing with the newest Keeper.

Fate had already propelled Kacey toward stardom, even though she was trying to dig her heels in and fight it, but Sibyl could deal with that. Nothing could break a woman's barriers like fame and fortune. Sibyl had seen it time and again throughout the many centuries she'd been chasing her book. Keeper after Keeper had succumbed to the awful power of success and money.

And love.

Love could utterly destroy a woman. Long ago, Sibyl decided she wouldn't allow love to enter her heart again.

Success, money, and love—the trifecta of ambition's demise.

After an officer told Kacey to stay put on the curb until he questioned her, Sibyl placed an arm around Kacey's shoulder. "Shhh, it's okay. Everything is going to work out."

"I can't imagine what went on in there. Well, I guess I can since the shooter was Paul's wife." Kacey looked like she might throw up. "I swear, I never led him on. I wasn't attracted to him in the least, and until a few days ago, he never hinted that he was attracted to me." Kacey wiped at the drying tears under her eyes. "Yet, when she visited me this morning, I had a feeling—this foreboding dread that I couldn't shake. I even wondered if she had a gun. It's like... It's like I knew..."

Sibyl narrowed her eyes, but she said, "No, you couldn't have really known. You were being careful. An angry wife was at your doorstep first thing this morning. Anyone would have been apprehensive."

Even in her haggard state, Kacey looked stunning. Sibyl glanced down at the badge Kacey wore, the little square in the corner featuring an old photo of her. It barely looked like the same woman. Sibyl marveled at the way the book manipulated reality.

"Sip your coffee. Maybe the warmth of it will help." Sibyl handed her the drink and took a sip of her own coffee. "You know, you can't take responsibility for what other people do. I can see it written across your face, Kacey, but Paul messed up all on his own."

Just then, the EMTs rolled out Paul's gurney and placed him into a waiting ambulance. Kacey sighed, and her shoulders drooped in relief at seeing that Paul was the only victim.

"I'm not saying he deserved to get shot, but he messed up his marriage all on his own." Of course, Sibyl knew the influence of the book was to blame, at least partly, but she didn't need Kacey melting down, taking the blame, and ending up in an asylum.

When an officer strode toward them, the two women stood. Officer Henderson smiled as he took Kacey's statement, even when she told him about Paul sending her flowers and his wife finding out about it. "I never showed him any interest. I just can't help but think what the woman could have done to me if she'd had a mind to," Kacey told him.

"We have her in custody, and I don't think her husband will bail her out—that is, if he makes it. Still, you might want to consider changing jobs. If Paul is so infatuated with you that he considered ending his marriage over it, then you may want to put some space between you two." Officer Henderson gave her a look of genuine concern.

"Yes, that makes sense." She shook her head. "No, it doesn't. I should upend *my* life because he can't control himself? I mean, I'm sorry he got hurt, but please tell me why *I* should be the one to change careers."

"Unfortunately, there's not much the law can do to protect you from someone who has a crush on you, whether he's married or not. He has broken no laws by sending you flowers, so you can't even get a restraining order until he escalates. And to be honest, they aren't very useful anyway." He pursed his lips with sympathy. "Anyhow, thank you for the statement. I have your number if I need to ask any more questions. We'll probably give you a call later to have you come in to write a formal statement." He tipped his police cap, stuck his notepad in the pocket of his body armor, and walked away.

With the flick of her hand, Sibyl moved the fog away, and the gray and purple clouds slid across the sky, sending sunbeams down upon them. "Ah, look at that. The day is already looking brighter." She gave Kacey's hand a reassuring squeeze.

Kacey glanced up at the sky, a frown on her face. "Well, as much as I hate to do it, I have to go inside and see what kind of damage there is."

Kacey showed her library badge to an officer at the door, and she and Sibyl entered the dark, cool lobby. Everything looked as it should, as far as Sibyl knew, but Kacey drew in a breath as she rounded the front desk. Sibyl came up behind her and looked over her shoulder. Blood spattered the books behind the desk, and a few posters on the wall, and a pool of blood marked the carpet where Paul must have fallen after his wife shot him. The smell of blood was strong, and Kacey pressed the back of her hand to her nose and mouth before she turned and pushed past Sibyl. She leaned against the front desk with her back to the gory remnants of the shooting.

Sibyl stared at the blood for a moment, the bright red color so vibrant against the tan carpet. It reminded her of Joan. For a moment, she was back in France beside the young maiden who burned with a desire to complete what she believed was her divine purpose.

Prophecies across the French countryside had spoken of a virgin maiden who would restore France. Joan claimed to have had visions from what she believed were an angel and female saints, but Sibyl knew it was the Mágos still trifling in human affairs. Though it didn't happen often in the Middle Ages, they hadn't yet completely abandoned the Earth at that point. Word of Joan's influence brought Sibyl to France to search for the young woman.

With the red book in Joan's breastplate and her Bible on the other side, over her heart, she boosted morale and turned the Anglo-French conflict into a religious war. Sybil was there when Joan was wounded in Paris. Sibyl held her and stopped the bleeding until help could arrive. She still remembered the virgin's blood on her hands. It was so red, it looked unreal.

The day she saved Joan of Arc's life was the day she realized Joan did, indeed, have her book. Having saved her life, Joan trusted Sibyl completely. It didn't take long for Sibyl to hand Joan over to the Burgundians at Compiegne, who burned her at the stake in the city of Rouen.

The book disappeared again before Sibyl could get her hands on it, but Joan's death, with the purity of her conquests in her short life, steeped into Sibyl's diary, giving it much more power.

In fact, in 1431, Sibyl stopped chasing the book so relentlessly, as she realized the benefit of letting the book's power grow from absorbing the energy of each Keeper. After all, Apollo had granted her many thousands of years. What were a few millennia when she could gain an untold amount of power from them? The world would be completely under her thumb one day soon.

For hundreds of years, Sybil relented—until she grew impatient once again.

How had over two millennia passed without discovering the secret to getting her book back? No matter how close she was to the book when the Keeper died, it disappeared just out of her grasp and reappeared somewhere else. She hoped that once the book had enough power, it would willingly return to her.

Sibyl clenched her teeth and feigned compassion, knowing the book was inside the bag slung over Kacey's shoulder. Kacey took a few deep gulps of air to calm herself. Then, she picked up the phone, completely ignoring Sibyl, as she set about dealing with the aftermath of the shooting.

Sibyl meandered around the library while Kacey spoke with her boss and hired a cleanup crew. Kacey's admission that she knew something bad was going to happen concerned Sibyl. However, lots of people said those things without really meaning them. As a powerful seer, Sibyl could usually tell if a person had any amount of psychic ability, and she didn't read that kind of energy from Kacey.

She dismissed Kacey's claims of premonitions and thought about how she could use this situation to her advantage. If she could talk Kacey into giving up her library career, at least for now, she could probably convince Kacey to work with David Fiore on that film. Anyone else would have jumped at the chance already. What was wrong with this woman? Sibyl thought that the stuffy old library would soon be a distant memory when Kacey saw the amount of money David would throw at her in the contract.

And that was good for Sibyl. She needed to get Kacey out of her comfort zone and into the arms of a man who could utterly destroy her.

CHAPTER 20

SIBYL, 30 B.C.

The war against Octavian had been brutal. So many people died. Cleopatra and Mark Antony's combined armies had been decimated at the Battle of Actium the previous year. They were worn down from the effort involved, and it had cost

Cleopatra untold amounts of the fortune she intended to leave to her children.

They'd hunkered down in Alexandria since then, but in her prophetic waters, Sibyl saw Octavian coming. Cleopatra's death was imminent. Sibyl looked up from the bowl of water and herbs. "There's no changing the course of Fate, my dear Queen," Sibyl said.

Cleopatra's eyes shined with tears, but she said nothing.

Almost all of their armies and old friends from the "Society of Inimitable Livers" had abandoned the lovers to what everyone saw as certain doom. Even Cleopatra and Mark resolved themselves to the inevitable, though Sibyl knew Cleopatra hoped that fate would side with her again.

Cleopatra, along with her few servants who stayed, Sibyl, and Mark with his closest companions, renamed themselves "Companions to the Death." Beside the temple to Isis at her palace, Cleopatra had a two-story mausoleum constructed. If Cleopatra was to die, she would go out with a flourish, as any goddess-queen should. Sibyl suspected that Cleopatra really believed that she might become a transcendent being upon her death. No, Cleopatra would rot as any other human does when death steals away the essence of life.

In July, word came that Octavian would soon land in Alexandria and would storm the palace any day. Cleopatra readied the mausoleum for her impending suicide rather than waiting to be killed by a mere man, one that she'd come to despise with all of her being.

Knowing that Sibyl needed to hurry things along in case Cleopatra had a moment of doubt and fled Alexandria instead, Sibyl went down to where Mark Antony was watching for Octavian's arrival with a few of his men.

"Mark!" Sibyl screamed, tears in her eyes. He ran to her, leaving his men watching Octavian's ships on the horizon. He grasped her by the shoulders. "My queen is gone. It is done," she said. "Oh, that the gods hadn't been so envious of her earthly power and had let her rule on earth longer." Tears streamed down Sibyl's face as she willed them forth.

Mark Antony's face crumpled in agony. "No!" He took off toward the mausoleum.

"Stop!" Sibyl ran to catch up to him, knowing she couldn't let him find Cleopatra alive. "She made me promise upon my life that you would not see her lifeless visage this side of Elysium." Sibyl grabbed his arm. "She is no more here on this Earth than the mists that swirl in the winds. Please do not make me break my word to her, old friend."

Mark looked up the hill toward the mausoleum and then back at Sibyl. "We were to go to Hades together. Companions to the Death, remember?" His friends were coming up the hill.

"Of course." Sibyl pulled out a poisoned dagger from the leather bag she carried. "Meet her there now! I'll follow."

Without another thought, Mark Antony grabbed the dagger with both hands and plunged it into his own stomach. Sibyl stepped back, triumph in her eyes. Stupid mortal men and their big, dumb hearts.

As his men neared, she put her head into her hands in mock despair. "Carry him to the Queen. Then, stand your ground with courage as Octavian disembarks. Tell him that Queen Cleopatra has snakes in her tomb. If he wants to enter, beware the asps." Then, she followed the men carrying Mark Antony up the hill to tell Cleopatra that the love of her life had committed suicide without her.

When the men brought in a dying Mark Antony, Cleopatra ran to her lover. "What happened?" Her voice was so angered that the men shrank and looked to Sibyl to answer.

The men laid Mark Antony at Cleopatra's feet and hurried out. Cleopatra wailed with sorrow, knelt, and held her lover. Mark's breathing was labored, and he could no longer talk. His eyes were wide, and he shook all over. His skin was sallow, and blood pooled under him.

"My queen! The worst has happened. Fearing Octavian's fleet, who are now arriving, Mark Antony stabbed himself outside the city." Without saying so, Sibyl implied that he'd died with shameful cowardice, which she knew would be another dagger through Cleopatra's heart.

The light died in Cleopatra's dark eyes. A single tear escaped before she turned to her two servants. "It is time," she told them, her voice flat with resignation.

The servants changed her blood-stained clothes, cleaned her skin, and covered her in perfumed oil. Meanwhile, Cleopatra had other servants bring in a beautiful gold couch. Sibyl gathered the opium, hemlock, and wolfsbane and prepared the poison. Then, Iras and Charmion, Cleopatra's favored female servants, sealed the four of them into the tomb.

"How much time do we have?" Cleopatra sounded more dejected than Sibyl had ever heard, and she almost felt bad for the woman. She spied the red book beside the queen, and she set her jaw. Now was not the time for weakness.

"Octavian's men won't immediately come in. I told them you'd have deadly asps in here to bring about your demise. Men are terrified of snakes." It was quiet outside. Their voices echoed in the dark tomb, lit only by candles.

"Very well. Administer the poison when you're ready, my darling Sibyl," she whispered as though the very act of speaking was too heavy a burden for her broken heart to manage. Cleopatra had barely spoken since Mark died in her arms. She rested on the gold couch, her eyes closed, as the poison coursed through her body. Her two servants laid down at her feet, poison flowing through them, as well.

When Sibyl reached for the crimson diary under Cleopatra's hand, the book vanished. She screamed in frustration, the sound bouncing around the chamber. She'd waited so long to have her hands on her book again, and it had evaded her as soon as the life left Cleopatra's body. Why? What had Sibyl done wrong when she created the magical book? Why did it always seek other Keepers and not return to its rightful owner? She shook her head in frustration as real tears stung her eyes.

Sibyl heard the men at the door. As the men forced themselves into the entrance, she dissolved into a mist and blew through the doorway in a rush. The men fell back, fear in their eyes.

"Gods! Stand back! It is the essence of Isis leaving this damned tomb."

"Be bold, men," Octavian bellowed deeply behind them. "Cleopatra was no more the goddess Isis as I am Zeus." As Octavian pushed through them to stand triumphantly over the dead body he finally conquered, Sibyl materialized behind them and simply walked away.

Sibyl decided she needed to get to the ocean to see where the book might lead her. She'd spent decades serving its last master, and her anger bubbled at the surface. Clouds rolled in from the choppy ocean as she threatened a tsunami with the tantrum she wanted to throw.

"What have you been up to lately, dear Sibyl?"

Sibyl stopped on the road and looked around. She couldn't see where the voice was coming from, but she'd know it anywhere.

"Apollo?" she called out hopefully. He hadn't revealed himself to her in so very long.

Sibyl heard the tinkling twangs of a lyre floating through the balmy late afternoon air, and she smiled at the familiarity of the notes. The winds died down as her anger abated.

"I don't like the things I've seen you doing, little one." His voice seemed to be all around her, but he was nowhere in sight.

She turned around and around, expecting to see him at any moment. "What do you mean?" she asked as innocently as she could muster.

Sibyl saw shining golden eyes in the growing gloom of the coming evening before she heard him. A huge golden wolf bounded out of the shadows and leaped on top of her, throwing her to the ground. She cried out, but the force of impact knocked the wind out of her, cutting her cry short.

When she could breathe again, she whispered, "I'm so sorry, my dear Apollo. I only wanted what was mine."

The wolf morphed into the handsome man she hadn't seen in hundreds of years. Despite the darkness from the clouds above them, his skin was golden, as if he made his own light. He'd never glowed so brilliantly before.

"What is happening to you?" Sibyl asked. She couldn't take her eyes off him.

"You know I have a soft spot for you, prophetess," he murmured into her hair. He sat up so he could look into her eyes. "But I am also the averter of evil."

"I am no more evil than you are."

"You have their blood on your hands," he growled, pointing toward Cleopatra's palace. He shook with rage, and his golden eyes flashed fire.

For the first time, she was afraid of Apollo, and she trembled as she scrambled backward, away from him. "The waters confirmed what would happen. I only helped it along. That's all. I need to get my book—"

"What book?" he interrupted. "Do you honestly believe that any book is worth the lives you ruin?"

A crack of thunder rumbled in the sky over them. "You have no idea, Apollo. No idea." Sibyl smiled.

CHAPTER 21

SIBYL, 30 B.C.

Sibyl spent the night in the arms of Apollo, his gentle luminescence the only light other than the Pharos Lighthouse, far out in the harbor. Heavy clouds still blocked the moon and starlight, but the winds had died down as Sibyl's fury abated. She was still angry that her book had disappeared once again, but Apollo's sudden appearance made the sting of it less painful. The grain barges coming down the Nile had stilled and silenced for the night, and she could only hear Apollo gently breathing beside her.

The two of them had retired to a tent to get drunk on wine and fill themselves with fish and fruit. It only made Sibyl long for days past. The dulled ache of separation worsened when he was so near. She couldn't wholly enjoy his presence when she knew he would soon leave again.

Sibyl tugged at one of his curls before dawn, waking him from his dreams. Truthfully, she could have stayed in his arms forever, but Apollo would never settle down. She'd sought that knowledge long ago and mourned losing the possibility of possessing his heart.

"Now that I've told you about my beloved, cursed book, tell me why you're illuminating the night, Apollo. What is this soft golden glow that surrounds you?"

He sighed. "I'm not sure, but I think my time is drawing nearer."

Sibyl's heart beat faster. "Already?" She thought she'd have much more time with him, many more nights like the one they'd spent listening to the ocean and making a delicious rhythm of their own.

"Your story is just beginning, my dear prophetess. You have thousands of years left. I've lived for thousands of years already."

She had to admit that he didn't look as youthful as he once did, but Apollo would look handsome at any age.

"My magic is weakening. I can feel it. And this golden aura about me... Artemis says she's read that it's an indication of Ascension. I probably only have a few hundred years left, at most."

Sibyl looked up at him bashfully. Oh, to spend those years with him, if he'd allow it. Tentatively, she said, "You could spend the rest of your days in Greece with me." She would even give up looking for her book, for a time, anyway.

Apollo ran his fingertips along her arm, his touch so light that it tickled her skin. His golden eyes shone in the predawn gloom as he gave her a smirk, not one full of arrogance but a look that seemed amused with her. "Little seer, can you not see that we are not meant to be together? That I've fallen in love with someone else?"

Sibyl hadn't consulted the waters about him for quite some time. He'd used her again. Or maybe she'd used him. She knew that his heart wouldn't ever belong to her, but somewhere in the back of her mind, she'd always hoped. It was that way with a person's first love. She swallowed the lump in her throat and laughed to quell any rising tears. "Of course. Who is she?"

"A nymph. Daphne, one of Artemis' servants."

Sibyl pressed her lips together and narrowed her eyes. "Apollo, you aren't destined for her, either," Sibyl told him. It gave her great pleasure to see the pained expression on his face. She was stabbing him in the heart as he'd stabbed her moments before.

"I know," he whispered as he watched the waves crest one after another, the white foam highlighted by the fire inside the lighthouse's cupola. "I love her still."

Sorrow bubbled deep in Sibyl's soul. Though she was sad that he would never love her, the agony in his voice also pained her. To love another is to want them to never suffer. She'd only ever felt that way about Apollo. "Are you here to say goodbye?"

Apollo nodded. "I may not see you again. This business with the book," he said with a stern expression, "let it go. It's going to drive you crazy. Besides, don't you want to end up in The High with me someday?"

"You know that my light won't burn brighter. It will dim. I'll never be one of the Effulgent."

"You are young, prophetess. You don't have to become a Gloomeer if you don't want to." When he stood, a golden aura bathed his beautiful body. It enticed her like an insect to a candle in the darkness. She wanted to burn herself in him.

"My light will fade, radiant Apollo, but before it does, I will happily rule this world and all who walk the Earth."

"I will never understand your damned ambition," he said as he clothed himself. He didn't look at her anymore.

"I know," she whispered. "When you are born with so much power, you can't know what it's like to have almost none." She refused to let more tears fall for him. She would harden her heart against it.

After Apollo left, she watched the crest of the waves beyond the harbor as the sun lightened the horizon, first to a deep plum, then to pink and orange.

Just as dawn crept into Alexandria, Sibyl transformed into a mist and boarded Cleopatra's treasure ship that Octavian's fleet now guarded. The purple sails fluttered in the warm breezes against a darkening sky that blocked out the morning rays. She was angry and frustrated, and the sky reflected her rage.

"Evil portents!" she heard some men cry as they looked up at the sullen black sky. "The gods are angry that Isis has been conquered."

Some of Cleopatra's sailors and servants still manned her ship, but others onboard were no doubt Octavian's military. They'd probably all heard that the Queen of Egypt was dead.

The mist rose and swirled, thickened into a smoky fog, and Sibyl materialized on deck in front of them. Men cried out and bowed at her feet. "Rise, faithful crew. I am here to save you. From this moment forth, you are no longer prisoners of war or under the conqueror's employ. Your Queen is dead, as was I. We are truly immortal now," she lied. "You will do our bidding. Octavian's fleet surrounds us, but I am calling forth a storm that will allow us to escape."

The men, fearing for their lives, stayed down.

"Rise! Mind your stations. We'll need all hands ready as the seas rage against the tyrant Octavian!" she yelled at them.

No doubt, some of these seamen would worship her as a goddess after seeing her powers over the next hour. That's what humans did—assume that the Mágos were deities and create cults around them.

"Dear Poseidon," she murmured, "hear my call. Allow me to control this sea today. Give me power over its currents as we escape the harbor. Forever your faithful granddaughter and servant." Sibyl's powers were limited, though they grew as the years passed by, but Poseidon could help her now, even if he wasn't near.

Once they were out of the northeastern harbor, Octavian's warships would never catch her. Sibyl didn't really care about taking out Octavian's fleet, though she knew she could if she wanted to. The point was to get away safely with Cleopatra's treasures. Sibyl was storing up plenty of valuables for the many years that stretched before her. Not only would she someday be the most powerful person on Earth, but she'd be the richest, too.

She raised an arm as the crew scrambled about. The sky darkened to almost night as winds and waves battered the ships in the harbor. Octavian's crews were focused on trying to keep their ships upright. Every time one of his ships would try to overtake Cleopatra's treasure ship, Sibyl would gather her rage and use it to send a wave of water crashing into the ship. Lightning streaked the sky as her ship moved out of the harbor. Sibyl watched dolphins jumping out of the water ahead of them, and she knew Poseidon guided her ship.

Sibyl tried to smile at her triumphant escape from Alexandria and from the servitude of Cleopatra, but she was weary and heavy-laden. The book was gone, and she'd have to figure out where it was. And Apollo... He was never with her for more than a few fleeting moments, but his touch left an impression on her that lasted much longer.

Sibyl winced. This must have been how Cleopatra felt about Mark Antony. She'd told Sibyl that it was almost unbearable when they were apart, and Sibyl felt that ache like a desperation, as though she were slowly dying of thirst.

Maybe she should abandon her search for the book for a while and follow Apollo. She had his love and attention once. Maybe he could love her again? But she knew in her heart that Apollo wasn't in love with her. And whatever he was going through as he slowly transformed into one of the Effulgent in his process of ascension, he'd have to experience alone. No one made the journey to The High with a companion—not twins, not lovers, not mothers with children. It was a solitary journey.

As the winds whipped the sails and carried them toward Greece, Sibyl strategized. Somehow, she'd figure out why her book evaded her each time it left a Keeper.

One day soon, she'd have so much power that even the Effulgent would tremble.

CHAPTER 22

KACEY

Kacey smiled gratefully as Sibyl set a warm cup of tea in front of her. Kacey's hands trembled as she sipped the warm chamomile. Sibyl had walked her home after she dealt with the fallout of the shooting, and Kacey was grateful for her presence.

She couldn't imagine coming home to silence when so many tumultuous thoughts and fears were churning in her mind.

The library was closed temporarily while the San Diego PD finished their investigation. She'd been surprised they let her leave without an interrogation. Then, a restoration company was coming in to assess the damage and clean the library. It would be days before they opened back up, and when they did, Kacey wasn't sure she'd ever feel safe there again. The library had been her haven for so many years. Now, it wasn't, and she felt like she'd lost something very important to her. It was a little like losing a friend.

A low growl reverberated from behind the couch. Sibyl looked sideways and inched away. Kacey didn't know what had gotten into Jareth, her Maine Coon cat. He was usually so affectionate to new people—or, at the very least, indifferent. He'd certainly never growled at a guest.

"Jareth, calm down." Kacey tucked her hair behind an ear and pulled up her legs to cross them under her. "I don't know what's gotten into him. Maybe he senses my anxiety from this morning."

Sibyl gave her a thin smile and a shrug. "Listen, Kacey," she said, "I think what happened today might be a message from the universe. You have a producer offering you an incredible opportunity at almost the same moment that all hell broke loose at your job."

"It's not a job, though. It's my career. I love the library, the books, the people who also love books—"

"But will it be the same now?" Sibyl interjected gently. "Truly the same?"

Kacey shook her head. She knew it wouldn't be. She slumped back on the couch.

"If you take this job with David Fiore, there's nothing that says that at some point in the future, you can't go back to being a librarian. You have plenty of years to do that. Why not try this new thing that might change your life?"

Kacey shrugged. It would be nice to make more money for a change, and the extra attention she was getting across social media was flattering. She'd never had much attention at all growing up. Her parents had always been too busy with their careers to pay much attention to her, and since she was well-behaved and made good grades in school, she'd made it easy for them to ignore her.

Throughout high school, she found it hard to make friends. Eventually, she just gave up. In college, she'd dated a few men, but they were never lasting relationships. They mostly just fizzled out. They'd stop calling and coming around after a few months. She'd even run into one of her old boyfriends at the movie theater once, and he didn't remember her. That had hurt.

That's when she adopted Jareth, her beloved Maine Coon, soon after grad school. At least he depended on her. She might be utterly forgettable to everyone else, but she mattered to one living soul, at least.

"Yes, I could always go back to the library—well, *a* library. I don't know if I'll ever go back to that one." The smaller branch library where she'd worked for several years wasn't really the one she wanted to work at, anyway. She'd always dreamed of working in one of the larger libraries with extensive collections and lots of daily patronage. Maybe this would be her opportunity for advancement. If the book she'd found truly was magical, maybe she could get a better placement after they wrapped this film. It was doubtful that she'd do more with a film career. *Little, timid me, a film star?* she thought. Kacey shook her head at the absurdity of the idea. "I suppose I should put in my notice." Nervousness stirred her stomach, but Kacey ignored it. "Yes, that's what I'll do today."

"Let me take care of it for you. I'm your P.A., after all." Sibyl smiled and made a note in her planner.

"What kind of movie is it, anyway?"

Sibyl waved her hand. "Oh, some kind of Arthurian legend retelling. It's called *Out of the Mists*. I read a bit of the script last night, which a friend of mine sneaked me an early copy of for you. I'll send it to your email."

Kacey sat forward. She loved the King Arthur legends. The quests, the magic, the noble knights. She'd grown up reading those stories. What wasn't to love? "Who would I play?"

"You're supposed to be reading for Guinevere, of course. You're leading lady material now, at least in David Fiore's eyes, and he's all that matters with his film. Anyway, the story takes some unexpected turns, and Guinevere isn't construed as the one who ruins the idyllic Camelot, as she is so often portrayed. There's lots of magic in this particular version." There was a twinkle in Sibyl's eye as she said, "Except in this story, she has some magic of her own."

CHAPTER 23

KACEY

T hree weeks later, Kacey stood in the posh Thompson Hotel in the Vinyl District, just off Sunset. The hotel had a very 50s vintage Hollywood feel, which made her think of Norma Jean again and how a girl like her would have become enamored with the glitz and glam of Hollywood, probably not very far removed from how Kacey herself was feeling at the moment. She thought it must be a sign that the Thompson was where they were staying, as if fate was telling her she was on her way to a stardom that even she couldn't anticipate.

She set Jareth down in his cat carrier as the bellhop wheeled her suitcase into the room from the hallway. Sibyl came into the room last, carrying a garment bag, which she draped across the couch. Kacey turned around and around as the bellhop took his leave. The yellow king-sized bed with white linens looked plush and relaxing, and the roomy studio featured a balcony with a little table and two chairs.

"Wow! I mean, I knew I'd insisted on some nice negotiations in your contract, but I seriously didn't expect them to splurge this much on your accommodations. It just goes to show you the quality of this film. This is going to be a blockbuster success, with buzz about it already. Quite a bit of the cast will be staying here for the next several weeks, so it'll be perfect for getting to know them, rehearsing lines, and such." Sibyl glanced out at the balcony and turned her blue eyes back to Kacey. "What a view. This is a beautiful room."

"It is. I should be very comfortable here. Thanks, Sibyl." Kacey took a deep breath. She had assumed she'd get a little trailer on some lot at the studio, not a beautiful room in a new hotel.

"Word is, David Fiore is staying at the hotel, too. Just thought I'd let you know." Sibyl gave her a sly smile.

Kacey pursed her lips. "Thanks for the warning."

"Oh, come on, Kacey. He isn't so bad. Yes, he came off troublesome at first, but surely anyone can have a bad first impression."

Kacey thought about meeting David in the library before he even knew she existed and how dismissive he was of her then. She shrugged. She wasn't ready to let him off the hook about his sudden infatuation with her, no matter how much he was changing her life for the better. The fact that she attributed his infatuation with gaining the diary didn't help. He'd have to show her a whole new side of himself before she forgave him for assuming she'd sleep with him the first night he took her out to eat.

"It all happened so fast." Kacey tucked a strand of her hair behind her ear.

Sibyl grinned. "It has, but you're going to do great tomorrow." She held up the garment bag and unzipped it. "I've got a little surprise for you. I've brought a few designer dresses and a beautiful pantsuit, and I've hired a photographer to do a photo session. The sweet pictures of you and Jareth on your social media are great, but you also need some professional photos, too. I'm telling you, it'll ratchet up your following to unbelievable heights."

Kacey knew nothing about marketing herself, but she trusted Sibyl to take good care of her. She'd already scored Kacey a commercial spot with a perfume company that she shot the week before, and Kacey was grateful for the paycheck.

As Sibyl pulled out the items of clothing, Kacey touched the fabrics. "These are beautiful. But when will I have a chance to do a photoshoot with all the film work I've got lined up?"

"The photographer is coming tomorrow, which is your day off. I've hired makeup and hair for the morning, too. I'd say starve yourself and hydrate, but you never gain an ounce, so I won't bother." Sibyl smiled.

Kacey knew the book had something to do with that because she'd always had trouble keeping the weight off before it'd landed in her hands. Over the past few weeks, she'd indulged in pizza, ice cream, and cinnamon rolls just about every morning (because why the hell not). She'd also been devouring her favorite chips, and chocolate, and she hadn't gained an ounce. It was truly amazing. Her eyes wandered to her bag, where the book was hidden. She ached to hold it suddenly, and she wished Sibyl was already out of her hair.

"I can't help feeling I'm in way over my head." Kacey unzipped the carrier, and Jareth poked his head up and looked around. He let out a low grumble and jumped out of the carrier, sniffed the couch she'd placed it on, and hopped through the hotel room, his tail straight up and twitching with curiosity. Kacey couldn't help noticing Sibyl stepping back. *She must not like cats,* Kacey thought.

"Anyone starting a new job feels that way." Sibyl watched as the cat disappeared into the bathroom and then said, "Something tells me you're the kind of person that catches on quickly. Don't worry. Besides, I've dealt with Hollywood plenty in the past, and I'll guide you." Sibyl gave her a wink.

Kacey had that feeling in the pit of her stomach, a buzzing that radiated to her head and left her a little lightheaded—the same feeling she'd had the morning of the shooting at the library. She couldn't shake the feeling that something bad was going to happen again, but he couldn't explain that to Sibyl. She'd sound like a lunatic. Maybe it was just a reaction to the trauma.

"Well, I guess this is home sweet home for the next few weeks, at least until we start filming on location." David told her when she read for the part that some scenes could be filmed in the studio, but that much of it would be filmed in the Scottish lowlands and in Wales. Kacey couldn't help the excitement of that prospect. She'd never been to either country, but her father had once told her much of his Wiltson family came from Wales.

She just had to make it through this first round of terror, er—filming, to get her chance to travel. And the travel would be worth every bit of the awkwardness of learning how to act.

In a major feature film.

With dozens of people way more experienced than her looking on.

While they filled her bank account with more money than she'd ever had access to.

Kacey gulped. She was lightheaded. Oh, what had she gotten herself into? She sunk into the couch near the balcony door.

Sibyl pulled up the planner on her iPad and read through the list she'd jotted down. "After our photo shoot, Mr. Fiore has requested that you attend sword and fight training. You're a little behind on that since most of the cast has already been trained. Here's your agenda for Monday," Sibyl continued while hardly taking a breath, "which I'll email to your phone: 6 a.m. costume fitting, 7 a.m. makeup and hair, 9 a.m. test shoot, noon lunch, and 1:30 p.m. to around 6 p.m. will be for filming, though the stage manager advised it might go longer depending on lots of different variables.

"The studio will bus the cast over Monday morning, so you won't be by yourself trying to find where everything is at the studio." Sibyl pulled out a printed map of the studio buildings. "But I've got you covered there, too. This is where you'll go first to get ready," she said, pointing. "Then, this is where they'll set up the test shoot that morning. I've got lots of media stuff to attend to, but I'll check in with you at lunch on your first day, okay?"

Kacey smiled weakly and nodded.

"It's going to be fine. The producer absolutely dotes on you, so you shouldn't have anything to worry about."

Kacey thought of the hungry way David Fiore looked at her every time he set eyes on her, and she thought she probably had plenty to worry about. Just then, Kacey's mood shifted, and she wished Sibyl would stay to give her someone to talk to. She was filled with nervous energy, but she didn't want to meet new people right now. "Won't you stay and hang out for a while tonight?" Kacey pleaded.

"Can't. I have lots to do." Sibyl turned, her long hair flowing behind her. "Besides, you need to get to know the cast members." She paused at the door as she tucked her iPad into her bag. "Get out of here and have a drink at the bar, go grab a bite to eat at that beautiful brasserie here in the hotel, or lounge around the rooftop pool. I assure you, wherever you choose to spend your time tonight, people will *flock* to you. Do get some rest for your photoshoot in the morning, though." Sibyl gave her a reassuring smile and went out the door.

Kacey knew Sibyl was right, but she lingered in her room for a while longer. She peered out the windows at her balcony. Maybe she'd hide out here tonight, read through her script, and get some extra rest for the big day tomorrow. She heard laughing and talking faintly from the hallway, and she wondered what the rest of the cast was doing tonight. They'd already had a week or two to get to know each other, and she felt like the odd one out. No acting experience, no training, and coming into the project late. They would probably all hate her. She sighed.

Except maybe not, now that she had her magical book. Attracting people had become so effortless. She'd never in her life been liked—much less adored—by so many people.

Kacey busied herself unpacking and putting away her clothes, setting up a dish of water for her cat, and making sure that there was a litter box in the bathroom as she'd requested. Jareth hopped onto her bed, sniffed at the coverlet, circled, and then curled into a ball to sleep. The room was cozy, but she already missed her little house in San Diego. Nothing interesting was ever going to happen to her there, though. And she couldn't hide out in this hotel room forever.

As she pulled the book out of her bag, she ran her hands over the red cover of the diary, and a jolt of confidence filled her, making her stand taller. She tucked the book safely into her room vault. She didn't own expensive jewelry, but this was more precious than any jewel, and she didn't plan on parting with it anytime soon.

Kacey ran a brush through her shiny hair and pulled it up into a high ponytail. She assessed her outfit, which was her favorite new pair of jeans and a yellow off-the-shoulder top, and grabbed her bag before heading out the door.

"Jareth?" While she was getting ready, the cat had disappeared, probably napping under the bed in the cool darkness. "See you later, kitty."

CHAPTER 24

KACEY

A man in his early to mid-twenties with a reddish beard and piercing green eyes stood in the hallway as if waiting for someone. As she walked by him, he grabbed Kacey by the arm and guided her toward the elevator. "*Dwt*, I thought I'd never get you alone for a minute!" He was tall and thin but surprisingly strong, and he wore a nondescript oatmeal-colored linen shirt over dark pants.

Kacey opened her mouth to respond, but the man shoved her into the elevator and let go of her arm. He hit the buttons on the panel behind him without looking. She took a few steps back as the doors slid closed, her mind frantic. Was this man abducting her? Why had he been looking for her? Who was he? Why did he have an accent? Where was he from? She had too many questions and couldn't seem to get even one out. "Wha-what—" she stammered as he turned to face her.

"You are one difficult person to pin down, Miss Wiltson. Always someone around these days. Let's see the book."

Kacey narrowed her eyes. Was he talking about her diary? "Excuse me?"

He turned his head, appraising her. "You look different this way. The book. I know you have it." His green eyes widened wildly. "You don't need all this. And you're in grave danger." His accent sounded like a song, as though he were simply singing a nursery rhyme, not telling her that something was wrong with her beloved book. The accent sounded like it was somewhere between British and Scottish, but neither was quite right. It differed slightly from both.

Kacey gulped, and her palms were sweaty. Who did this guy think he was? And how did he know anything about the book? Was the book his? That thought made her the most nervous of all. She played dumb because she had no intentions of giving it up.

"I don't know what you're talking about." She crossed her arms over her chest and clenched her jaw. "And I don't appreciate being manhandled." Kacey wondered if this guy was a stalker, and she worried that he might have a weapon. After the incident with Paul's wife, it was hard to trust any stranger who came up to her now. Her throat tightened, and her heart pounded at the thought.

"What is its significance to *you*? I've gotten desperate. Listen, *lush*, I shouldn't even be—"

The elevator doors slid open, and Kacey looked past the guy's shoulders to a person standing in the lobby. "Justin! What are you doing here?" Kacey rushed forward and pushed past the guy in the elevator, happy to see a familiar face—and relieved to no longer be alone with the strange guy.

Justin flashed her a look of surprise. "What are you doing in L.A.?" He gave her a quick hug and then stepped back, a warm smile on his face.

Justin's smile was a relief. She was afraid that he was still mad at her. When she heard the elevator door close, she glanced back and was relieved to see that the wiry guy with the red beard hadn't followed her out.

"I'm acting in this film, and uh..." She faltered, wondering if mentioning David Fiore would bring back memories of their last conversation. "Well, Fiore brought me into the project."

"The King Arthur retelling? So am I!" Justin laughed when Kacey's eyes widened. "Well, not acting. I've been hired by the writing team to make sure historical details are authentic and such. We're about to finish up the final details of the screenplay. I was just leaving a meeting and thought I'd go up to the bar and have a look around."

Kacey's heart leaped. Maybe she was getting a second chance to make things right with Justin. Fate had brought them together again. "Mind if I join you?"

"Not at all. It's good to see a familiar face in an unfamiliar city."

As they stepped into the elevator, Kacey wondered where the guy with the green eyes went. What if he'd gone to look for her book? With her palms sweating, she asked, "Mind if I stop back by my room first? I forgot something."

Justin shrugged. "Sure. The rest of my evening is pretty open. I'm in no hurry."

Kacey punched the button for her floor, and they stood in uncomfortable silence until the door reopened. She and Justin were still practically strangers themselves, but she hoped she could change that.

She exited the elevator and turned toward her room but stopped in her tracks. "Jareth!"

Her cat sat at the door as if patiently waiting for her to return. Had he slid past her legs when she left a few minutes ago? Maybe she hadn't seen him come out, what with the stranger pulling her into the elevator. Her heart pounded as she scooped Jareth into her arms. She frowned. What if the stranger had gotten into her room and let the cat out? An uneasy feeling settled into the pit of her stomach. At least Justin was with her. If the guy was in there, the two of them could surely deal with him. Her hands trembled as she pulled out her key card.

"Not sure why my cat's in the hallway," she said over her shoulder.

"He's beautiful," Justin said as he rubbed the cat's head.

Kacey stepped into the room and glanced quickly around. Nothing seemed to be out of place. She set Jareth down as Justin followed her inside. "Nice room," he said, walking over to look out the window at the balcony. "They're treating you actors well." He glanced back at her. "We're not staying in anything this nice."

Kacey shrugged. "One of the perks, I guess."

Justin nodded and turned back to the view.

Kacey checked her vault, which still contained her book. She heaved a sigh of relief. "Okay, everything's fine. I guess maybe housekeeping let Jareth out by mistake. Good thing I came back up. No telling how long he would've been out there. I'll make sure they don't do that again, right, Jareth?"

She bent down to pet him, but his tail twitched, indicating he was distracted. He padded over to the window beside Justin to watch a blackbird, which sat perched on a small tree in a pot outside. Its black eyes followed the cat's movement.

Kacey clapped her hands. "Let's go check out the hotel, shall we?"

Justin followed her out of the room, and she spied Jareth still at the window, intently staring at the bird that was now cleaning itself with its beak. She made sure her door shut and locked this time.

CHAPTER 25

SIBYL, 535 A.D.

Sibyl combed Guinevere's strawberry-blonde hair. "You know," she said to the queen, "I've seen Lancelot's adoring glances at you when he thinks no one is looking. He's quite handsome, isn't he? All muscles and dark eyes and seriousness."

Sibyl felt Guinevere stiffen. "I wouldn't know. My eyes are always on the king."

"Come now, Guinevere, it is only you and me here," Sibyl said as she ran the fingertips of her left hand delicately across Guinevere's scalp as she brushed with her other hand. "I've known you for a while now. I know you like no one else does. Maybe even better than you do. Did I not foretell that Arthur would fall in love with you and that you would be queen?"

Guinevere touched the red cover of the diary with the tips of her fingers as Sibyl combed her long, wavy locks. Her shoulders fell. "Yes. My life has certainly changed these last few years."

"Every knight of the Round Table fancies you, my dear. Even the married ones." Sibyl watched the queen in the mirror. A small smile teased the corners of Guinevere's lips. "It's the way it should be. No one wants a mean, ugly old queen."

No matter the age, people were as shallow as the pools of water along the River Usk.

"Lancelot fancies you the most, though. He adores Arthur, so he'd never ask anything of you, but he does need a favor. He'll go into battle soon. I've seen it in the waters." She gave Guinevere a concerned look in the mirror. "Can I send him a lock of your beautiful hair as a symbol of your appreciation for his devotion to Camelot? I know it would embolden him on the field."

Guinevere examined a piece of her hair that fell across her breast. She rubbed her fingers against the strawberry-blonde strands. "I'm not sure that would be proper." Concern washed over her pretty features, though she looked at Sibyl as though she hoped Sibyl could find some excuse for it.

Sibyl laid a reassuring hand on Guinevere's shoulder. "I would not tell a soul, and Sir Lancelot can be trusted to keep secrets. He's proven his devotion over and over."

"Do you really believe Sir Lancelot, the bravest of our knights, needs anything from me?"

Sibyl leaned in, whispering what she knew would affect the queen the most. "I fear that if you do not, he will not live to see another battle. I've seen... hints of his demise." That part was the truth, but it wasn't this battle that would kill Lancelot du Lac.

"Oh," Guinevere said as she covered her mouth with her hand, the same hand that had protectively held onto the crimson diary. Her countenance turned serious. "We must, then. Whatever it takes to save the brave knight's life."

Sibyl leaned back. "Very well, my queen. Your generous favor has saved a noble life." She tied a red ribbon around a piece of Guinevere's hair and snipped it off above the knot. She held up the lock of hair. "Sir Lancelot will be overjoyed to wear this under his armor near his heart." She placed the lock of hair at her own breast to hide it from sight.

Guinevere hummed to herself as she opened her diary. Sibyl noted it was the tune she'd danced with Lancelot just the night before at a feast Arthur had held for his brave knights. Sibyl's smile broadened. She bowed and left the lady's chamber as the lady's maid entered with a basin of warm water with fragrant yellow gorse blossoms floating in it.

Sibyl hurried down the corridors. Lancelot was already lovesick over the beautiful Guinevere. The book's spell was working its way throughout all of Camelot—but especially on those who were closest to her. Arthur had fallen in love with Guinevere well before she'd obtained the crimson diary, though. As far as Sibyl could tell, the only way the book wouldn't affect someone's devotion was if they'd already fallen in love with the person before the book worked its magic. The book created a kind of lusty obsession with the bearer, but it didn't affect true love, the kind that remained devoted beyond the effects of the magic from the book. The obsession, in contrast, tended to end poorly, usually with some demise.

As much as Guinevere loved Arthur, her lust for Lancelot du Lac would burn much fiercer. It would be easy to push her toward adultery, which would lead to the queen's death and the freedom of the book once more. Now, Sibyl's task would be to show Lancelot the possibilities of the desire that smoldered between them.

"Sibyl," a voice in the darkness called out. There was an edge of suspicion to it. Myrddin stepped from the shadows.

Sibyl's pulse quickened at the sound. She'd first met Myrddin before he helped Arthur claim his rightful place as Uther's successor. He was a talented seer, but he didn't have half the power of sight that Sibyl did. His prophecies were usually jumbled and vague, notions of futures possible instead of the lucid visions she pulled from the water. He was much stronger in other types of magic, though. She'd seen him use it a time or two when it was really needed.

She smiled at him as he neared. Myrddin was handsome with piercing green eyes that twinkled with mischief. They were the kind of green that startled a person. His beard had been fully gray when they'd first met, but it now looked reddish in tint, as though instead of turning gray, its color was returning to its youthful hue. The crinkles at the edges of his eyes were softening these days, too. He appeared to be in his fifties, but age meant nothing to people like them.

"Ah, good evening, my Lord," she said, looking up at him through her lashes. It had been a long while since any man made her heart flutter, but Myrddin had that effect on her. She rarely got the chance to be alone with him at court. She typically avoided it, if she were honest with herself. There was a pull that she couldn't deny, and it scared her a little. Though she had a very important errand to run, she couldn't help but spending a moment with him.

"Is it?" he asked. He stepped closer, his eyes dropping to the swell of her breasts.

Was Myrddin finally returning the affection she felt for him? She'd flirted with him at court, but he'd only shown her a reserved version of himself in front of others. Now, something dark clouded his eyes. Was it a deep, passionate lust that clouded his otherwise bright green eyes? It was as if he could see beyond the clothing that covered her, as if he'd peeled back the cloth with his eyes and saw her standing there naked. She could feel the heat rise to her skin as it flushed under his intense gaze.

Terror seized her. The lock of Guinevere's hair. Could he see it beneath her dress? Her hand went to the place she'd stowed it as if to cover it from his vision.

"What are you hiding, Sibyl?" He glanced back up at her eyes.

She laughed to obscure her surprise that he might know she'd hidden the lock of hair in her dress. "Well, if you'd really like to see what's under my dress, I'm sure we can find a nice little private alcove somewhere around here." Sibyl bit her lower lip seductively, knowing that Myrddin wouldn't be deterred by her playful advances. He was much too serious for casual sex.

"Don't play with me, seer." His voice was harsh, but his eyes reflected a tenderness that confused her.

Sibyl narrowed her eyes and dropped the smile. "You know as well as I do what is about to happen. Don't act like you don't. You can't stop it now. They're too far gone."

"It's never too late to change someone's fate."

"Is that what you told Vortigern? Or Uther when you assisted him in impregnating a married woman to sire Arthur?" Sibyl smirked at the twitch of Myrddin's eye. "At what point are you going to stop playing with kings and let their fates take them as it will?"

"And what are *you* playing at?" He'd thrown her own insult back at her. He circled her like a wolf, his eyes sharp, and she turned to follow his movements. "What is it that motivates you, Sibyl? All I know of you is that you are Guinevere's most trusted advisor and that you have no future that I can see, which must mean that you are a true oracle. Beyond that, I know nothing of where you came from or what you want here."

"The same as you—power. We're much the same. I have a different avenue for it, though."

"No, we're not the same, Sibyl, because I don't want power for myself. I never have. I've always built others up, those I see so much potential in. It's never for myself; it's for the people."

"So in putting these men in seats of authority, you gain nothing from it? Come now, Myrddin. I'm not an idiot. You prosper as the most revered prophetic advisor to the king. Your every curious whim is attended to."

On the kingdom's money, he'd traveled far and wide when the mood struck him, and he'd entertained some of the smartest theologians, academics, cartographers, and historians, sparing no expense to treat them to the most lavish meals and the best wine the castle could offer.

Sibyl was surprised to find that he'd backed her against a wall. His eyes narrowed as he placed a hand on the wall beside her head and looked down at her. His lips parted slightly, and she ached to touch them. He smelled of leather and fire and the faint scent of juniper. "*Dwt*, we are not the same." He didn't sound as sure when he said it this time. "My mother was a nun, taken by an incubus. My gifts were *not* chosen, but I chose to use them with integrity, unlike you. You are selfish, ambitious, and vain. That is a dangerous combination for a prophetess."

Sibyl recognized the stormy battle behind the twinkle of his eyes. Though he despised her, he also knew that she was one of the few people in the world who understood what life was like as a seer—lonely, sometimes confusing, and always frustrating. She ached to manipulate his hesitancy and convince him he needed to ravish her at the moment, but she had more important matters to attend to than the desire that they both felt for each other.

Sibyl broke eye contact as she swung out of his reach. "Well, this will be a matter we'll have to ruminate over another night. I have beauty sleep to get to. Unlike you, I'm not getting any younger."

She smiled when he cocked an eyebrow at the remark. Most others hadn't noticed the tiny changes over the years, but she had. Myrddin was growing younger instead of older. Yet another reason that anything between them would end up going nowhere. She had an eternity stretching before her, and he'd eventually become a child wizard. His curse was absurd.

Sibyl had seen what was coming for Arthur and his knights. She'd had plenty of time to study the waters as she bid her time with Guinevere. In the next year, a volcanic winter would envelop the land, darkening the skies, turning the sun blue, and bringing snow in summer. The prolonged frost and a drought would harden the apples and sour the grapes. Widespread famine would spread discontent throughout the kingdom. Another volcanic eruption a few years later would herald the death of Arthur and many of his noble knights. She hoped Myrddin wouldn't be stupid enough to stick around through it and get himself killed. Even he wasn't powerful enough to stop the horrors coming to Camelot.

Sibyl left Myrddin standing in the corridor watching her. She turned down another hallway as if headed toward her quarters, but she quickly took another hallway and headed down the staircase and out of the castle. She waved her fingers, and a heavy mist shrouded her as she moved through the darkness.

CHAPTER 26

SIBYL, 573 A.D.

Sibyl ran through the edge of the bog, hoping she didn't slip—or worse—end up in quicksand. Her boots did little to keep her feet from getting wet. The silly updo of the times was coming undone and obscuring her view more than if she'd let it fall naturally, as hair should be able to do. She missed the old days.

She almost laughed aloud at the thought as she swatted away grasses that were nearly as tall as her in this wild land. The old days. The really old days. It'd been almost two millennia since she'd made her bet with Apollo. She'd smiled as each grain of sand tumbled from her palm. Now, she frowned at the thought. Even thinking of Apollo made her heart ache with missing him. No one would ever replace him. A lump formed in her throat, but she pushed it away before melancholy could weigh down her shoulders and make her quest seem inconsequential. She trudged on, humming an ancient tune—one older than her.

Though the path was rough, she knew the way like the back of her hand since she'd come here many times over the past few decades after she finally found someone like herself, someone caught up in a life that lasted much longer than mere mortals. Catching the scent of wood burning and seeing the grove of apple trees ahead, she knew she was near his hut. She climbed up a craggy bank, and his home came into view. She let out a huff of relief.

A few weeks ago, as Sibyl looked into the waters of the river, she'd seen him covered in the blood of his countrymen and their opponents at the Battle of Arfderydd. War had broken out, and he was in the middle of it. He'd knelt there, surrounded by bodies and looking up at the sky, rays of light illuminating his bright green eyes.

She'd left immediately. Only, it had been too late for her to intervene with her magic. Too late to save him from the madness of war.

People called him a wild man, crazed and consumed by the occult, talking to animals and holed up in the hut like a hermit. A far cry from the revered seer, wizard, and advisor of King Arthur, as she'd known him before. She hoped it wasn't too late for him.

"Myrddin," she called out, making sure that he was aware of her presence. "Hello?"

A man with an auburn beard mixed with silver stuck his head out the door. He was tall and thin, and he munched on an apple. His appearance, one that flowed backward in time, but much slower than a mere mortal's age progressed, always startled her. He'd appeared older when they'd first met a half-century ago. There'd been more silver in his beard then, and the laugh lines at his eyes had been deeper. Though her unchanging youth probably startled him as well after all these years. They were both anomalies of time.

He narrowed his green eyes at her. "There you are, there you were, though where will you be?" As he rattled off his rhyme, his eyes roamed around as if he was confused. He took another bite of his apple, drops of juice dotting his beard as his teeth crunched the fruit.

A heavy dread settled into the pit of her stomach. So he'd gone mad after all. She'd asked about him in the nearby villages, and they'd warned her of the man they were calling Lailoken. Still, she'd hoped they were only rumors of an eccentric oracle. She pressed her eyes closed for a moment. When she opened them, he was staring at her thoughtfully.

"I can't see your future, Sibyl-seer. Can you see it, dear?"

"Myrddin, I'm sorry that I couldn't get to you in time. What happened out there?" She stepped closer but didn't touch him.

His words were like a sad ballad sung after a tragedy, the rhyme off-putting with a flat note of dismay. "The clouds opened. I saw God up there. He gave me visions of possible futures and laid eternity bare. A gold chariot pulled by ravens is how he crossed the sky, glowing gold like money in the sun, so bright it made me cry."

Sibyl's eyes widened. She'd never be able to see Myrddin's future, but she could see what was happening to him, that which could not be changed. She'd seen him kneeling on the battlefield, looking up at the sky and crying, his tears running rivers through the blood and mud covering his cheeks. But what she couldn't see in the vision was what he was looking at. And what he described certainly sounded a lot like Apollo. Her heart fluttered with hope, though she was wary of allowing it to blossom and grow. Hope was a dangerous thing. Still, was it possible? Maybe Apollo wasn't gone after all.

Myrddin frowned at her. "So much blood on you, too. Your hands are covered with it. Don't you ever think it should have been you?"

Sibyl feared he'd never forgive her. Though his rhymes sounded like child's play, there was a cutting edge to the words he chose. She'd finally made a real friend, maybe something more, and even in his madness, he dwelt on her misdeeds in Camelot.

"Yes, well," she said, looking down at her palms, "we all make our choices, don't we?" She picked at a dirty fingernail to avoid looking at him in the eye.

Myrddin tossed the apple core into the bushes, and a few chickens fluttered out, warbling either their surprise or their thanks. He turned his head a little to the side as if listening to them. "Yes, you're quite right," he said in their direction. "What a dismal sight."

Sibyl frowned. Was he talking to the birds or to her? He finally returned his gaze to her, his green eyes as bright as they'd been in Camelot. They still held the spark of danger and the sternness of a powerful wizard who had the Sight, but they also held the comfort of someone she'd come to know and love.

"Can I rest here a while, old friend? I've come a long way to see you."

Myrddin motioned for her to enter his hut, and Sibyl was glad to get out of the cold. Her feet were nearly frostbitten, and her fingers were numb. Though she might live ten thousand lifetimes, she could still be injured or fall ill. She sat by the fire, removed her boots, and set them on the hearth to dry. Then, she removed her stockings, hung them, and wiggled her toes near the flames. She sighed as the delicious heat returned feeling to her numb feet.

Sibyl glanced at Myrddin, who'd sat down at his desk to examine the maps and books he'd scattered across it. He looked as though he hadn't bathed in a while. His hair was wild and matted. He was thinner than normal. All the results of the terrors of war. Sibyl didn't know why he continued worrying about politics. It was a futile battle, she'd come to realize long ago. And this was the first time she'd ever known of him entering the battle as a soldier. He usually used his magic from the rear. She wanted to ask him why, but his incessant rhyming was grating on her nerves.

Carefully, Sibyl asked, "Tell me about the figure in the chariot?"

"The High or the Below, here or Witheryn, I know not where I belong in this damned reality that unfurls."

Would he only speak in riddles and rhymes in his madness? It was beyond frustrating.

"We're going to take a trip in the morning," she told him. "There's a magical waterfall a few days south of here. We'll leave tomorrow and acquire horses and food for our journey." He ignored her as he scribbled on paper. "I can't leave you like this, Myrddin. You think me a monster, but I do have a heart."

Myrddin hummed to himself for a moment. "A heart as black as obsidian stone," he sang, "is a heart all the same. Hard and dark and all alone with no one but yourself to blame."

CHAPTER 27

SIBYL, 573 A.D.

Sibyl glanced back at the cloaked figure riding on the horse behind her. He sat with his eyes skyward, murmuring who knows what in sing-song rhymes. The hood of his cloak had fallen from his head, and his reddish hair looked crimson in the gloom of the early morning dawn. Her poor Myrddin was so sick, and it pained her to see him this way.

She looked down to ensure that she had secured the lead rope of his horse to hers. Then, she proceeded up the dirt path through the woods, searching the road for the great black-leafed tree where they would veer off the trail and into the forest—the home of the magical waters. She hoped it wasn't too late for him, that he wasn't too far gone. Sibyl spied its dark leaves amidst the bright green a kilometer ahead.

"Almost there. Brace yourself for the rough terrain ahead," she called.

"Over and under, and through the wood, none of this matters, for 'tis all that I could, and now I cannot, no, never can I, for all is out, and so is the eye."

Sibyl shook her head. His ramblings were getting worse. He was stark-raving mad and with centuries, or maybe a millennium, ahead of him. What kind of life would that be if she couldn't cure him? She set her teeth and prodded her horse forward. This had to work.

Sibyl turned her horse toward the tree, and the mare resisted for a moment. Horses can sense magic, and this was a doorway to a very magical place. If not for the persuasive braid of Helen's hair plaited into hers at the nape of her neck, the horse might have never turned into the wood. She patted the horse's neck before prodding her forward, and under the great, reaching limbs of the dark tree, they trekked into the forest toward the Waterfall of Hollow Tears.

The terrain was rough, and they made slow progress. Sibyl looked back every so often to make sure Myrddin hadn't fallen off his horse, but mentally, she was preparing for what lay ahead. She whispered her own prayers, and she enveloped them in mists to protect them from the wraiths that inhabited this land. The moans of the wraiths echoed through the dark forest. They gave her goosebumps and even hushed the mad mumblings of Myrddin.

Sibyl could smell the magic of this forest. It was heavy like incense and bonfire smoke and ocean water all mixed together. Despite her cloak, a cold settled into her bones, and apprehension and foreboding filled her, the body's natural instinct urging her to run away from powerful magic.

They veered to the right, around a great stone that jutted from the earth in the hooked shape of an eagle's beak. Sibyl spotted the rowan tree she was searching for. The waterfall would be just up ahead. The red berries of the rowan were purple on this special tree, and the fruit hung heavy and plump. She dismounted and tied her horse to a tree close by, and she had Myrddin do the same.

His eyes looked about wildly as though he was only now realizing that they were in the middle of the magical forest. "Oh, me. What strange things there be," he whispered.

"Come, friend. I've brought you to this place to make you better." She grasped his arm and urged him toward the rowan tree. She pulled the purple berries from a low-hanging branch and held them up. "Eat up. It'll make things much easier." She put the berries to his mouth, and he accepted them.

His eyebrows shot up at their sweetly delicious fruit, and he grabbed a handful more and popped them into his mouth, purple juice dribbling down his red beard.

"Good," she encouraged him as he chewed and swallowed the magical fruit. His eyes grew heavy almost instantly, and she knew that she'd need to get him to the Waterfall of Hollow Tears quickly, or she'd end up having to carry him. "Let's go." She led him forward through the protective mists surrounding them.

"Oh, what do I see?" he asked as they neared the basin of the waterfall. Its waters were multicolored, like a flowing rainbow. His head lolled back as he looked up at the tree branches above them, caught up in whatever hallucinations the berries had given him. The hallucinations would save him from the anguish and pain he was about to endure in the Waterfall of Hollow Tears. Not only did the waters envelop you in the miseries of all your regrets and fear, but Sibyl was going to have to drown him.

The colorful waters sang out like a chorus of heavenly beings at first, beckoning them to come near, enticing them, each gurgle a promise and the rising vapors a gentle caress on flushed skin. Even though Sibyl had her own control over water, her power was put to the test as she resisted the urge to jump in with abandon.

She turned to Myrddin, who'd knelt and was intently studying tiny purple flowers at the edge of the rocks on which they stood. "It's time."

Myrddin looked up, and his face softened. "You are stunning. I've always thought so. Yet, there's something in your eyes that always makes me say 'no.'"

"Listen to the water. Come for a dip." She tugged at his hand to pull him up, and then, with all her strength, she hurled them both into the pool at the bottom of the waterfall.

The cold water pulled them down as she held onto him. Suddenly, Apollo appeared to her, all golden and beautiful. Then, it was Cleopatra, crying in her temple. Helen. Dido. So many others in between whose lives she'd ruined. Sibyl screamed into the water to escape the visions of regret. Because she did feel regret, no matter how driven she was with desire for the book and for power.

Myrddin fought against her, but the hallucinogenic berries weakened him. She had to bring him to the brink of death, to make him face his fears and his regrets before he could heal. She felt his warmth against her as visions of the future flooded her mind.

Sibyl was lying in bed with him entwined in her legs. Myrddin was screaming at her. Sibyl stood at the ocean with a short sword pointed at her own chest, but try as she might, she couldn't bring herself to drive it into her broken heart.

Her eyes shot open, and she kicked upward, bringing Myrddin with her. She had no sense of time, of how long they'd been under. She pulled him out of the water, which was no easy feat. His clothes were saturated. He lay lifeless and pale across the stones. Her heart was heavy, but it beat wildly at the prospect of losing him.

"Myrddin," she said, stroking his face. She lowered her mouth to his, touching her lips to his, something she'd thought about from the time she'd first met him in Guinevere and Arthur's court. Summoning all of her power over water, she sucked the water from his lungs in a sudden whoosh that she blew out of her mouth like smoke. When she stopped coughing up the water, she watched his lifeless form. She lay her head on his chest and cried, "I'm so sorry, Myrddin. I tried. I wanted so badly to save you."

CHAPTER 28

SIBYL, 573 A.D.

Tears filled her eyes as Sibyl turned away from Myrddin's pale face. He looked at peace, at least. That might give her a small measure of consolation in the years to come.

She fluttered her fingers in a circular motion, and the water weighing down her clothes lifted from the fibers into a great ball of writing water. And she hurled it back toward the waterfall with more force than she meant to use, where it crashed in a splendid splash. Her mouth was a hard line. She was angry. At herself. At magic. At Myrddin for losing his mind and abandoning her. There were so very few people she liked in all the time she'd lived on this Earth. Myrddin had been one of them.

Suddenly, she didn't care if the wraiths heard her. She screamed out her frustration like a petulant child with her hands fisted at her sides. She screamed again, the force of it shaking her body until she had nothing left. Her shoulders slumped, and she closed her eyes. She needed a moment. Just a moment to grieve and to suffer through the pain.

Then, she'd head back to the convent where Guinevere had locked herself away after her infidelity with Lancelot du Lac years before. Guinevere's self-exile came after Arthur condemned her to die—but before Lancelot and Arthur fell on the battlefield. Nearly a lifetime ago for regular mortals, but to Sibyl, it was as if very little time had passed.

The book had given Guinevere enough influence to keep her head, but she'd never used the crimson diary as it was intended, locked away as she was with the holy sisters. Guinevere didn't deserve the book, and Sibyl intended to be there with her hands upon it when Guinevere finally passed away of old age, as the waters had revealed to Sibyl.

A sound behind her made Sibyl freeze in place. It reminded her of meat sizzling over a fire or the last wheeze of a dying person. Whatever it was, it made the hair on the back of her neck stand on end. She carefully turned her head toward it, her body taut with apprehension.

"God's blood!" Myrddin croaked. "What are you going on about with all that screaming?" He held his hand to his chest, and he winced as he tried to sit up.

Sibyl ran to him and threw herself on him with a hug. "I thought you were dead." She kissed his forehead, which felt warm. "I'm truly thankful I didn't kill you in the water."

"Ha, I'm cursed, woman. I can't die that easily. It was just a rough bath, right?" He raised up on one elbow to look at her as she sat back on her heels beside him. "Do you think I'm so filthy that you needed to drown me?" His green eyes crinkled at the edges as he teased her.

His teasing alone gave her reassurance that he was back to his old self, and she smiled. "Your brain was filthy."

"Aye, it's been filthy all my life," he joked and gave a hearty laugh.

Sibyl put her palm against his temple. "You were very ill, so I had to clean your mind of the madness," Sibyl explained with gravity.

"I suspected, though I don't remember you coming for me. I don't even know where we are," he said, looking around.

"We're at the Waterfall of Hollow Tears."

Myrddin frowned. "Those are dire measures. You could have lost yourself in there. And here, I thought you only helped yourself, not other people." Though it sounded like another joke, there was an edge of condemnation in his words. He'd said similar things to her before, namely when she stood by Guinevere's side through the queen's adulterous affair that stripped her of her crown. As far as Sibyl knew, though, he'd never learned of the book or just how big a part she played in making the affair possible.

"What kind of thanks is that?" She crossed her arms. Joking or not, his words hurt. "I saved you from centuries of suffering."

He scratched at his beard. "Not one, I suppose. Water under the bridge. I apologize. And I do truly thank you for saving me from the madness."

Sibyl stood and held out her hand to help him up. He rose and fell forward into her. His arms went around her so suddenly that her mouth fell open in surprise.

"You know, Sibyl," he said into her hair, "we're two of a kind. Both living out long, lonely lives with powers others only dream of." His eyes softened as he looked down at her, the water still dripping from his red beard. "Whatever has you always running off after Guinevere, you could just leave it alone. She isn't coming out of the convent. She'll die there."

"I know. I've seen." She swallowed hard. Was he offering her something here? It sure seemed like it. And her heart ached at the hope of it, which she tried to ignore. Myrddin was more than a friend. They'd shared a bed together once, and it had been a memorable experience. Was he wanting more from her now?

"Is that why you came for me?" he asked with a hint of a smile.

Yet, she had to put herself in check. She was forgetting herself, something easy to do with a handsome magician whispering into her ear. She'd hardened her heart toward love long ago. Love ruined women. She'd seen it time and again. Though she'd allowed herself to melt into him for a moment, she pulled herself back.

He seemed to notice her shift under him, and he held her tighter as if trying not to let her go. "Come back to the cottage with me."

Sibyl shook her head. "No." She'd seen what that future would bring. The waterfall had given her that. And it would destroy her. Maybe the both of them. She couldn't. Tears filled her eyes again, and she swallowed the lump in her throat. "I have other plans for my life."

Myrddin released her. "Of course you do," he said with disappointment. He turned away from her.

This is for the best, she thought. No matter how much it hurt them now, it would save them from the misery that would come from their being together.

Their horses were still tied to the trees where they'd left them hidden among the dense fog, though both were touchy and visibly spooked. Myrddin spoke softly to his horse in a murmur Sibyl couldn't hear as he rubbed the horse's crest and shoulder.

Sibyl's horse was jumpy, and the mare pranced and shied at her touch.

Myrddin mounted his horse. "Until we meet again, then." He turned back before the fog enveloped him and said, "By the way, if you want to find me again, ask for Merlin. A new lease on life calls for a new name, and it's time mine's changed." He gave her a wistful look. "Though I think I'll keep Wyllt as a surname. It can't hurt these days to be seen as a bit wild, right?"

He kicked at his horse, disappearing into the surrounding mist.

"Goodbye, wild man," Sibyl whispered as the fog swirled.

CHAPTER 29

SIBYL, 573 A.D.

Now that Sibyl had taken care of the most pressing matter, attending to Myrddin's—er, Merlin's mental state, she resolved to seek out a man she hadn't spoken to in quite some time. She would return to Guinevere as quickly as she was able, but she had more pressing matters at the moment. When Merlin had revealed what he'd seen on the battlefield, the thing that had driven him mad, Sibyl couldn't help wondering about Apollo. And as they'd traveled to the waterfall, it had dawned on her who she needed to question about it.

Lugh had been called by many names, but he was another of the Mágos, favored by his foster father, Manannán mac Lir, one of the Mágos of the sea. To Sibyl, she'd first known Lugh as Mercury. His powers revolved around light and the sun, though he was also a gifted magical weapon creator. She'd heard that Lugh had become a sort of Mágos guide to the afterlife, though she didn't exactly know how that worked. He could be a trickster, one to be avoided if possible, and she wanted nothing to do with him. He hadn't been kind to others, at times. Yet, if he knew what had happened to Apollo, she'd chance it and go see him.

It took her less than a day to travel to Ireland. That was one perk of being able to manipulate water, which she was becoming more and more powerful over. As she arrived in Ninch, an ancient town on the eastern side of Ireland, a heavy fog shrouded the buildings and the hills. Sibyl spent a few days traveling around the countryside and asking about him. The people here were distrustful of her, as they were of most foreigners, and because she didn't know the land well, her powers of sight weren't very helpful.

On a grassy hillside, she found his faithful wolfhound Failinis. The dog's big brown eyes peered at her from the morning mist, glowing yellow in the predawn darkness, and he panted in the cold morning air as if he'd run far and fast to meet her. It looked like he was grinning at her with each foggy exhalation.

"Good morning, Failinis," she said as she held out her hand for the dog to sniff. "Where is your master?"

Far away from any town, Failinis brought her to a little thatched cottage with a smithy behind it. Failinis guided her to the smithy, a wooden structure with a large fireplace where she could see Lugh hammering out a sword, the blade glowing orange in the dim light beneath the building as sparks flew from it with each solid hit. The wolfhound lay down at his master's feet and closed his eyes.

"Hello, old fellow," Sibyl called out as she neared.

Lugh grunted but continued pounding at the sword, ignoring her as he finished his work. She didn't mind because she was curious about the place Lugh called home. She looked around, admiring the beautiful countryside as the morning sun lifted the dense fog. There was no greener land than that of Ireland.

"What are you here for?" Lugh finally turned his eyes upon her, and their amber color almost glowed in the dark under the smithy.

"Merlin told me he saw a golden chariot in the sky pulled by ravens above the Battle of Arfderydd. It sounded like Apollo. Do you know anything about that? Apollo had been glowing when I saw him last, and he talked of Ascension."

"Belenus, Apollo, Grannus, or whatever you want to call him, has been gone for over a hundred and fifty years. Why are you looking for him, prophetess?"

Sibyl's shoulders slumped. "I just wanted to know what happened to him. Did he return from the High? Could he have?"

"Doubt it. Those who Ascend typically don't care what happens down here anymore in this forsaken land."

"But—"

"Look here, I took him myself to the High. It's part of my job here and in the After. I help the Mágos Ascend. And it's heaps better than this place. I can't think of anything, or anyone, to make him come back." With this comment, he looked her up and down.

His words stung her harder than he probably meant for them to. Or maybe Lugh was cruel. So many of the Mágos were.

"He's gone, little Sibyl. Forget him."

Tears stung her eyes, but she refused to let them fall while Lugh's luminescent gaze still rested on her face. She turned and looked into the water, where he cooled his blades. Sibyl gripped the stones so hard that her knuckles turned white. When he looked away from her, she allowed two tears to drop into the water. Ripples from the tears turned to swirls and then to colors until she could see scenes before her eyes.

In the vision, Lugh held a shortsword with golden accents inlaid in the blade and a beautiful hilt of gold, citrine, and steel. Sibyl gasped. She'd seen that sword before in the vision at the waterfall—the one of her and Merlin by the sea. She'd held it at her breast, the blade pointed at her heart. In this vision, the fog swirled around their legs at the edge of a calm body of water. Then, it was a tossing sea behind them.

And in this vision, Lugh handed her the blade. Then, he thrust it into her.

CHAPTER 30

SIBYL, NOW

W hen Sibyl rounded the corner to enter the upstairs lounge, she paused in her tracks. Kacey was with some guy Sibyl didn't know. Was he a member of the media? Was the little mousy Keeper actually having a conversation with someone in the news?

Her eyebrows shot up in surprise. She'd put in a call earlier, but she hadn't expected a reporter to show up this quickly.

Sibyl took a step back so Kacey wouldn't notice her watching them. She couldn't get a good look at his face, but she assessed his outfit. He didn't look like a reporter. For one thing, he wasn't carrying a camera, and he was better dressed than the typical entertainment photogs she'd come across in the business. Most of them looked sloppy these days. And the way he sat close to Kacey made Sibyl think that there was some kind of intimacy between them.

Was shy little Kacey already getting involved with someone? A smile spread across her face. She could use this against the naïve woman. A good love triangle could crush a person. She'd seen plenty of that in the past.

When she saw the actual reporter coming, pulling his camera from beneath a jacket, Sibyl grinned even bigger and left the lounge. Let the media get a hold of that—their beloved Kacey having drinks with someone other than the dashing womanizer, David Fiore. Sibyl's work was done for the day.

As she wandered the halls of the big hotel, Sibyl wondered what else she could get into. She'd booked a studio room in the Thompson, near David's room. She only stayed in the best, and the few studio rooms were immaculate. But as comfortable as her room was, she didn't feel like sleeping or being lazy. One would think that with a near eternity yawning before her, Sibyl could take the time to relax, but it just wasn't her personality. She was itching to go out and live a little. She spent far too much of her life running after the book and doing the bidding of the Keepers to get as close to her enemies as she could.

California was one of her favorite places on Earth. The people were so vain and cutthroat around L.A. It suited her. She'd spent a lot of time here over the last century. The people hadn't changed, but the media had. Sometimes, she missed the days when indiscretions could go mostly unnoticed, but she'd also learned to use the media to her advantage when needed. It was a powerful tool and had knocked down several Keepers so far.

Sibyl made her way to the front lobby and asked the concierge at the desk to call her a cab. She wanted to spend a little more time at the beach before she left for the chilly, overcast clime of the moors of Wales and Scotland next week. Tomorrow would be a full day with Kacey's photo shoot and lining up some sponsorships for her. Besides, Sibyl needed to consult the waters about Kacey and this new man, and the ocean always gave her better visions than any other body of water, probably because of her link to Poseidon, though he seemed to be long gone with most of the rest of the "gods" of antiquity. She wondered if he'd Ascended as she assumed Apollo had.

Thinking of Apollo put her into a foul mood. She got up from the chair she'd been waiting in and wandered out the front door into the evening twilight. Of course, the street was so lit up with artificial lighting that it was almost as bright as day.

Someone exited the hotel behind her, and when she turned to look, a man with reddish hair had turned his back to her and was walking away. She cocked her head to the side. A familiarity tugged at the edges of her mind. Then, the cab pulled up to the curb, and she shook off the feeling.

"Santa Monica Pier," she said to the cab driver as she settled into the seat. The cab driver turned right onto Santa Monica Blvd. "Take North Highland. It'll be quicker." As the lights blurred past her window, she closed her eyes. The next few weeks would be critical if Sibyl wanted to get Kacey into the predicaments that she knew could end the Keeper's miserable existence and free the book from being bound to her.

Her only other option, one she didn't even want to consider because it was too dangerous for herself, was a weapon that could kill even a Mágos. And if it could kill a Mágos, surely she could wield it against someone given power by a magical artifact. Sibyl shook her head as icy dread filled her at the thought of its existence. Though she'd been unable to destroy it, she'd vowed to never unseal the weapon. She could get rid of this Keeper some other way.

CHAPTER 31

KACEY

J ustin smiled as he brought Kacey her drink to the table where
she sat, looking out at the city lights as the day faded to orange
and red across the sky. They had a spectacular view from the bar
at the top of the Thompson Hotel. She could learn to love a view
like this.

He set down the two red cocktails in martini glasses. "I thought it was fitting that we have a King Arthur. I have no idea what it'll taste like." His eyes laughed as he grinned at her.

"It looks pretty, at least." She took a sip and tasted cranberry and a lot of vodka. "Not bad. I definitely couldn't drink many of these, though."

Justin took a sip and gave a face. "I think he would've preferred mead."

"Yes, I feel like we should be drinking from big, carved beer steins or something," she said and laughed. "Though you'd have to pick me up off the floor if I drank a huge mug of this stuff. Probably if it was filled with mead, too."

Her alcohol tolerance was decently high, considering she drank wine often, but she had her limits. She took another sip. The taste was growing on her. And the pleasant warmth that flowed down her chest was satisfying, like a warm hug. She relaxed a little.

"So tell me how you got involved with the film. I still can't believe you're here," she said.

"Well," Justin said as he twirled the skinny stem of the glass between his index finger and thumb, "I finished up grad school and graduated a few weeks ago. My research position was up, and I had no prospects for a career move. I honestly didn't know what I was going to do. So, in my job search, I came across an ad for a historical accuracy consultant for a film." He glanced up at her. "I thought, 'Why not?' I wasn't doing anything else with my degree. To my surprise, it was a film being produced and directed by David Fiore. So here I am.

"Actually, the writers want me to also travel once the project goes overseas to make sure the costuming and props and everything are true to history. So, this is turning into a much better gig than I originally thought. The production company is paying me a good bit of money to consult," he said.

"Wow! That's wonderful!" And that meant she'd get much more time with Justin this way. "And you'll get to see more of the world, too. That's part of the reason I took this opportunity." She took another sip of her drink.

"Well, it won't last, but you have to take opportunities where they present themselves, right?"

"Yes, exactly. After the shooting—"

"Right, I saw that on TV," he interrupted with concern creasing his brow. He leaned in as if his closeness might console her.

Kacey shook her head. "I couldn't go back there. It was a turning point for me."

"The guy—Paul something—they said he survived it, though."

"Thankfully," she nodded. She swallowed hard. It was still difficult to talk about. How would Justin look at her if he knew that the whole thing was over her? "I just hope he and his wife are okay now. For their children," she added in a quiet voice. She wanted to drop the subject. She'd tried not to think much about that day. "Anyway, it's wonderful having you here—" A camera flash distracted Kacey.

When she glanced in its direction, she found a photographer taking pictures of her and Justin as the bar attendant came around the bar, yelling at the man. "Hey, dude, we don't do that in here." The two argued loudly.

Kacey ducked her head and smiled sheepishly at Justin, who was staring wide-eyed at the photographer like a deer caught in headlights. "Sorry about that. Maybe we should take our drinks outside by the pool? We can let the staff handle that."

"Okay," he agreed. Justin picked up his drink and hers, and he followed her.

They stepped into the balmy afternoon. The sounds of the city below, punctuated by a horn beep or rev of an engine occasionally, mixed with the sounds of hotel guests swimming in the pool and calming instrumental music floating from hidden speakers around the pool.

"This is beautiful!" Kacey exclaimed. "I can see why Sibyl wants me to have a photoshoot up here this weekend."

Justin appraised her as they sat down at a table far away from the bar area. "You seem to have really taken to this kind of life. You fit here."

Kacey suddenly felt very self-conscious. The large green leaves of potted banana trees shaded them from the sunset's last rays. "Do I? I don't feel like I do." She pulled at her top. "It's probably the clothes. Sibyl picked them out for me." Not to mention how much the book had changed her overnight. But she couldn't explain that to him. She didn't want him to look at her again like he'd looked at her that day in the coffee shop when she'd shown him the pages of it, which had all appeared blank to him. That look of wariness and confusion he'd given her still haunted her. "Sometimes, I think about how utterly forgettable I was as a librarian, and all of this seems like a dream."

"I never thought you were forgettable, Kacey."

His words made her blush. She took a sip of the King Arthur to hide her smile. "Well, I've had no formal acting training, and I'm sure I'll feel like a sham in front of the camera."

"All you can do is your best."

"Oh, there you are!" a demure voice from behind Kacey said.

Kacey turned to find a tall brunette wearing sunglasses that covered half her face and completely obscured her eyes. She pulled a chair to their table and sat.

"Allison. Everyone calls me Allie, though." She stuck out her hand to shake Kacey's. "Nice to meet you, Kacey. I've heard so much about you."

Kacey swallowed, the rising fear . This must be one of the other actresses. "Nice to meet you. This is Justin. He's on the project as a consultant."

"For historical accuracy," Justin added as he shook Allie's outstretched hand.

Allie turned back to Kacey. When she pulled her sunglasses up and rested them atop her head, Kacey saw Allie had piercing blue eyes, almost the color of a cloudless day—not quite gray, but almost. "I'm cast as Morgan le Fay, enchantress extraordinaire. My word, you are as beautiful as they're saying."

Kacey tucked a strand of hair behind her ear and avoided Justin's eyes. "Who's 'they'?"

"Everyone. The media. The celeb magazines and news stories. The rest of the cast. Even our director bragged about what a beauty he'd found. And they aren't lying. Don't look so humble," Allie teased as she gave Kacey a wide smile.

Kacey found it hard to swallow, and she avoided Justin's gaze even harder. "Oh, but can she act? *That* should be the question."

"Movie magic, darling. Even if you're not very good, it can make you look great." Allie squeezed Kacey's hand as if they were old friends. "Though I bet you *will* be great, so don't worry."

Kacey glanced at Justin, who also gave her a reassuring smile. It was almost as hard to embrace the confidence others saw in her as much as it was to accept the beauty the book had given to her. Maybe things were going to be okay. Maybe, just maybe, her new life could be something great.

CHAPTER 32

SIBYL, NOW

S ibyl stepped into the Ferris wheel car on Santa Monica Pier and sat as the attendant snapped her in. As she inched upward into the sky, she watched as, one by one, each seat accepted its riders, usually couples. She'd never ridden the Ferris wheel with someone she loved, or not in the romantic sense, anyway. Besides, she'd only loved three men in her long lifetime. She'd found it rare, but the love between women can be stronger than the love between man and woman when sex isn't an influencing factor, and losing that female bond can be just as devastating.

As Sibyl inched up higher and saw the lights of Santa Monica and L.A. beyond to her left and the Pacific Ocean to her right, she remembered the first time she'd ridden a Ferris wheel. It was 1898 in Vienna, Austria. The Ferris wheel had just been built, the tallest in the world at the time, for Franz Joseph's Golden Jubilee, the celebration which marked the fiftieth year of his reign. Sisi had already been assassinated on a trip to Lake Geneva the prior year, and Sibyl rode it in memory of her dear friend. Sisi would have loved the adrenaline rush of soaring high above the city. That's what Sibyl dwelled upon as she swallowed her fears in the wheel car high above Vienna so many years ago. And as she closed her eyes on the Ferris wheel on Santa Monica Pier in the present, she imagined her best friend there beside her, the warm, salty ocean air tousling their hair as they laughed and joked like old times. Sometimes, you welcome the ghosts that haunt you.

Sisi had been the closest thing she'd ever had to a best friend. No, she was more like a sister. They'd had an unbreakable bond. If anyone was worthy of the diary, Sibyl was sure it would have been Sisi. And Sisi had held it in her possession for a time. She could have done great things with the power the book gave her. However, it wasn't meant to be.

Emperor Franz Joseph of Austria fell in love with the lively fifteen-year-old Elisabeth, better known as Sisi, in 1853. And it was the book's fault that she loved no one to the extent that she was loved. Though she had three children by the time she was twenty-one, she wasn't the doting mother type, nor did she enjoy the constraints of being Empress of Austria and Queen of Hungary, always under the thumb of the Emperor and caged by the expectations of the court. The crimson diary didn't always bring happiness to its Keepers.

Sibyl met Sisi when the free-spirited Empress traveled to the Greek island of Corfu in the Ionian Sea. She was as good a horsewoman as Sibyl, and they became fast friends. Sisi already had the crimson diary, and Sibyl kept her eye on it as she tutored Sisi in the Greek language. Their friendship was so close that they sailed the seas together and even got matching anchor tattoos on their shoulders. They would always have the freedom of the ocean. Its wild waves and wide-open spaces anchored them in a way that nothing else could. Sisi said it was spiritual, and Sibyl agreed.

Sibyl never wanted nor needed to get the book from Sisi. From the moment Sibyl met her, Sisi's world was crumbling by her own hand. Some women can thrive, at least for a time, with attention, riches, and power. Sibyl had seen that over and over again in women like Cleopatra. Some cannot. Sisi was the type that found the lifestyle too difficult. Too constraining. She was a sad bird in a gilded cage.

Not that Sibyl blamed her. Ruling under a patriarchy, or sharing power with anyone, wasn't something Sibyl would do herself. When Sibyl began her reign over the Earth, she most certainly would not have a man by her side.

Year after year, Sisi grew older while Sibyl did not, and Sisi noticed. She was vain, especially about her weight and appearance, so she wouldn't allow anyone to paint her portrait after she turned forty. She hid behind veils and fans if she left her room so people couldn't see her aging visage. The book allowed her to age beautifully, but Sisi's confidence in her own beauty faltered. Even the smallest of changes in her looks made Sisi uneasy. Their friendship, it seemed, was taking its toll on Sisi, though the book made her irresistible and beautiful even as she aged. And her aging friend brought Sibyl back to the reality that any kind of relationship with mere mortals was fleeting at best.

Sibyl didn't know how she would have reacted to aging had she been a mere mortal, like Sisi. Maybe Sibyl would have been the same as Sisi as she aged—doing everything in her power to stop its toll on her body. After all, she'd asked Apollo for many lifetimes. Aging was such a strange idea to Sibyl now. She felt as young as the woman who sat in the sand beside Apollo over three thousand years ago. If that much time could pass without a person feeling old inside, no matter what happened outwardly, then imagine how a woman must feel as short decades swiftly turn them into old women with gray hair, wrinkles, and sagging, atrophied muscles. Even the book couldn't stop that. Old age eventually crept up on everyone.

Well, not me, Sibyl thought. But as Apollo promised, it eventually would. That would be quite a few millennia away, but she'd turn old and gray, too. And instead of growing old for a short time, she would be old for a very long time. She shuddered at the thought.

The only death she'd ever witnessed of herself in her own visions was the one she'd seen in the vision under the Waterfall of Hollow Tears. And that sword was buried and lost to anyone who might wield it against her.

The screams of glee from the rollercoaster beneath the Ferris wheel pulled her from her memories. These thoughts had thrown Sibyl into a sour mood, despite the bright flashing lights of the rides, the smells of delicious food, and the sound of the waves hitting the beach and pier. Why had she held onto so many memories from her long life when so many were filled with regret and sorrow? She supposed it was part of her humanity, what was left of it. People naturally dwelled on the past as they aged, and she was no different. Her past was so much more vast than a normal person's was, though.

She looked out at the ocean as the Ferris wheel slowed to let passengers off. She knew she needed to feel ocean water on her skin soon. And she needed to see, to deep dive into her powerful sight. She wouldn't waste away decades on this newest Keeper, and she needed to know how Kacey would die.

CHAPTER 33

KACEY

After spending the evening meeting and chatting with a few other cast members, Justin walked Kacey back to her room. They paused outside the door as she unlocked it.

"I better be getting back to my hotel," Justin said. "I've got some things to look over tonight."

"Okay, thanks for having a few drinks with me," she said as she pushed against the handle and opened the door a bit. "It helped take away some of my nerves." She smiled.

Justin paused, and her heart hammered in her chest as she wondered if he was going to ask to come in. He swiped his hand through his hair. "After your photoshoot tomorrow, can I take you out for a meal?" He looked down. "I mean, on an actual, proper *date*?" He stressed the last word as if he was unsure that he should use the word.

The fact that he'd just asked her on a date instead of assuming she'd invite him into her room was enough for her to fall utterly and hopelessly in love with him. Justin was one of the good ones, and she felt lucky to have met him and even luckier that he wanted to spend more time with her. But she pulled herself back from those feelings because feelings like that had only left her a sobbing, depressed mess of a woman in the past. When he glanced back up at her shyly, Kacey allowed herself to smile, despite her reservations. "That would be nice. You have my number."

Justin nodded and turned toward the elevator. "Goodnight, Kacey," he said before stepping away.

Hope had persistence, and it bubbled back up almost as fast as she'd squashed it. Kacey allowed herself to grin as soon as he disappeared, though she suppressed the squeal bubbling up in her chest.

Kacey pushed open the door to her dim room, only lit by the lamp by her bed. She saw Jareth's tail curling out from behind the curtain. It disappeared, and a dark shadow rose higher and higher until it was the size of a person. Kacey opened her mouth to scream when a man stepped out from behind the curtain. It was the same man from the elevator earlier. It surprised her so much that the scream caught in her throat.

"Don't scream." His voice was quiet but firm.

Kacey took a step back, her heart pounding. "Why shouldn't I?"

"I'm here to help you," he said with that same foreign lilt from earlier.

"Help me? By removing my skin? Taking my eyeballs as trophies?"

"I'm no killer, *beaut*. And you have a vivid imagination," he said with a smile.

Her fear was entertaining him, Kacey realized. His smile seemed to belittle her, which made her even more furious and defensive. "I watch horror movies," Kacey said. "I know how these things go. How did you get in my room?"

"You let me in," he replied.

"No, I most certainly did not," she said. "I think I need to call security." She pulled her phone from her pocket.

"Please," he said as he held up his hands. "Talk to me first. I have no weapons, and I'll keep my distance. Just a conversation, okay?"

Kacey sighed, and against her better judgment, she put her phone away. She pointed to a chair. "Have a seat there." He sat down, and she remained close to the door.

"Let's start over," he said. "Sometimes, I forget how much I know and how very little you know." When he saw her frown, he lifted a hand and said quickly, "No, don't take that the wrong way, Kacey. Where do I start?" He folded his hands in his lap, and his eyes took on a faraway look. "I'm your cat. Er—I mean to say, your cat is me. Well, what I mean is, Jareth is a form of me."

Kacey blinked, confused by his train of thought. "Uh—a what? Come again?"

"Your *cat*. And I resent being named Jareth, by the way. He was a Goblin King. His magic was parlor tricks. His real power came from intimidating others. Couldn't you have picked a better character's name?"

"It came from one of my favorite movies, okay?" Kacey closed her eyes and pressed two fingers to her temple. She was getting a headache. She was obviously dealing with a crazy person.

"That's lush, that is, but I still don't like being named after such a *twp*. Have you ever heard of shifters?"

Kacey shrugged. "Sure, I've read fantasy." She gave him a smug smile. "Even Jareth was a shifter in the Labyrinth movie." When he scowled back, she shrugged. "He's the owl. But shifter stuff is fiction."

"No. It isn't as common as writers would have you think, but it's a very real thing."

Kacey put her hand on her hip and narrowed her eyes. "If you're my cat, why are you just now revealing yourself?"

"That's a complicated question. When I found you, I didn't know if I'd need to reveal myself at all. I rather like being in cat form, actually. I mean, I get to sleep all day, be petted and cared for, and don't have to make meaningless conversation."

Kacey laughed. "Yeah, I guess. If you don't like Jareth, what do you call yourself?"

"What does it matter? A name is a name. All these people, all throughout time, are connected in so many ways through shared history. You think of them as one name, but they have many. Take, for instance, the Greek gods. Romans gave them different names. Heroes and demigods are no different. They're called by different names according to the group of people they came into contact with at a given point in history. They were no more a god that I am. Just magical. Like me, you see?"

She shook her head. She didn't see. He wasn't making much sense at all.

"Just call me Lin." He waved his hand in the air as if annoyed with this line of conversation. "Never mind names right now." He leaned forward. "My visions were coming true. Then, Sibyl arrived, and I knew you were in dire danger. I came to protect you, *dwtty*. When I saw you and when I saw what was coming, I *had* to do something."

"What's coming?" she asked dully.

Lin said in a singsong voice, "I saw you in a dream, your skin so pale and cold, I saw you covered in water, ne'er to grow old." His eyes had that spacey quality about them again. He seemed to snap back, to refocus on her. "It's the red book. I saw the changes, I did. And I saw what could be."

He continued without giving her a chance to explain.

"When Sibyl came 'round, I knew that it was no good. But she's been with you virtually every day since, and I haven't had a chance to reveal myself. She can't know about me, Kacey. Trust me in that. It would be bad for us both. Besides, I needed to see exactly what she was up to and to figure out how I needed to get things sorted, and well, I didn't know how you'd react to the fact that your pet is really a man."

"Ha! Tell me about it." Kacey frowned. Was she really considering this as the truth? Maybe she'd had one too many King Arthur cocktails. "What has she got to do with any of this?"

"Sibyl is bad news. Sibyl is... evil—as close to evil as ever I've seen."

Kacey thought of her new friend. Nothing indicated Sibyl was evil or even ill-meaning toward her. She'd done nothing but help Kacey from the moment they'd met. Kacey shook her head. None of this made sense. "No, I—" she stammered, terrified that this fellow was going to hurt her if she said the wrong thing.

"Look, I'll show you." Lin twirled his fingers, and wispy smoke gathered around him.

How is he doing that? she wondered. She stepped forward to get a better look. He was apparently a magician. What was he using to create the smoke, though? She moved her head to the side to see if Lin concealed anything in his palm.

"That's a good trick," she said, "but—"

"No trick, my dear Kacey." The smoke coalesced into a dark matter. It became shiny and bulbous. It stretched and widened until it was a gaping hole hanging in the air. Kacey took a step back from it. It stretched and yawned open like a black mouth, and Kacey covered her own mouth with her hand, terrified of what she was seeing. She glanced at Lin, who gave her a leer before he pushed her in.

CHAPTER 34

KACEY

K acey fell. It was that heart-jumping, weightless tumble that she sometimes felt right as she was drifting off to sleep and starting to dream, only to find herself startled in bed instead of falling. Except in place of the relief of it ending quickly with waking, the bottomless feeling continued until a bright white light blinded her so much that her eyes hurt, and she shielded her face as she found the solid ground beneath her. She let out an 'oomph' as she landed, and her right hip ached from the jolt.

She was lying in a grove of trees with thick brambles that created a wall around a space about fifty feet wide. The light was strange here. It glowed a hazy orange like a sunset during a storm. The scent of juniper berries hung heavy in the air. In the middle of the space was a green book laid open on a black marble dais. Green vines snaked up the dais as if they were trying to reach the book.

Lin appeared over her and reached down to help her up. He had a strong, sure grip and pulled her easily to her feet. There was a sparkle of mischief in his eyes, and Kacey thought she saw a smile at the corners of his mouth.

"Where are we? And why did you push me?" she asked. Kacey gave him her best accusatory face. If he thought this was the way to get her to trust him, he was wrong.

"This, dear Kacey, is Witheryn. Well, my piece of it. I created this little space with magic to protect that book." He pointed toward the book.

She moved toward the green book on the dais. The pages were old. They looked like they might crumble in her fingers if she touched them, so she didn't. The writing was nothing like she'd ever seen before. It had intricate symbols instead of letters in a green ink that looked iridescent. They moved on the page, and her eyes widened as they rearranged.

"Oh, don't try reading it. It's written in my own language. When you're as old as I am, you have to keep a catalog of spells, people, events, and so on. Creating a language was the best way I knew to protect the knowledge of the book. The Viridian Journal, made from the Round Table of old, is for me."

He waved his hand, and the book slammed shut, with a shimmer of magic floating up from its pages like sparkling dust flying.

"If I didn't bring you here, if I didn't show you that true magic exists, I'm afraid you'd have never believed me. Or not until it was too late, at least."

"Who *are* you?"

"Lin Wiltson."

Kacey's mouth fell open, and her eyes widened. "Wiltson?" Was this man part of her family? She'd never known another Wiltson in all her life other than her own parents and her grandfather.

"Do you know how few Wiltsons are in the world, Kacey?"

"Um, no." Once, Kacey had made a friend at school with the Wilson surname, and she'd asked her dad if she might be kin to the girl. There were lots of Wilsons, but her father had been adamant that their Wiltson family wasn't connected to them. He'd never elaborated on their genealogy, though. He'd only told her that Wiltson was a Welsh name.

"Five people—four in the United States and one in Europe. It comes from my name. Wyllt. It's a very old name."

"But I thought you just said your name was Wiltson. Which is it?"

"It is Wiltson *now*. It *was* Wyllt for a time." Lin spoke to her as though he were trying to explain surnames to a child.

Kacey pressed her fingers against her eyelids. This man never made sense. "Didn't you tell me that names don't really matter?"

"They don't, but they *are* a clue to history, and that's what I'm trying to get you to see," he explained.

"So you want me to understand history?" she asked.

"What's Sibyl's last name?" Lin asked.

There he goes, switching gears again, she thought. "Uh, Marlowe, I think."

"Correct. She never changed it after her marriage. To one Christopher Marlowe." He paused as if for dramatic effect. "Have you heard of him?"

"It seems like an innocuous enough name," she said with a shrug.

"Not familiar, though?" Lin raised an eyebrow. "Come now, you're a librarian."

"Well, I mean, there was the famous Elizabethan-era playwright, but—"

Lin nodded. "Yes, him."

Kacey snorted laughter. "Okay, and you're George Washington."

"No, though I did meet him once."

Kacey's eyes widened. *Magical or not, this guy has mental problems.* She grimaced and took a step back.

"Sibyl is older than I am, and I'm pretty damn old. I age backward, you see, but she ages very slowly. She'll probably outlive me. She told me once that it was a deal she'd made with Apollo, though I'm not sure I believe that. I never met him specifically."

Kacey gave him an incredulous look but kept silent. He spoke as indifferently about historical figures and mythological gods as she did about current politicians or actors.

"Anyway, back to Kit Marlowe. That's what people called Christopher. The two of them fell in love while Sibyl was in the employ of Queen Elizabeth I. She swore she'd never fall in love with another man after Apollo Ascended, but Kit had a particular hold on her. When I say she was madly in love with him, that's exactly what I mean. It wasn't hyperbolic.

"Their marriage was secret. He saw to that. He was a spy, but she didn't know it. She was blind when it came to Kit. She truly believed he loved her, and maybe Kit did. He even wrote of Sibyl the famous line, 'O, thou art fairer than the evening air clad in the beauty of a thousand stars.' It was a perfect description of how wonderful Sibyl could be when she desired to be so."

There was a hint of regret in his eyes that he couldn't hide from Kacey. She knew regret when she saw it.

"But more important to him than matters of the heart was getting the throne away from the Protestant monarchy. Marlowe was paid well by Lady Arbella Stuart for information," he continued. "She was the niece of Mary, Queen of Scots, who was Catholic, and Lady Arbella was the cousin of James VI of Scotland, who became James I of England much later. Things came to a head when Queen Elizabeth didn't want to award Kit Marlowe a degree from Cambridge because she knew he was involved in espionage. Then, Sibyl found out about his dealings with the Stuarts.

"Here's where the plot thickens. He faked his death in a bar fight in Deptford in 1593, I believe it was. Sibyl thought he was dead, and when she realized he was still alive and well in Wales a few years later, she got him drunk and stabbed him to death outside a tavern. I know because I was there that night, though she never saw me. I've never witnessed so much savage anger in a woman. It was definitely a crime of passion, but I know now that she'd cut the throat of anyone who crosses her, if given half the chance."

Lin sighed. He looked sad.

"You may think you know your new friend, but you don't. She has a sordid past, a long and terrible one that even I don't know the half of. I thought I knew her heart once before she betrayed me. She's ruthless, and you're in grave danger."

Kacey swallowed hard. She had a terrible feeling in the pit of her stomach. So Sibyl was immortal? And a ruthless killer? "Why are you telling me all this? All this history, all these stories? What does my life have to do with the dealings of kings and queens?"

"The women she befriends always have terrible fates. I know she has something to do with their demise, but I'm not sure what. I've never been able to figure it out. It's like... she sees to it that they rise to great power before they are ruined. Is it a game to her? Is she that cruel?" He shook his head. "I just don't know. And I can't *see*." He looked at her. "But you're special, Kacey. You are *my* descendant, and you have something all those other women didn't have."

"What's that?"

Lin smiled. "Magic."

CHAPTER 35

SIBYL, NOW

T he ride on the Ferris wheel was ending too slowly, and
Sibyl grumbled with impatience. She glanced below her car.
Though she was high up, she wasn't all the way at the top. She saw
the attendant far below, letting the riders out of their car before
moving the wheel forward to let the next car stop at the bottom.

Sibyl raised a hand and summoned all of her focus on turning into a mist that floated up and out of the car and down toward the Pacific Ocean.

She swept down and soon stood on the beach at the shoreline. It was quiet and dark here, away from the frenetic energy of the Santa Monica Pier. The sound of the waves hitting the beach calmed her momentary frustration, and the salty air cleared her mind of the cobwebs of memories.

Sibyl raised her hands and blew a thick fog with her mouth that shrouded her from curious eyes that might look on. When it was so thick that she could only see a few feet in front of her, she knelt in the wet sand. She grabbed two handfuls and crushed them in her palms as the next wave slid up the sand toward her, crashed into her feet, and stole the sand from her hands before sliding back into the ocean.

"Oh, water, hear me now," she said as she slipped out of her sandals and waded into the cool water that lapped at her feet. "Give me the visions I seek. Show me the trajectory of one life and how it will end. Reveal what you will."

She was up to her knees now. Her skirt floated on top of the water, and with each wave that rolled in, it swept behind her before returning to her legs again as the water went back out. When the seafoam reached her waist, she closed her eyes and concentrated all of her energy on Kacey Wiltson, the newest Keeper. The sound of the ocean ceased, the smell of the saltwater disappeared, the chill of the water against her warm body diminished, and she found the visions.

Scattered scenes of sword-fighting, magic, and Kacey on horseback, her hair flying with the wind, swam in Sibyl's vision. The young man Kacey had been having a drink with earlier red-faced and screaming, David Fiore screaming, too, papers flying, and a man in a green cloak with green eyes who turned from her. It was only the eyes she could see of him now as he watched. Fire leaped up, smoke swirled, and the wind scattered ashes, which turned into tiny yellow butterflies. The green eyes again, glowing in the darkness. Sibyl felt an overwhelming sense of being seen, of being found out and known, and it pulled her from her visions.

She sputtered as she resurfaced and dragged herself from the water to sit on the beach to think about what she'd seen. Her visions hadn't been clear at all. She frowned. It might take multiple tries to get a lucid vision about Kacey, but she'd been sure that the ocean would have given her more than the fragmented scenes she'd conjured tonight. And those eyes. She couldn't make sense of that. An icy dread filled her, and she wrapped her arms around herself as she watched the waves move in and out under the cold starlight.

Her oracle powers weren't set in stone, unfortunately. That would be too easy. Magic always had its drawbacks. However, it showed her the current trajectory of things, and her visions gave her at least hints that whatever was to come would have to do with the King Arthur movie Kacey was about to work on. And the two men she'd intended to put up against each other were already in place. But the green eyes...they haunted her.

CHAPTER 36

KACEY

"Magic?" Kacey repeated. She thought of the crimson diary still locked away in her hotel room and wondered if that was the magic Lin sensed in her. It pulled on her, even here in—*where did he say they were? Witheryn?*—was so strong, and she longed to be back in her room in the hotel and nearer to it.

"Yes," Lin said. "I was married once. We had a child but kept it a secret from those who would do me harm. That child inherited some of my magical powers but not the curse that I live with. On and on down the line, generation after generation, each child in the Wyllt family has been granted some form of magic. And now you have it within you. I've watched you for a while. You see, before I came to you in my cat form, I watched you from afar."

Great, she thought. *I have a magical stalker. One who can open portals, too, apparently. That can't be good.*

"You're my kin, Kacey. I care about what happens to you. And,"—he looked down and back up through his lashes at her almost timidly, though she thought there was nothing timid about the man who stood before her—"I've seen visions where you were in trouble. Sibyl was always in them, too. So I sought you out, became your cat, and waited for her to show up in your life."

"But what magic do I possess? I can't do anything special."

"Oh, on the contrary, you have powerful magic. Have you never noticed how so easily people seem to forget you?"

Kacey scrunched up her nose as she thought about the boyfriends who'd stopped calling or the friends who would ignore her almost as soon as they showed any interest in being her friend. Even Paul at the library would forget she was on the shift with him. She'd spent her whole life feeling invisible.

"Well, yeah, I'm forgettable, but I thought that's because I'm a boring person." She looked down at her feet. She'd never felt like enough. Even her parents ignored her most of the time.

"You're not boring. You have the power of imperceptibility. When things get tough or uncomfortable, you make people forget you. I think you've probably been doing it all your life without even realizing it, but it's truly a unique gift. I've only seen a few people with that particular power throughout the ages."

Kacey thought back to those times. Maybe she had unconsciously wanted people to forget about her. That was a weird revelation, and she couldn't quite process it yet. She had a flashback of her parents leaving her at Disneyland. It had been fun at first, but as a seven-year-old, she'd quickly become terrified. Had she made them leave her there? Had she really created her own loneliness throughout her life? She shook her head. "I don't see what's so great about it," she mumbled.

"It's defensive magic," Lin said, as if that explained everything.

"Okay, have you got anything else? Because if that's my only magic, then I'd be useless in a comic book movie. Things get tough, and I what—think really hard about being forgotten and just walk away from the fight? That's lame."

Lin gave a hearty laugh. "It isn't lame. It's bloody brilliant."

"Does my dad also have magic, then?"

"Possibly. He may have it and not realize it, like you. Or it could have skipped him. That happens." Lin eyed her warily. "You also have a power that I gave you directly, though you've never used it before. I can sense it in you, though. It is a magic you'll have to develop over time. It doesn't come naturally like imperceptibility because it's offensive instead of defensive. We are naturally defensive, but we have to practice our offensive skills to develop them." He picked up a stick lying in the grass. "Make this a bunny."

Kacey laughed. "You may be a magician, but I'm not."

"Concentrate. This is a bunny. Imagine its soft fur, pink nose, and floppy ears. Its warmth, the gentle tremble in your arms, the animal smell. Got it in your head?"

When she nodded, imagining the bunny she'd had as a child, Lin suddenly hurled the stick at her.

"Ah!" she said and flinched as a brown bunny with a white streak across its head landed in her arms. She widened her eyes in wonder as she pulled the animal close to her. It looked exactly like Cocoa, her bunny, when she was ten. But Cocoa had died long ago. "How did you do that? How did you know what Cocoa looked like?"

Lin stood there with his hands in the pockets of his trousers. "I didn't do that. You did."

Kacey had done nothing other than focus really hard on the stick and imagine the bunny she remembered from her childhood. Surely, this was another magic trick. Lin had to be messing with her. "So, are we the only magical people?"

"No, there's been lots of us through the ages—the gods and demigods of myths, those heroes who seem too extraordinary to be normal people, powerful prophets and seers, like Sibyl."

"Sibyl can see the future?"

"Yes, and more than that. She has her own bit of magical powers. And those of us who are magical are called the Mágos. Think of us as a different kind of being with different rules. Take our afterlife, for example. It isn't the same as humans'. Some day, you'll either Ascend to The High and join the Effulgent, or Descend to the bowels of The Below and waste away with the Gloomeer. I've seen the shining glory of the Effulgent with my own eyes on the battlefield. It drove me mad for a time. It was too much for my mind to comprehend."

As he talked, Kacey petted the bunny's head, but she suddenly held a stick again. She looked down, baffled.

"If you don't concentrate, it won't stay as you imagine it," Lin said. "It takes a lot of mental power to warp reality."

"Oh," she said, feeling foolish for holding the stick lovingly in her arms. She dropped it to the ground.

"And you'll need it if you end up fighting Sibyl, which I believe you will. I see images of the future, but unlike Sibyl, my visions are less vivid and more symbolic."

"What did you see when you had a vision of Sibyl and me?" she asked.

Lin sighed. "There was a wall of water and glowing red words in the air. Crows, too, but that might be for me. I'm fascinated by them." He blinked and looked at her. "You two were fighting each other."

"Who won?" Kacey asked.

Lin shrugged. "That's to be determined. The reason I'm telling you about any of that, dear Kacey, is that I hope you'll use your magic to benefit others, not just yourself. What we do to others creates ripples. I need you to understand that before I tell you about your other powers."

"What if I make her forget me?"

"That won't work for long. She'd come back. Now that you have the book in your possession, I'm afraid there's no getting rid of her."

Kacey's eyes widened. With all this talk of magic, she guessed he *did* know about the book.

"Sibyl doesn't know it, but I've been watching her throughout time concerning that book. If it ever becomes hers, we're all in grave danger. But this is the first time in history that the book has chosen a Mágos Keeper, and with your powers, well, I'll be frank with you. You're just as dangerous as she is. Or potentially. I fear the book has chosen you precisely because you are my descendent, though I have no proof of how sentient it is. Will you use the power it gives you for good or for evil?"

"For good, of course," Kacey said.

Lin shrugged as if he wasn't so sure. "I've witnessed a lot of good people do terrible things for a myriad of reasons." He picked up the stick. "This is child's play. You have one of the rarest, most powerful, and most dangerous powers at your command, though it takes some practice and some getting used to. Reality warping is something I didn't even know I possessed until I was locked away for a time. Until then, I only thought I had the power to shapeshift. But learning to manipulate reality is how I'm able to come to this place," he said with a motion to the little enclave of the forest they were standing within.

"Locked away?"

"Sibyl, again." He frowned. He gave her a sour look as though it was a story he didn't want to relive.

CHAPTER 37

SIBYL, 1152 A.D.

S ibyl followed Eleanor and the other ladies-in-waiting through the market square in Rouen, France. She looked toward where the new Cathédrale Notre-Dame de Rouen was being erected. They'd recently traveled from Poitiers, where Eleanor was almost kidnapped and forced into marriage by Theobald

V, Count of Blois, and Geoffrey, Count of Nantes. The book's influence on the lovely Eleanor was growing, as was the desire for Eleanor's lands, and men were flocking to the newly available queen after her annulment from King Louis VII. When Eleanor requested the marriage of the younger Henry II, Duke of Normandy, he came running. Eleanor wanted to find a present for her new love, and Rouen had exquisite gifts that would impress her betrothed.

Sibyl stood in the market beside a booth selling onyx jewelry. She touched a gold and onyx ring engraved with a waterfall.

"Sibyl? Is that you?"

Sibyl turned toward the voice with a familiar lilt and timbre. She narrowed her eyes as she cut them toward Eleanor and the other ladies in the market. They were busy looking at the fine jewelry and art, but she couldn't tell if they were listening.

"Nay, sir. 'Tis Lady Vivien of Calais," she said for the benefit of the surrounding women, but by the curve of one side of his mouth, Sibyl knew Merlin recognized her. How could he not? Other than the fashions of the times, she'd changed very little since he'd seen her last. He, however, had grown a good bit younger and now appeared to be in his late 30s. His hair was fiery red, and his eyes were bright and as green as the moss on a tree.

"My apologies. I thought you were an old acquaintance of mine." He bowed slightly and kept walking.

It was hard to watch him go. She wanted to catch up with him and find out what he'd been up to all these years since their time in Camelot together. Perhaps another time.

The next day, a letter arrived from Merlin, signed by Lord Wyllt, asking to call on Lady Vivien. Sibyl smiled. She, of course, replied at once, almost giddy, wondering what her old friend had been up to over the past six hundred years. Had it really been that long? It was strange to think that it had been six centuries.

Sibyl dressed in a blue floor-length tunic over her linen chemise with intricate silver detailing around the sleeves. She wore a long white belt with silver tassels cinched at her waist.

Instead of asking him into the chateau, she asked him to meet her in the gardens, where they could talk in private. Nosey eyes and ears didn't need to witness their conversation.

As they walked side-by-side among the hedges and rose bushes, Sibyl asked, "How have I not run into you in all these years?" She assessed his appearance. He differed greatly from the wild man of the forest as she'd last seen him. Merlin wore a rolled-brim hat and a green tunic with wide crimson-colored cuffs over dark green leggings. He looked very much the 12th century European gentleman.

"I've spent quite a few centuries in the pursuit of arcane knowledge, spiritual enlightenment, and... celibacy."

Sibyl stopped in her tracks, but Merlin kept walking. "You've become a monk then?" She raised an eyebrow. "I thought there was a special twinkle in your eye," she teased as she caught back up with him.

Merlin smiled. "It's called clarity. You'd be surprised what it clears from your brain."

"I'll take your word for it." She raised her cheeks toward a break in the clouds and let the morning sun warm her face. "Lord Wyllt, why did you call on me?"

"When I saw you in the market, I realized how much I missed your teasing." Merlin looked back toward the dark windows of the chateau and the dark gray clouds beyond its roof. "You know, they're calling you the Lady of the Lake these days."

"Is that so? So the legends persist," Sibyl said. "Well, I think the Lady of the River would be more appropriate around here. It's where I see my best visions." She wrinkled her nose. "The lakes around the city aren't very clean. Anyway, the river is connected to the sea, which is where my best sight comes from." She knew she was rambling, but it was easier than talking about the hard things she knew were coming.

"Why do you surround yourself with these political fools? Didn't we learn that it all falls apart, even the most honorable of hearts, back in Camelot?"

Sibyl gave him an amused look. "What else would I do with my time? I'm not going to sit in some cave and practice magic by myself and talk to the birds. I'm certainly not going to ignore the yearnings of my youthful body. That's a fool's way to live when you have virtually forever stretching before you." Sibyl shrugged. "I'm having fun. I'm enjoying all that life has to offer. You run away from it now, all because your beloved Arthur disappointed you hundreds of years ago. How can you still be so concerned with one man's life?"

"How can you not be? He had all the potential in the world, and his heart was righteous. Arthur believed that mankind should not be oppressed by those wielding magic. He loved his kingdom, probably even more than I can understand. Besides, he was your friend once upon a time. Does life mean so little to you?"

"It costs too much to have such an honorable heart," Sibyl said.

"Maybe try it sometime, Sibyl. Being honorable might surprise you." When she scoffed at his comment, he grew serious. "I helped turn the tide when the Spartans stood up to the Persians at Thermopylae, even before my influence over Arthur. I know you cannot understand, and it's something I cannot fully explain to you, but it was my mission to affect certain events throughout history."

Merlin looked so distraught, so miserable, that her resolve softened, and Sibyl caressed her cheek. "I know you believe that, though I wish you didn't," she said.

Merlin seemed to be holding back a tumult of emotions. "I wish it weren't so."

Sibyl dropped her hand and picked a lily from the garden. "Pretend for a while, then. Spend some time here and have a little fun. Forget whatever mission you have, and enjoy life a little."

"I'm a bit wayward with my mission presently," he said.

Sibyl eyed him suspiciously. "Was it fate that you were in Rouen, or did you come looking for me?"

"I've been following you for a little while, after I heard stories floating throughout Europe of the wise woman of the waters. I owe you my life, Sibyl, Nimue, Vivien, or whatever you're called around here. I'd still be stark-raving mad and roaming around the forests of Wales talking to squirrels if not for you."

They were now walking down a path flanked on each side by a line of European Beech trees that were vibrant green but would soon turn flaming orange.

"When I sided with Guinevere through her betrayal of Arthur, you could have had me thrown in prison or killed. You were mad enough to kill me yourself, and you easily could have. You spared me then, and I repaid the debt."

Merlin stopped her as he placed his hands just above her elbows and turned her toward him. "Ah, why must you always bring everything down to its most basic construct? It isn't that simple at all. Can the heart beating within your breast no longer love? Can it not feel the pull we have toward each other, Sibyl?"

A tear rolled down her cheek, the bit of water she didn't have the strength to control as she stood in front of the man she felt more for than any man since Apollo. She refused to show him any other indication of emotion.

Merlin pulled her to him and kissed the tear from her cheek. "Don't cry. I cannot bear it."

"I've seen. And it won't end well," Sibyl whispered.

"You know as well as I do that our visions are what might be, what the course of fate the current path takes, but futures aren't set in stone. They change as the course of a ship changes on the ocean—a storm here, a navigational detour there." He'd moved his hands up to her shoulders like he wanted to shake some sense into her, but he held her there as though she might run away instead. "Surely, you, of all people, know how changeable water is. Let me be your storm. Some things are worth fighting for, aren't they?"

Sibyl's heart raced with the intensity of feeling in Merlin's words. She knew he meant them. Of his sincerity, she had no doubt. It was her own heart she didn't trust. "I have a path, as you say, that I must travel," she whispered, "and you aren't on it." If she repeated it enough, she'd come to believe it.

"Aye, you've said that before, but with much more resolution that I hear in your voice now."

"Eleanor will soon be Queen, though, and we'll leave this place. She has future kings to bear and people to rule. She'll do a lot of good with the power she's gained after so much scandal in the arms of King Louis VII. That should set you at ease."

"She doesn't need you right now. Take a little side quest with me." He waved a hand over her face, and her eyelids fell. The last thing she remembered was falling into his arms.

CHAPTER 38

SIBYL, 1152 A.D.

The sound of the ocean reached her ears. It called to her in its
comforting, familiar way. For a moment, not only did she
not know where she was but *when* she was. Then, it came back to
her. Eleanor now had her book. Yet, Rouen wasn't on the ocean.
The chateau wasn't even on the River Seine.

Her eyes shot open, and she sat up despite the grogginess of being under a spell. Sibyl knew that Merlin had used magic on her. As she looked down at the white bed gown she wore, one sleeve falling off her shoulder and down her arm, she touched her hair, which he'd plaited before laying her down to rest. She could smell the ocean from the breeze at the window by the bed and could hear the seagulls searching for breakfast in the hazy dawn. Sibyl felt more rested than she had in a long time. She heard Merlin humming to himself as he cooked breakfast. He had his back to her in the one-room cottage.

Merlin glanced at her rising form. "I hope you like goose eggs," he said.

She swung her legs off the side of the bed as she sat up, but her head was swimmy. "That was some powerful magic you hit me with," she accused.

"I also have some honey and butter you can have on bread if you'd like," he said.

"Merlin," she said. Sibyl stood tentatively, shaking off the magic and finding her footing. She took a few steps toward him and toward the warmth of the fire in the hearth. The smell of wood burning was sweet, and her stomach grumbled with hunger. "Did you put a sleeping spell on me?"

He turned his green eyes to her with a look of amusement. "Well, you didn't appear asleep. You should have heard the talking you did back at the house. In fact, you told them I was your cousin, and you and I were going on a trip over some family affairs. You were very genuine and so very sad to leave so suddenly."

"Oh!" she said with vehemence as she raised a hand to slap him.

Merlin grabbed her hand as it swept through the air toward him and deposited something into the palm of the hand he restrained.

"What's this?" she asked as she opened her palm to reveal the little onyx and gold ring with the waterfall engraving that she'd been looking at in the market a few days ago.

"A peace offering. A reminder that you once saved my life. Does it mean so little to you now?" A twinkle of amusement brightened his eyes.

He was in much too good of a mood for having stolen her away without her consent. "Of course not, but I have things to—"

Merlin cut off her words with a passionate kiss that bent her backward with force and hunger. Sibyl didn't pull away. She reveled in his warmth, his smell, and his taste as she reached her fingers up into his red hair. He was the first to pull away from the kiss.

"I'm sorry I had to trick you to bring you here, but I knew you wouldn't come on your own, and I wanted a little time away with you. I didn't want to have to call you Vivien or pretend to be a cousin."

Sibyl slipped the ring on her finger and buried her fingers in the curls at the nape of his neck again. "I don't like it when you use your magic on me." She pouted.

"It was just a little reality manipulation." There was humor in the twinkle of his green eyes.

Sibyl stared at him. Did Merlin even realize how powerful he'd grown over the centuries? Did he understand the possibilities of manipulating reality? "I thought you'd given all that up after you allowed Uther Pendragon to transform into his enemy Gorlois so that he could sleep with the man's wife, Lady Igraine. Nothing good comes from trying to change reality." *I should know,* she thought. *I've tried it time and time again, to no avail. All it ever gives me is heartache.*

As if reading her mind, he said, "You know, you never have to go back there if you don't want to. As I had to learn, kings and queens will get along just fine without us. Wouldn't you like to live inconspicuously by the sea in a little cottage like this one and let the years pass us by?"

Us. "That's not my dream. That's yours." Even as she said it, though, the thought of existing without some driven purpose teased at her heart. It would be so easy to let all her cares go for a while and just exist with Merlin, to lie in his arms as the moon and sun took turns in the sky while they listened to the ancient melodies of the ocean against the shore.

"Well, maybe I won't let you go," Merlin said. He said it with gravity, but his piercing green eyes softened as he looked deep into hers. "Maybe I'll keep you here forever and love you so much that you'll never want to leave. Maybe you'll lose all sense of time and place until none of it matters except for what's between the two of us."

Sibyl could have melted into him. In fact, her body tried to, but her head pulled her back from it. "Are you using your magic on me right now?" she asked with suspicion.

"No, love. The warm fuzzies you feel inside are natural and healthy stirrings. Let it thaw that cold, fearless heart of yours," he murmured into her hair.

As frustrated with him as she was, she *did* want to bathe in his warmth, in his love. And why shouldn't she? She'd been falling in love with Merlin—and denying it—for centuries.

So for a time, that's what she did. Living together in a little cottage by the sea, they talked, laughed, walked hand in hand along the cliffs, and let time slip away. They searched for sea shells and tended a garden. They swam in the ocean and lay together at night, lulled to sleep by the sound of the waves.

Eleanor of Aquitaine got along fine without her. She had the book, after all, and it took care of all her desires. Eleanor became queen again. She had babies that would become kings.

For a short while, Sibyl gave up pursuing her book and allowed herself to love again. Eventually, however, the need to find it came over her so suddenly and so powerfully, she tricked Merlin and sealed him in a cave without explanation. Love wasn't enough for her to abandon her pursuit of power. Imprisoned there, he wouldn't be a temptation to her any longer, and he couldn't use his powerful magic against her.

Merlin howled in fury and sorrow as she walked away from the cliffs—and back toward her destiny.

CHAPTER 39

KACEY

Kacey woke to her phone's 5 a.m. alarm Sunday morning, a tinkling little melody that wasn't too obnoxious. It was still dark at her hotel window. She glanced down and found Jareth—or Lin? How should she think of him now?—staring at her with his big green cat eyes.

"Good morning to you," she mumbled.

She remembered being in the magical place with Lin, but she didn't remember returning here. Maybe he'd somehow slipped her a narcotic? The more reasonable explanation was that someone had slipped something in her King Arthur drinks the night before. That was more likely than her cat turning into a man and taking her to some weird plane of existence that normal people couldn't get to. She squeezed her eyes shut for a moment. She didn't feel groggy, and her head didn't hurt, though. It all felt like a weird dream. How could any of it be true?

"Right, cats don't talk back."

She sighed and threw back her covers as Jareth jumped from the bed and went to do his own morning business in the litter box. She'd rather stay in bed, but today was officially her first day of work, though shooting wouldn't begin until tomorrow. Sibyl had lined up the photo shoot for the morning, and Kacey had sword fighting practice in the afternoon. And the date with Justin after that. She couldn't help smiling as she pulled her hair up and washed her face with cold water. As she brushed her teeth, she continued to smile. She spat the bubbles into the sink, rinsed her mouth with water, and patted her mouth dry with a hand towel.

Last night must have been a dream, she decided. Wasn't it normal for anxiety to produce lucid dreams? She looked at herself in the mirror. If it wasn't a dream, it was a mental illness. As she exited the bathroom, the dark figure of her cat morphed into a man, and she yelped in surprise and stumbled back, clutching her chest where her heart pounded.

"Good morning. I forget myself sometimes," Lin said with amusement on his face. "It's so simple being a cat."

"I'd begun to think I was losing it and had made all that up," Kacey said as she rounded the bed and went to her closet for her robe. It was strange having a man in her room, and she felt self-conscious in her pajamas. "You know, Sibyl will be here soon, as well as hair and makeup and the photographer, too."

"I know. I just wanted to remind you while I've got the chance that you should be on guard." He glanced toward the door and whispered, "We'll talk more later."

Kacey looked to it, too, and when she heard a light knock, she glanced back at Lin, but he'd already turned himself back into Jareth. He laid down with his head between his paws and stared at the door.

Kacey pulled the door open, and Sibyl swept into the room, looking around. "Is someone already here? I thought I heard a man's voice."

"Oh, uh," Kacey stammered and glanced at her phone on the nightstand. She picked it up. "Audiobook. Forever the bookworm," she said with a quick smile. She wasn't sure how much she believed about what Lin had told her last night, but she wasn't about to tell her new friend and publicist that she had a magical cat who was also a nearly immortal ancestor. *Wow,* she thought, *that would sound exceptionally delusional.*

"Okay," Sibyl said as she clapped her hands together. "We've got a busy day today. The stylists should be here at any moment, so I ordered you an early breakfast, which should be here soon. We want early morning light for these photos." Sibyl pulled the outfits from the closet that she'd bought for the photoshoot.

"I'm glad we're getting it done early. After I'm finished with fight lessons, I've got a date," Kacey confided.

Sibyl clasped her hands in front of her. "Oh? Who?" she asked.

"Justin. He's the historical accuracy consultant for the movie, but I knew him before in San Diego. He came to the library often."

"Was that the handsome man I saw you with at the bar last night?" When Kacey nodded, Sibyl added, "I didn't want to interrupt what looked like a cozy thing."

Kacey found it hard to keep from smiling. She was absolutely giddy about her date later. She couldn't help but tell Sibyl about it. It's all she wanted to talk about. She felt like a schoolgirl again. Lin's warnings about Sibyl made her reign in her glee a bit, though.

"Well, keep your options open, Kacey," Sibyl said. "Some people aren't made for the love of one man." When Kacey frowned, Sibyl added, "Like me. I was always too ambitious for only one man. Let me tell you, there are some sexy, gorgeous, rich men out there who would fall at your feet if you gave them half a glance. And you don't have to stop at just one."

Kacey shrugged, knowing she didn't see relationships the same way. She wanted someone to grow old with, to come home to, day after day, and to love with all of herself. She couldn't have those things with a plethora of men. Kacey believed that's what Norma Jean had never understood, and look where it got her.

Jareth gave a croaky cry and jumped off the couch to find a softer spot to curl up on the bed.

Another knock at the door brought a tray of assorted fruit, yogurt, bagels, and muffins to her room. Kacey grabbed a piping cup of hot coffee first, though, and she thanked the hotel staff as she closed the door. She'd surely need caffeine to get through the day ahead of her. She added sugar and cream to it while Sibyl let in the stylists next, who immediately got to work on Kacey's hair and face while she snuck bites of fruit and a warm cinnamon raisin bagel between sips of coffee.

In no time, Sibyl was letting in the photographer and introducing him to Kacey. Then, they rushed her to the top of the Thompson Hotel and out onto the swimming pool area. The sky was lightening to a peachy pink color, and the photographer's assistant had set up huge white umbrella-looking things that Kacey assumed helped with lighting. The photographer, a man in his fifties named Gregory, snapped a few test pictures to get the setting correct on his camera while the assistant showed Kacey where to stand.

As the sun peeked over the horizon in the distance, Kacey turned toward the photographer, the high-rises of L.A. to her right and a dark mountain sloping gently up on her left. Kacey stood in a white ankle-length dress that accentuated her womanly curves. These were going to be some amazing photos. She felt too giddy to stand still. She took a deep breath and tried to concentrate.

"Gorgeous!" he said. "Turn your head to the left, chin up, and your left hand up like you're trying to touch the sky ever so gently. That's right." He continued to direct her on how to pose as the wind gently tousled her hair. "Exquisite, Kacey. Look straight in the lens now. Stunning!"

With his constant encouragement and precise direction, he made it easy for her to feel confident. When the sky had lightened considerably, he had her return to her room for a chic gray pantsuit. Sibyl helped her change. Kacey noticed Jareth sitting on the patio watching the sky lighten, as well. He paid no attention to them. He seemed more engaged by the birds flitting by every so often.

Quite a few people had gathered near the pool to watch as the photographer took more photos of her. Though the hotel was efficient in keeping the general public at bay, hotel patrons were free to come watch the action. It was surreal having people watch her every move. She tried to ignore the growing crowd.

It was getting hot, and the makeup artist touched up her makeup and changed her lip color before the next set of photos.

Again, Gregory coached her through the poses he needed for the shots. "You're doing great, Kacey," he said. "One more outfit change, and I think we'll be done."

Before she could make her way out of the pool area, people were asking for her autograph. Apparently, word had gotten around about who she was, which surprised her because she hadn't even begun filming yet. Besides, there were actual movie stars on this project, and she wasn't one of them. She was a nobody, but then again, while she signed her signature on napkins for strangers, she had to admit that she enjoyed their smiles and kind words. It felt good to be the center of attention this morning. She could get accustomed to that.

"Okay, Ms. Wiltson has to finish her photo shoot," Sibyl told the crowd as she pulled Kacey from them after only a minute or two. "This one is the moneymaker," Sibyl said with a smile as they walked back toward her room.

Kacey wondered what the next outfit would be.

Inside, Sibyl pulled out a garment bag Kacey hadn't looked inside yet. She had a wicked grin on her face. "Are you ready for this?"

Kacey's eyes widened as Sibyl pulled out a dusty rose-colored two-piece swimsuit. Rhinestones outlined the top, and a rhinestone collar of sorts came down between the bust. Rhinestones also covered the entire front of the high-waist bottoms.

"Oh, wow!" was all Kacey could say. She couldn't even dwell yet on the fact that she'd be in front of strangers in this. It was so pretty. The sunlight from the window hit the stones and dazzled her eyes. "How many rhinestones are on this thing?" she asked as she touched it.

"Not rhinestones. These are a mixture of Swarovski crystals in blush rose, moonlight crystal, rose gold, and silk shimmer, and they're highlighted by strategically placed diamonds. This is on loan from one of my favorite designers, who owes me a favor. I have a fashion magazine interested in these photos of you, so we may have more than just social media content here."

"Wow, you're good at this PR stuff."

"Told you." Sibyl handed it to Kacey and pushed her toward the bathroom. "Now, go put it on. You're going to blow their minds in this."

CHAPTER 40

SIBYL, NOW

The swimsuit hugged her body perfectly, as if the designer had made it specifically for her. When Kacey timidly stepped out of the bathroom with a grin on her face, Sibyl said, "Yowsa, you're a superstar now, woman!"

Sibyl was confident that the shy librarian wouldn't be under the radar any longer. Even her annoying, lazy cat, who'd been with licking his paws after a can of tuna, sat up and looked at the dazzling crystals and diamonds bouncing light all around the room. Kacey slipped on her silk robe while the hairstylist touched up her curls.

Sibyl promised the swimsuit's designer that Kacey wouldn't get into the water, but if Sibyl had her way, Kacey would drown in it today, and they wouldn't have to take the trip overseas at all. Sibyl adored California and would rather stay there than travel to dreary old Wales any day. Once the book was in her hands and she had its power, she'd gain control of the United States first. The rest of the world would soon follow suit.

Sibyl thought of the pool, trying to conceive a plan for Kacey to drown. She faltered, though. Where was that damned book? Where was Kacey hiding it? She glanced around the room. If Kacey was smart, she was keeping it in the vault. And since Sibyl didn't have the code, she wouldn't be able to get to it before it disappeared. So no, Kacey couldn't fall in and drown today.

Sibyl let out a sigh as she and Kacey headed back up to the rooftop pool. Quite a few more people had gathered, including some of Kacey's coworkers. Sibyl smiled to herself. This would probably put them off about their newest cast member, and that could be a good thing. Loneliness and animosity on set might push her into the arms of the men wanting to sweep her off her feet.

To Sibyl's delight, David Fiore was among the crowd now. He wore khakis and a blue shirt that showed off his broad shoulders. Though his eyes were covered at the moment behind dark sunglasses, Sibyl saw the smile tease his lips when he turned toward Kacey.

David stepped forward from the crowd. "Good morning, Kacey. You're up early and working hard, I see," David said.

Kacey gave a quick nod but looked cautious and worried. And she should be because when David saw her in that swimsuit she had covered up, it was going to be impossible for her to keep him away from her. Sibyl was so delighted that she nearly giggled. This was perfect.

"Okay, Kacey. Let's not keep the photographer waiting." Sibyl pulled at the robe, and Kacey stepped out of it. There was an audible gasp from the crowd, and David's mouth fell open as he removed his shades.

"I think I put her in the wrong movie," Sibyl heard David murmur to himself as the makeup artist ran to get Kacey ready for the next shots. The makeup artist added a bit of extra blush to Kacey's cheeks, some bronzer to her shoulders and decolletage, and a pink gloss to her lips that matched the dusty rose color of the swimsuit. David watched every move Kacey made with the intensity of a man inexorably smitten.

While the photographer took some photos of Kacey lying on a chaise lounge chair by the pool, Sibyl leaned toward David and said, "Isn't she stunning?"

David nodded, at a loss for words.

Sibyl smirked. "She told me how much she appreciates you bringing her into this project and how indebted to you she feels for changing her life with this movie."

David finally peeled his eyes away from Kacey to look at Sibyl. "Is that right?"

"Oh, yes. Kacey plays coy," Sibyl said, pursing her lips and knowingly widening her eyes.

David turned his eyes back to Kacey and watched her intently. She was now walking around the end of the pool to lie on the edge. Sauntering, actually. David licked his bottom lip. Sibyl could practically see the indecent thoughts running through his head.

"Of course, after her fighting lesson today, she's got a date with some guy," Sibyl added.

David's head jerked to Sibyl's face. "Who?"

Sibyl didn't want to tell him who Justin was just yet. The last thing she needed was for David to fire him from the project before things got incredibly awkward between the three of them. She shrugged. "I'm sure it's nothing. Of course, if her fight training were to last too long, they'd have to cancel their date, wouldn't they? That'd be a shame. And next week, she'll be far too busy and too tired to be going out with anyone."

Sibyl let David stew in those thoughts as she turned her attention back to Kacey, who was now standing thigh-deep in the pool with her fingers lightly grazing the surface of the water as the photographer took shots above from a ladder.

She was glad to see Kacey so at ease in the water. Standing in the pool in that beautiful swimsuit, Kacey reminded Sibyl a little of Marilyn, but she was much more comfortable than Marilyn ever was in the water. Sibyl had tried to drown Marilyn on several occasions, but the book protected its Keepers from magic used against them, and because the book became a part of them when it chose a Keeper, Sibyl wasn't able to destroy the Keeper directly. They had to die by other means. It was frustrating, to say the least.

On a whim, mostly because she was so vexed after chasing the book for so long, she closed her eyes and imagined the water roiling under Kacey's feet—not enough to break the surface but enough to make her lose her footing and plunge the woman into the water. When she opened her eyes, Kacey was gone. The photographer stood on the ladder with a confused expression, and the assistant yelled and ran toward the pool.

Sibyl's heart pounded as she realized Kacey had gone under when she saw her head bob up out of the water. Kacey, of course, was only in a few feet of water and not in any real danger, but an amazing revelation dawned on Sibyl. The book had chosen its Keeper, but something about the process hadn't been completed yet. What was different here? Whatever it was, Kacey wasn't safe from Sibyl's magic—not yet anyway, and if Sibyl had her way and could catch sight of the book, she'd kill this woman with her bare hands to get it.

CHAPTER 41

KACEY

Kacey came sputtering back out of the water after finding her footing again. Her heart pounded, and heat rose to her cheeks to have all these people witness her clumsiness in three feet of water. How had a calm pool knocked her off her feet? Perhaps the current of the pool's filtration system hit her feet with just the right amount of force.

"I'm sorry. I don't know what happened."

"Pause, Kacey," the photographer said with his hand up. "I know that wasn't expected, but the way the sunlight is hitting the droplets of water on your face, it's magical! Give me just a slight smile. There." He pulled the camera back up and clicked away. "Perfect! These are going to look amazing. Sometimes, happy accidents are the real money shots in modeling."

Acting, modeling, and walking the runway. *My, how my life has changed*, she thought as she made her way carefully up the steps at the end of the pool.

The assistant photographer had grabbed a towel from somewhere, and she rushed toward Kacey as the photographer came off the ladder.

David was beside her in an instant. "Are you okay?" he asked.

Kacey felt foolish, but she was fine. "I just slipped, I guess," she said with a shrug and a dip of her head.

Gregory said, "I've got some great shots here. You did an excellent job today, Kacey. Thank you for the pleasure of photographing you." He moved the camera to his left hand and held out his right hand.

Kacey gave his hand a firm shake, and she noticed David shift toward her at the other man's touch.

Sibyl walked toward them, an odd look on her face. She must have been worried, too.

"I'm fine. Really," she said to Sibyl. "Just a little clumsy."

Sibyl had narrowed eyes, which, today, in the morning sunshine, matched the color of the pool water. She said nothing.

"Well, let's hope you aren't clumsy at our fight practice today. The last thing I need is for my favorite actress to get injured before filming begins." David grinned. "Or after, for that matter.

We'll be sure to go over lots of safety procedures, and we can hire a stunt double for anything you don't feel comfortable doing." David draped an arm around her shoulder and guided her back toward the inside of the hotel.

Sibyl followed them and let them into Kacey's room with the room key. David made himself comfortable on her couch while Sibyl helped Kacey out of the swimsuit in the bathroom.

"I hope I didn't ruin it," Kacey said with a frown.

"Oh, no, don't worry. I'll get this water right out of the garment. There won't be a drop left in it." Sibyl smiled. "Let's talk tonight about some collab opportunities. I've been getting lots of requests from companies who want you to sponsor their brands. And they're willing to pay you a lot of money." Sibyl waved a hand at David as she went out the hotel room door.

Kacey stepped into the shower to rinse the pool water from her hair. The steam of the shower felt nice. She almost forgot David was sitting on her couch. She shrugged on her robe and tied it before she came out. Knowing now that her cat was Lin, Kacey didn't think she'd ever walk around without a robe again.

David still sat on the couch, texting on his phone. "Achoo!" David sniffled.

"Bless you," Kacey said as she picked up a comb and ran it through her wet hair. No tangles whatsoever. It still amazed her. "Hope you aren't catching a cold."

David eyed Jareth, who rested with his eyes closed in the golden sunshine streaming in through the patio door. It made Jareth look ethereal, bathed in amber light. "I'm allergic," David said, motioning his thumb toward the cat. "We'll take the bus in the morning for filming, but today, I'll drive you over to the gym where we're working on fighting and swordsmanship. I know a great sushi place near here where we can grab an early lunch first." When Kacey gave him a look, David raised his hands. "No strings!

I want to make sure you're well-fed before you burn a bunch of calories today. It's going to be intense, especially in the beginning. I hope you're in shape."

She didn't like the way his eyes slid down her body. "So, no other actors will be working on fighting today?"

"Only one. You'll be working with Allie."

Kacey nodded. "She's playing Morgan le Fay. I met her last night." At least she'd be working with someone nice.

"Everyone else has been through weeks of training, and you and she will be in a scene together fighting, so it made sense to ask her to work with you through some of the choreography. She'll meet us a little later. The trainer is going to take you through some basic stage combat techniques first and get you loosened up for sword fighting after."

Kacey pulled out an activewear outfit from her closet. "Okay, then, I'll meet you downstairs in a few minutes," she said pointedly.

"Right," he said, standing. "Achoo!" He sniffled after she blessed him again. "It'll be better for me to get out of here sooner rather than later, anyway. See you downstairs."

Kacey dried her hair and got dressed. As she picked up her bag to leave, she glanced toward the safe. Kacey didn't like the idea of being so far away from the diary. While Jareth slept, she pulled it out of her safe and caressed its cover. It felt warm to her touch, and she hugged it to her chest. She'd been so busy that she hadn't read any more of it.

She picked up a pen lying on the table by her bed. Maybe she should write her own first entry in the diary. After all, it was hers now. What would it hurt? Her new life had begun today, and a new beginning deserved to be recorded.

Kacey opened the book and thumbed through its pages. She stood there for a moment, fighting the intense desire to share her own amazing story. However, she closed the book and set the pen back down. Maybe tonight. David was waiting for her, and she had lots of training to do today. She stuffed the book into her bag to have it nearer to her.

Kacey took a deep breath. Time to learn to fight.

CHAPTER 42

SIBYL, NOW

S ibyl watched Kacey leave her room. She waited until she saw Kacey and David exit the front lobby together. Then, with the key card still in her possession, she entered Kacey's hotel room and glanced around, hoping the book was sitting out somewhere.

She glanced around, peeked under the bed and in the nightstand, then huffed in frustration. That'd be too easy.

Sibyl sat on the edge of the bed and tapped her fingers against her knee. In all her years watching Keepers, they'd always been protective of the crimson diary. She'd gotten close to it when it was unwatched a couple of times, but the book generated some type of protective force field around itself so that anyone who would attempt to pick it up simply couldn't make themselves do it, no matter if they were Mágos or human. Someone else could only hold it if the Keeper offered it.

However, the book wasn't bound to Kacey yet, so the force field shouldn't be around it. Though its influence was already working in Kacey's favor, Sibyl's magic worked against Kacey that morning, which was proof enough that Kacey wasn't fully protected by the book yet. That gave Sibyl hope. It blossomed in her chest like a beautiful pond lily reaching for the sun.

If she was lucky and Kacey hadn't taken the book with her, then it might be in the room safe. Sibyl went to the safe and tried a few number combinations, but none of them worked. She pulled at the little braid of hair plaited at the side of her neck underneath her hair. Perhaps she could persuade one of the hotel staff to give her the master code.

Sibyl heard a low growl coming from somewhere in the room. She searched for Kacey's feral cat. It had never liked her, and if she got close enough, she might give it a good, swift kick. She saw its shining green eyes flash in the dark bedroom as it gave a hiss. "Mind your own business," Sibyl hissed back. "This is between me and the book. And if I get my hands on it, it's all over."

Sibyl turned her attention back to the vault. There had to be small cracks in the door's seal, cracks so small that a mist could enter and take a peek, at least. With a wave of her hand, Sibyl dissolved into a mist as Jareth gave another low growl. She found nothing in the vault, and had she been in a solid form, she'd have let out a shriek of anger. Instead, she shot out of the room under the door in a whoosh of fury.

Back in her own suite, Sibyl paced, trying to decide what to do. On the one hand, she knew she could still affect the Keeper, and she suspected that meant she could kill Kacey. Her heart pounded, and she wrung her hands as she paced. Why? Why wasn't Kacey protected from Sibyl's powers by the book yet? What was different than any of the other Keepers she'd come across?

And if killing Kacey was her only option, the book would have to be in hand so that Sibyl could finally grab it and claim her rightful place as its Keeper. She didn't want to go chasing it down yet again. She twisted the black onyx ring on her finger absentmindedly as she considered the possibilities.

Sibyl paused. She'd never seen Kacey write in the diary. Perhaps the act of writing in it was the key. Her mouth fell open in disbelief. Maybe *that's* why the book had never really been Sibyl's, either. Before she'd ever written anything in it, the book was lost. It'd disappeared from her cave by the sea, and for hundreds of years, she wasn't able to find it. Finally, Sibyl had found it in the hands of Elyssa, later known as Queen Dido.

Thus began her journey to pursue the book through time and space. She'd traveled the entire world and lived hundreds of lives searching for her book. And here, it was essentially unchained from anyone. She wanted to cry and laugh hysterically at the same moment. Yes, it had chosen Kacey, but it hadn't completely bound itself to her yet. Sibyl marveled at that revelation. And she marveled at the influence the book had already released for Kacey. It had grown incredibly powerful through the years, even more so than Sibyl had realized. In fact, she didn't think it'd ever worked quite this quickly before.

Sibyl tapped her fingers nervously against her lips. Interesting. Could she intervene and take the book back now? She needed to find Kacey and try.

Sibyl jumped as someone pounded on her door. She frowned. Who would come see her at the Thompson Hotel? Very few people knew she was here. Perhaps it was the Vogue editor she'd befriended and asked to feature Kacey. Or maybe it was the Mercedez rep who'd come to her seeking a collaboration with the up-and-coming superstar.

Sibyl pulled open the door and gasped. She blinked as her mind tried to make sense of the man standing before her. "Lugh?" She blinked in confusion. "What are you doing here?"

CHAPTER 43

KACEY

Kacey stood with her back to the trainer, a tall, thin man with a friendly smile. "Now, turn, grab my opposite arm, and twist." She'd done this move at least six times already, all perfectly, but the trainer told her they were trying to work on muscle memory, which would keep anyone from getting hurt.

They'd spent a half hour on safety procedures before Allie got there. He'd practiced a few fight scenes she would have with other characters. Then, they'd worked on the scenes that the two women were in together.

"Good, now do that move with Allie," he instructed. Allie hopped up from her seated position on the floor where she'd been scrolling on her phone and moved into his position while Kacey completed the same sequence with her as the trainer watched.

David paced as he talked on the phone in the hallway outside the gym's training room. He glanced every so often toward them, but he stayed out of their way. Kacey was surprised he was sticking around this long. She and Allie could get back to the hotel on their own.

"I was just checking my social accounts," Allie said as Kacey turned her attention back to the movement the trainer was having her work on. Allie pulled up her sword and brought it down, but Kacey blocked the blow with hers. "People are calling you 'The Dark Bombshell,'" she said with a raised eyebrow and a smile. "It could be your superhero name." She moved through the rest of the choreography seamlessly, and Kacey met her move for move.

Kacey glanced back toward David. It was so weird that people thought of her as a sex symbol. She was still the shy, modest woman who'd hidden herself away for so long in the library. Though she'd lost her contentment with being invisible, she'd never anticipated this much visibility. She dropped her guard.

"Kacey, pay attention," the trainer told her. He gave her a stern look.

"Right, sorry," she mumbled. They went through the sequence two more times. Kacey swiped a sweaty strand of hair from her face, expecting him to demand they do it once more.

"Okay, take a break. Get some water."

230

The two women sat down on the floor beside their bags. Kacey leaned back against the wall-to-ceiling mirror and drank half a bottle in one swig. Fight sequences were harder than they looked, and she could tell that her muscles would be sore by morning. Kacey glanced at David, who was still deep in a phone conversation in the hallway outside of the training room.

"Getting distracted by the hunky producer?" Allie asked with a little smile. She tucked a strand behind her ear before taking another drink from her water bottle.

"David? No, those are just rumors. We aren't seeing each other," Kacey said defensively.

Allie shrugged. "I wouldn't blame you if you were, though I'd caution you that he's known to be a bit... promiscuous," she said delicately as if she thought she might offend Kacey. "I'm pretty certain he's interested in you. And usually, what David Fiore wants, David Fiore gets." Allie shrugged. "He's also known to be flighty. He doesn't tend to stick with one woman for long."

"So I've gathered," Kacey said. "I've actually got a date tonight." She couldn't help grinning. "With Justin, the guy you met yesterday?"

"Right," Allie said. "Justin. He's handsome in a guy-next-door kind of way. And serious. Is that your type?"

"I don't know if I have a type." Kacey had so seldom dated that she didn't know what her type was. "He's intellectual. Maybe that's my type."

Allie nodded. "Everyone has a type. If you haven't figured it out yet, you will. Justin is likely the cinnamon roll type."

"What's that?" Kacey asked.

"He's always going to do the right thing by you. He's considerate and romantic. He'll go to great lengths to please you," Allie said. "Basically, yummy." She laughed.

"Well, that sounds nice. How do you know all that, having met him only once?"

"I can read people really well. It's helped me quite a lot in this business." Allie grinned. "For instance, I can tell that you are capable behind the layer of self-doubt. You also like to go unnoticed. To a fault, I think. But look at you. No one can ignore you now."

At that assessment, Kacey's eyes widened. This woman really did have a knack for reading people. "So tell me about you, Allie. What are you like? And what kind of men do you go for?" Kacey asked.

Allie looked amused. "I'm an opportunist, so I look for the best opportunities that I can find, and I pursue them relentlessly. I guess I would say that I'm driven and ambitious. That's an understatement," she said with a grin. "As for men, I like the bad boys, which is why I'll probably never settle down."

Kacey looked sideways at Allie. "Bad boys like David Fiore?"

Allie shook her head. "Been there, done that, got the t-shirt," she said with a grim expression. "He's actually a decent guy, unless you're dating him."

Both women laughed as the trainer walked back over, interrupting their conversation.

Allie's smile faltered as she looked at David on the phone just beyond the windows of the training room. "Just be careful about getting involved in a love triangle involving David. He can be jealous, and as much as he can change your life for the better, he can also ruin it."

"Ready for a fight to the death?" The trainer smiled wickedly and handed them each a sword.

CHAPTER 44

KACEY

When they were finally finished with sword practice, Kacey slumped by her bag on the floor and drank some water, though her arms felt like jelly, and it was hard even to lift the bottle. She'd given it everything she had, and she had impressed the trainer with how quickly she caught on.

"You killed it today," Allie said.

"I think I killed my arms."

Allie grinned. "Definitely take some ibuprofen for the soreness tonight. Ah, here comes David, right on time." David was making a beeline straight for them after talking to the trainer.

Kacey made a face. "I don't want to disappoint him, but he's not keeping me from my date with Justin tonight," she said so he couldn't hear her.

Allie winked. "I'll make sure of it. Get out of here while I divert his attention." Allie stood and intercepted him before he could get to Kacey. "David! We had a great workout today, but I'm afraid I'm going to have to cash in on that meal you promised me. I've worked extra hard, and now I need carbs. How about it?" she purred.

"But I need to prepare Kacey—"

"I'll take care of things," Allie said as she grasped his arm and turned him away from Kacey. "Later. She'll be fine. Feed me. I'm starving!"

Meanwhile, Kacey made a hasty exit and waved over her shoulder as she slipped out of the training room. She hopped on a bus and made her way back to the hotel, where she took another shower to wash away the sweat she'd worked up while fight training. When she pulled her hair from the clip, it fell in perfect, glorious waves around her shoulders, so she shook her head and ran her fingers through it. She wondered if her magical mane would stand up to the powers of the damp weather in Wales in a few weeks.

When Kacey came out of the bathroom, she realized she still hadn't seen Jareth anywhere, and she guessed Lin had decided to leave the hotel room for a while. She couldn't blame him. She thought living as a cat must be boring.

Maybe he'd opened a portal to his netherworld lair for some peace and quiet for a while. Kacey wondered if the portal could be opened to anywhere. She glanced at the closed door, and then she closed her eyes, concentrating on her home in San Diego, thinking of the feel of her soft couch, the smell of laundry detergent, and her favorite candle mixing in the air. She pictured the way the sunset cast a beautiful orange glow across her kitchen in the afternoons. Kacey held out her hands as she'd seen Lin do, and she focused on creating that space right there before her. When she opened her eyes, a small orange mass was growing between her hands. Her mouth fell open in a gasp of surprise, and her concentration faltered. The portal swallowed in on itself and blinked out. She laughed with delight that she'd been able to do that much.

Kacey glanced at the clock. There'd be time to learn how to use her powers later. She didn't know what Justin had in store for her tonight, so she chose a pair of dark jeans and a black top with black lace trim that gave the casual outfit a hint of sexiness. Using a curling wand, she added a few extra waves to her hair, which was as lush and shiny as ever. While applying a pink tint to her lips, Kacey heard a knock at the door, so she pressed her lips together, surveyed herself, and smiled, giddy to be going out with Justin.

Through the peephole in her door, she saw him standing there in a plain green button-down shirt and jeans with mussed hair that was supposed to look effortless but probably took longer than she'd taken on her own hair. She couldn't help smiling, pleased that he wanted to impress her.

Kacey pulled open the door, and Justin's eyes lit up. If he looked at her that way for the rest of her life, she'd count herself a lucky woman. "Hi!" She leaned in for a hug, and he gave her a quick peck on the cheek as he hugged her. "I hope I'm dressed appropriately for tonight. What do you have planned?"

"You look perfect." He looked down at her feet. "And comfortable shoes, so you're all set. I thought we'd do a little sightseeing like proper tourists. The Hollywood Walk of Fame is only a few blocks north of here. Then, we can find something good to eat."

"That sounds fun! Let me get my bag." She slid the crimson diary into her purse and made sure she had her wallet. She turned and asked, "Ready?" He nodded, and she noticed he had a backpack slung over one shoulder. "What's in there?"

"A surprise," he replied mysteriously.

The two of them exited the Thompson Hotel and walked toward Hollywood Boulevard. It was still early afternoon, and the sun was high in the sky. Kacey told Justin about the fun she'd had with fight choreography and learning to properly use a sword. "Before now, I never could have imagined this would be my life."

"It's strange the types of skills you pick up in the movie business. I never thought my studies would land me here, either," he said, "but I'm enjoying it. It's fascinating to see all the behind-the-scenes stuff that goes on with a movie production."

Kacey had forgotten that Justin had been on the project for weeks now.

They quickly made their way to the Hollywood Walk of Fame. They laughed as they maneuvered around people to find the stars of the actors and actresses they were interested in seeing. As they walked, Kacey pointed out Ella Fitzgerald, Betty White, and Bing Crosby, to name a few. She imagined these revered film stars and singers standing on this very sidewalk with the warm California sun beaming down on them, the palms rustling in the breeze above, and the lights of cameras recording momentary flashes of their achievement, fuzzy little snippets of their lives and their legacies.

Kacey stopped and looked down at Marilyn's star. She found it hard to breathe as she glanced around, wondering if Marilyn's Hollywood looked anything like Kacey's Hollywood. It had probably changed a good deal in the sixty-plus years that had passed.

"Oh, look at that. Marilyn Monroe. I think she left her handprints and footprints at the Chinese Theatre. It's just up ahead." Justin began walking toward the theater, and Kacey had to make her lead legs move to follow him.

Instead of focusing on what she was about to see, she looked down at the names they passed as they walked. "Look!" Kacey said. "Minnie Mouse even has a star." They walked on further.

"And Godzilla," Justin pointed out.

He stopped, and Kacey looked up as she paused beside him. The iconic TCL Chinese Theatre, with its gold roof and trimmings in red and dragon artwork, stood before them.

"Let's go." Justin grabbed her hand and pulled her along until they were standing in front of Marilyn's prints. When they stopped, she noticed Justin didn't let go of her hand.

Sophia Loren and Steve McQueen were also above Marilyn's square, but Kacey couldn't focus on any of the others. There in the cement was the signature of the star, along with her petite footprints and handprints. Written across hers and her costar's squares of cement was the title of one of her movies, "Gentlemen Prefer Blondes."

Before the diary came into Kacey's life, she honestly hadn't been a huge Marilyn fan. She'd never even seen any of her movies that she could recall, and she'd wondered what the fuss was all about. But now, it was different. She knew of the inner turmoil Norma Jean's fame had caused. Kacey wondered if fame was like that for everyone. Norma Jean had written of the ability to step outside of her introverted self and be the blonde bombshell

Marilyn, which was exciting and fun until it became exhausting and troublesome: how she'd always felt criticized and not capable enough as an actress; how she'd wanted to be a mother but never could; how her relationships with men fell apart; how she'd gotten mixed up with all kinds of characters. Eventually, the negatives overruled any of the positives of stardom, and her light went out. It was sad.

"Put your hands in her handprints, and I'll take a picture." Justin raised his phone.

Kacey hesitated. Marilyn's handprints were nearly black from so many people placing their hands there. It almost seemed... disrespectful to dirty Marilyn's handprints like that. Kacey couldn't explain it to him because she'd have to explain the connection she now felt she had with the dead star, and saying any of it aloud would sound crazy. Maybe people still loved Marilyn because of traces of the crimson dairy's magical influence. That had to be some kind of influence if it still affected people so many years after her death.

Kacey sat down by the square of concrete instead. "No, I'll just sit beside it." She smiled up at the camera while Justin took a few shots of her. Then, he reached down to help her up.

"Let's grab some takeout, and I'll order us a ride. I have somewhere else I'd like to take you," he said as he pulled out his phone. "There's a good burger place just around the corner. Is that okay?"

"Are you kidding? I'd love a greasy double cheeseburger." Kacey grinned. "Make sure mine has bacon."

Justin grinned. "You got it."

While Justin ordered by phone, Kacey looked around at all the people converging on the tourist attraction. She wondered just how many people showed up each day to look at the Walk of Fame. As she watched the crowd at the front of the Chinese Theatre, someone touched her arm. Kacey smiled, anticipating that it was Justin coming back from ordering their food. However, when she turned, two women and a man stood before her.

One woman in huge, dark sunglasses pulled them down her nose to stare at Kacey's face. "Are you—"

"I told you it was her!" one woman said to the other woman.

"Kacey Wiltson?" the man in a blue sun visor asked. He already had his phone in her face.

A few more people moved in closer. More phones were held up.

"Yes," she said weakly, a little more than a squeak.

"Can I get your autograph?"

"Um, sure. Do you have a pen?" she asked the young man who'd requested her autograph.

As he scrambled for a pen, more people moved to the crowd gathering around her. By the time she was signing autographs, twenty or more people surrounded her. She didn't know how it'd happened so quickly.

"Kacey!" It was Justin calling her name, but she couldn't see him.

"Can I have a picture with you?" a young girl with braces and a pretty sprinkling of freckles across her nose asked.

Kacey smiled. "Sure." The girl leaned in close and held up her phone to take the selfie. Then, as the girl stepped away and others took her place, Kacey felt someone's hand slide across her ass, and she yelped and stepped forward, peering behind her at the strangers' faces, searching the group for the handsy fan. She shook her head. They were all leering at her. It could have been any one of them. She pulled her bag with the crimson diary closer to her body. "Okay, I have to go!"

No one was paying attention to what she was saying, though. They were more concerned with getting pictures to post to social media, and she couldn't see a way out of the throng.

"Kacey!"

More people gathered around her now. Someone touched her hair, and she swatted the hand away. What was wrong with people? You gave them a bit of yourself and your time, and they wanted to take whatever they wanted of it. The attention felt almost assaultive.

She felt panic rising inside her chest. She closed her eyes for a moment and did what she'd always done at school when things got stressful. Lin said it was one of her superpowers, so why not use it here?

"Go away," she whispered. She imagined a bubble around herself, impenetrable and concealing her in its protection. All of her senses went numb at once. She couldn't see, hear, taste, feel, or smell anything for a few beats. And when she opened her eyes a moment later, the crowd was casually moving away from her as if she'd never been there.

Kacey looked wildly about her, impressed that it'd worked so effectively when she set her mind to it. A nervous giggle bubbled up and threatened to escape. Her pounding heart slowed. It had never been that quick or absolute when she was younger. Of course, she'd never known she had that power in her, either. It had always been something unconscious. But now that she knew she had this power, she was determined to control it and use it to her advantage. She just needed some confidence using it. With confidence came better magical outcomes, it seemed.

Even Justin had turned away as if he hadn't been calling her name and trying to get through the crowd to her.

"Hey, Justin!"

Justin turned toward her again, blinked a few times, and the confused expression slid from his face as he broke into a grin. "I forgot what I was doing for a second." His brow creased with confusion. Then, he looked around at the people walking about as if remembering. "I turned away for only a few moments, and when I looked back, that crowd had swallowed you whole."

"Such is fame, I guess," she said with a shrug. Kacey looked over her shoulder. She wrapped an arm around his and said, "Let's go before it happens again."

CHAPTER 45

SIBYL, NOW

Lugh grabbed Sibyl by the throat, his large hand enveloping her slender neck as he peered at her through his long, wavy-blond hair, and he pushed her into the room as she scratched at his thick fingers. She was thankful he let go when the door closed behind him. "Where is it?"

"Where is what?" She pretended not to know what he wanted as she rubbed at the delicate skin of her neck.

"I'll send you straight to the Below right now if you don't tell me where it is." Spit flew through his clenched teeth.

"It's not here. It's hidden away," Sibyl said.

Lugh narrowed his eyes. "You hid *yourself* pretty well these last few hundred years. America!" He shook his head in disbelief. "I never would have guessed it."

Lugh had found her in 1534 with Diane de Poitiers, who had obtained the crimson book a few years earlier, and after the untimely death of Diane's beloved husband Louis de Brézé, was well on her way to becoming the royal mistress to King Henry II.

Lugh had asked for the shortsword back, but she'd refused him. He hadn't taken it well, but Sibyl reminded him that a deal was a deal. She'd tricked the trickster. After spending a while in Europe, she'd come to America, and the book eventually had, too. The shortsword, which was destined to kill her according to her visions, was hidden away where no one would find it.

"Sometimes, it's easier to hide in plain sight," Sibyl replied.

"Well, time's up," Lugh said. "You've had Fragarach long enough. The deal is done."

"I won it," she reminded him.

Lugh gave her a warning look. "You tricked me."

Sibyl smirked. One night, not long after curing Merlin of his madness and finding Lugh in Ireland, Sibyl convinced him over several cups of mead that she needed a powerful weapon.

"Aye, weapons, I know," he'd said.

"I need a special weapon, though," Sibyl told him. "One that can float in water."

Lugh had laughed heartily at her. "Then you need a wand, which I don't make because any weapon worth anything won't float."

"I'll make you a deal. If you have a weapon that floats on water, it's mine," she'd said. "I'll pay for it, of course."

"You have my oath then because all of my weapons would sink immediately."

As Sibyl had looked at his weapons cache, she'd spied the shortsword from her vision, the one inlaid in gold and citrine. She moved past it. "This spear."

"Ah, Gae Assail. Pick it up. You won't be the owner of that tonight," he'd said assuredly.

The spear was heavy in her hand as she handed it to him. "I'll take my chances. How about this warhammer?"

Lugh had laughed. "That's Hoard Shifter, and it's heavier than the spear."

Sibyl came back to the shortsword. "This one is beautiful. How about this one?"

"That's Fragarach. It may be smaller, but it's solid and will most definitely sink."

They took the three weapons to the pond near his house. In the shallow, she dropped the spear, which sank down into the brown water. Lugh retrieved it with a look of amusement on his handsome face. "I told ye."

"Fine, let's try the warhammer." It, too, sank, of course. Sibyl pretended to be perturbed. "And the shortsword?" She'd held out her hand for the weapon. She'd grasped it in one hand and held it over the water. With her other hand, Sibyl had altered the density of the water in the pond. When she dropped the shortsword, it'd plopped on top of the water and stayed there. "Ha!" Sibyl clapped her hands together in glee and then fished the sword back out, returning the water to its normal density before Lugh could test it with his own hand.

"There's something not right here. You've tricked me!" Lugh'd yelled. He plunged his hand into the water to make sure nothing was there that could hold Fragarach up, and he swore with anger.

"Nonsense," Sibyl had said. "I'm only a little prophetess."

And by his oath, Lugh had given her Fragarach that night, though he'd been so angry, she could see veins popping out on his forehead when he handed it to her. She'd left in a hurry before he changed his mind.

With the magical shortsword in her possession, she wouldn't have to worry about someone else getting the sword and using it against her. She just had to hide it and stay away from it herself so that there was no chance that she'd use it against herself—or that Lugh would use it against her, as her visions had revealed.

Now, Lugh had finally caught back up with her again. "You know you tricked me, and Fragarach is rightfully mine."

"You know plenty about that," she shot back. "How many mortals and Mágos have you tricked over the years?"

His face screwed up in anger. "Irrelevant! You've had it long enough. When I asked for it in France, you denied me. You won't deny me again. Take me to it, or I swear to you that I'll run you through with Gae Assail and watch your guts spill out. Apollo may have promised you a long life, but I promise you, it's a magical enough weapon to cut short your miserable existence."

That was something she knew to be true because she'd seen it in her visions, after all. As Sibyl turned, she wondered why Lugh needed Fragarach after over a millennium. Fragarach had been called The Answerer in legends because not only could it pierce any armor and always inflict mortal wounds, even in magical beings, but it was also capable of compelling truth when held against an enemy's throat. Why was he so adamant about getting it back now?

CHAPTER 46

KACEY

J ustin and Kacey picked up their food at the restaurant around the corner, and their Uber car arrived right after. Soon, they were headed into the Hollywood Hills.

As Kacey looked out the window of the car, she asked, "Where are you taking me?"

"You'll see soon." Justin's mouth twitched with a smile he tried to hide.

"I hope so because these cheeseburgers smell divine." The smoky scent of bacon made her salivate. Kacey guessed all that movement in training earlier in the day, plus walking along Hollywood Boulevard in the California sunshine, had used up a lot of her energy.

The driver pulled into a parking lot, and the Hollywood sign against the side of Mount Lee in the Santa Monica Mountains came into view.

"Oh, wow!" Kacey exclaimed. She'd always wanted to see it up close. They got out and walked down to Lake Hollywood Park. The white letters of the sign contrasted against the brown hill. The park below the sign was lush and green. A few clouds meandered across an otherwise clear blue sky. It was the perfect May afternoon.

"This looks like a good spot," Justin said as he stopped near the trees at the edge of the park and put down his backpack, which he opened. He pulled out a small rolled-up red and blue fleece blanket, which he spread out on the ground in front of them. Then, he pulled out two bottles of water, a thermos, two cups from the hotel, and a little box of chocolates.

"A picnic under the Hollywood sign. It's perfect!" Kacey knelt on her knees and opened the bag of cheeseburgers and fries. When she looked up at him, Kacey noticed Justin's smile of relief. She realized he'd been nervous that she wouldn't enjoy this. It was probably the most thoughtful date she'd ever been on.

Neither of them talked much as they enjoyed the good food and watched people moving around the park and taking pictures with the Hollywood sign in the background. Though there were people around them in the park, it was serene here. Kacey washed down her burger and fries with water as she watched a teenager run by with her German Shepard. A group of 20-somethings played a game of frisbee to her right. "This is exactly what I needed—especially after that weirdness at the Chinese Theatre. I don't think I'll ever get accustomed to big crowds of fans. I mean, what are they even fans of? I haven't made the movie yet. I'm essentially a nobody."

"You're *not* a nobody." As if sensing that his tone was too intense, Justin shrugged. "People are drawn to you."

Kacey remembered her book and reached into her bag to rub its familiar cover. "Well, maybe." *Because of the book,* she thought. No one had ever been drawn to her before she'd found it. Or it had found her. She wasn't sure which it was.

A tiny part of her worried the book was the only reason Justin was here. What if she lost it? Would she lose him, too?

The sun lowered in the sky, and it turned Mount Lee and the white Hollywood sign a beautiful orange hue.

"You want a picture in front of the Hollywood sign before the sun goes down?" Justin asked. "We can't be true tourists without it, right?"

Kacey smiled. She found it endearing that he was trying to give her the traditional tourist experience of Hollywood. "Sure." She stood as he pulled out his phone. "Make sure you send me all these." She held her head high and smiled.

Justin paused and looked at her intently before he raised his phone. As he took pictures, an elderly couple walked by them hand-in-hand. The old man stopped and said, "I'll take one of the both of you, if you'd like." He raised his thick eyebrows as the woman beside him smiled.

"Yes," Kacey said quickly. "Thank you."

Justin handed the man the phone, and he draped his arm around Kacey's shoulders. It was a casual gesture, but it felt good to be in his embrace. She leaned into him.

"Beautiful," the old man said as he smiled, handed the phone back to Justin, and took the woman's hand again.

"Thanks so much," Kacey called after them as they walked away. "What a cute couple."

Justin nodded as he knelt back down on the blanket. "I have a treat for you," he said. He opened the thermos, poured a caramel-colored drink into one of the hotel cups, and handed it to her.

Kacey smelled it before sipping the hot liquid. The familiar aroma warmed her before it even touched her lips. "Ah, chai tea latte. You remembered!" It was the drink she'd ordered the first time they went to the coffeehouse together. His thoughtfulness truly surprised her.

Both of them sipped from their cups and ate chocolate caramels and truffles as the sun dipped lower in the sky. They watched people and talked about all the new experiences they were having with their jobs in the movie business. Kacey thought she could stay here forever, but she knew they couldn't. When Justin ordered another ride for them to go back to the Thompson Hotel, she felt wistful about leaving. She hoped she'd get more special moments like this with Justin during the project. Maybe after it was over, she could dare to hope. Maybe, finally, she could settle down into the kind of beautiful life she'd always wished for.

Justin nudged her hand with his in the dark backseat and then wrapped his fingers around hers. His hand was warm and comforting. She looked up at him, and he smiled. A wave of shyness hit her, and she turned to look out the window as L.A. sped by. She didn't let go of his hand, though.

As she looked up at the twilight sky, polluted by too much city light to show many stars, she gasped as a streak of light crossed the sky. Her nose bumped the window glass as she watched it soar out of sight. "Did you see that?" she asked.

"See what?" Justin asked, ducking his head to see out her side of the car.

"I think it was a meteor." She turned to him, her eyes wide.

"A shooting star. Maybe it's a sign. Maybe it's showing you what you'll be—Hollywood's newest shooting star."

"I hope not," Kacey replied. "Shooting stars burn brightly before dying away."

CHAPTER 47

KACEY

Justin walked Kacey back up to her room like the gentleman he was. She'd come to expect nothing less from him. Allie was right—he was a genuine cinnamon roll, and apparently, that was Kacey's type.

Kacey turned as they approached the door. "That was one of the sweetest, most thoughtful dates I've ever been on."

Justin's brow furrowed. "Then, you haven't been treated as you deserve. I'll make the next one better," he promised.

"The next one. Tomorrow?" she asked with a smile as he laughed. "I could spend every day with you." She said this timidly, afraid he'd think she was a loser for revealing how much she liked him already. Wasn't there some rule against that at the beginning of dating?

"I might need a little more time to make the next one special. But I promise that I will."

"Well," she said as she stepped closer, suddenly emboldened, and looking at his lips, which were at eye level, "I can think of a way to end this one perfectly, at least."

As they embraced and kissed, Kacey could still taste the hint of chocolates and chai tea. She could also smell his cologne or aftershave, a fresh, citrusy bergamot scent. She swore she could feel the hammering of his heart as he pressed his chest against hers. Or was that her own heart hammering between them? The scruff of an afternoon shadow on his chin deliciously chafed her skin. It was as if all her senses were firing at once, and she was overwhelmed with sensation. The kiss was passionate but brief. It left her wanting more, and that was the best kind of kiss.

Kacey smiled as they parted. "There—perfection."

Justin grinned and nodded. "Goodnight, Kacey." He strode to the elevator as Kacey went into her hotel room.

When she flipped on her light, she noticed Lin wasn't there. No kitty tail poked out from beneath the bed or the curtains on the balcony. She searched the bathroom and behind the curtains. She shrugged. Still elated from her date, she pulled the diary from her bag and sat cross-legged on the couch, cradling the book in her lap. Her normal inner calm had transformed into a raging tumult of emotions over the past few weeks, and she never felt more grounded than when the book was in her hands. It was warm to the touch, even. She pulled a pen from her bag and turned to a blank page.

Kacey's pen glided across the page easily as her feelings about Justin poured forth onto the page. Every swipe of ink smoothed the frayed edges of anxiety that had been plaguing her. She'd never felt quite like this about a man before—comfortable and safe one moment, like being wrapped in a warm blanket; giddy and exhilarated, like she was flying down a roller coaster track the next. And that kiss! She pressed her fingers to her lips and smiled.

She wrote about the loneliness and fear she'd felt before finding the book, and she wrote about the adventures she'd already embarked on so soon after her life began to change. It'd been a whirlwind, and she was surprised that it'd all happened in only a month.

Writing these things down was a balm to her soul, as though putting them there kept them safe and ensured that she wouldn't wake up from this dream that had become her life.

This book had given her everything she'd hoped for. She'd met interesting people, she'd gained a career that gave her more than enough money to live on, and she'd found Justin. She paused as she finished the last sentence and closed the diary. Was it the book's magic that'd won over Justin's heart? Would he be interested in her if she didn't have the book anymore? She was pretty certain that the other fantastic things that had happened to her were due to the book's influence. Was his heart truly in it? She bit at her lip as she tapped her pen against her leg. And did she really care?

CHAPTER 48

SIBYL, NOW

L ugh shot into the night sky like a comet, a trail of light
blazing behind him as he kept up with the cloud Sibyl had
become, and they shot through the atmosphere toward Europe.
The journey was a long one, but it would only take them a few
hours to get there at the speed at which they were able to travel.

Sibyl arrived at Avalon, the hidden island surrounded by a magical lake, moments before Lugh touched down on its misty, rocky shore. She pulled her bag from her shoulder and set it down on the rocks. She dived down into the waters, searching for that which she hadn't seen in ages. The magical waters of the lake had preserved it well, just as they had Excalibur, which was also entombed there. Even in the water's darkness, Excalibur shone. And Fragarach, with its gold and citrine accents, gave its own golden glow in the murky depths.

Sibyl released the liquid fetters that held it in the ancient silt at the bottom of the lake. She grasped its beautiful hilt, but not without reservations. To bring it above the water meant that the vision of her death could still happen, but Lugh was backing her up against a wall with his threats. She knew he'd follow through on them. Lugh was neither essentially good nor bad. He just was. He was purpose-driven, and for whatever purpose, he was determined to get Fragarach back. There was no point in fighting him on it.

Sibyl walked out of the mists and stood on the shore beside Lugh. He was looking toward Avalon, no doubt trying to get a glimpse of the fairy island. Its pull was strong. Sibyl looked down at the sword in her hand as he pulled his eyes away from the glimmering purple haze surrounding the magical island and turned his own eyes to the weapon in her hand. She'd feared it for more than a thousand years, and letting it go was no easier now than it would have been when that vision of her death was fresh in her memory.

For a moment, she considered stabbing him with it. Wouldn't that solve her dilemma? Her hand tightened around the hilt, and her heart raced. Surely, killing the transporter of the Mágos to their end would be a bad idea, though. She'd certainly bring down the ire of the Effulgent on her head. And what would Apollo think of her then?

It was an impossible decision, so when Lugh stretched out his hand for the shortsword, she gave it up.

"What was the point of tricking me out of it to begin with, Sibyl?" he asked. "You just hid it away. That was a complete waste of its power."

She shrugged. There was no way she was going to tell him she believed it'd be the death of her. "I liked it. It's a beautiful weapon."

"Crazy swamp witch," he muttered under his breath. "It's laid idle long enough. We've work to do." With no more explanation, Lugh shot into the night sky and out of sight, leaving a trail like that of a shooting star behind him.

CHAPTER 49

KACEY

K acey's alarm had gone off at 5 a.m. so that she could board the shuttle to the studio by 6 a.m., but a mass text went out at 5:30 that a meeting was being called in the conference room of the hotel at 8 a.m. instead of the planned commute to the studio. She was a bundle of nerves. Had something happened to stop production? It would be her luck that something good would get canceled before it ever began. She shook her head. No, that was her old luck, her old life. She tried to stay positive as she waited for the meeting.

To kill time, she opened the crimson diary and reread the entry she'd written the night before. She smiled as she thought about Justin again. More than anything, it made her miss him more. She flipped back through the pages just before hers, and she landed on a print with big letters that curled at the ends. She noticed that the author of this entry talked about a pageant, and she suddenly remembered the news report of the young Korean woman who'd fallen from a hotel room in Canada.

Kacey closed the book and pulled open her laptop. She searched for news articles on the accident and found that it had been ruled a suicide. Kacey scoured the internet for pictures and articles about the young beauty queen. Sena had a large media presence, and Kacey found a multitude of pictures of her online.

Sena was stunning in every picture she took. Of course, she was a beauty queen, so that was to be expected. Yet, there wasn't one unflattering picture to be found, even from press and fan pictures. It's as if she was lit from within with a dazzling quality of perfection. And she looked happy.

Kacey glanced back at the first entry with this loopy handwriting.

"I was working in my parents' shoe store when I found this book in the back room where we keep extra inventory. I'd sat down with it and opened its pages, not knowing what I'd found. Its stories were intriguing, and it filled me with a hope and a desire for more out of life that this small town and this little store could give me.

"I was already advancing in the pageant circuit, but within a month, I had a PR assistant, contracts for modeling gigs and

sponsorships, and was well on my way to the big crown. It was the dream of a lifetime for a girl like me.

"Now, the main event is this upcoming weekend, and I can't help but think that I've been a little too lucky. Why do I deserve the crown over any other woman competing this weekend? I don't believe I do. We're all beautiful, accomplished females. However, I can feel it in my bones. I'm going to win it."

The next entry was dated a few weeks later.

"I'm being watched everywhere I go. I can feel it. And yesterday, I found a weird note in the house. IN my house. Sibyl says that it's probably a cleaning person that's maybe a fan."

At the mention of Sibyl, Kacey gasped. *Her* Sibyl?

"I turned it in to the police, but since nothing in the letter explicitly states that I am in danger of harm, there wasn't much they could do. I don't think it's anyone from the cleaning service. I just don't. Ah, I wish Clay could travel with me next week to Ontario. I don't feel safe anymore. We'll have plenty of event security when we get to Toronto, but what if something happens before that?"

Toronto. This was definitely from Sena, then, because Toronto is where the newswoman had reported that she'd fallen from her hotel balcony.

"I've gotten some pretty strange comments on pictures lately, too. I wanted to pull my social media accounts down, but Sibyl says it's part of my contract. Besides, she assured me that all famous people deal with this kind of stuff when they're trending. She's worked in Hollywood, Nashville, Atlanta, London, and Hong Kong with lots of famous people, so she'd know.

"I don't feel good about this trip. The only thing that keeps me going is knowing that the money I'm making through this organization will pay for a house for us when Clay and I get married next spring."

And that was it. Nothing else was written into the diary until Kacey wrote in it last night. Her stomach churned with worry as she lay her hand on the cover of the book.

Kacey scrolled back through the images of Sena, trying to catch a glimpse of her own Sibyl. Could they be the same PR person? It wasn't exactly a common name. It all seemed a little too coincidental.

CHAPTER 50

KACEY

K acey went into the meeting room early, anxious about the change of plans. She grabbed a cup of coffee and a cranberry muffin before sitting in one of the plush chairs. She was the first one there, so she picked at the muffin and gave a few tight smiles to those who entered the room after her. An assistant came in and placed folders on the table at each chair, but she didn't know if she should open them yet. She fingered the corner of the folder and sipped her coffee, which was getting cold.

Kacey was star struck over some of the faces around her. These were people she'd only ever seen on TV or in magazines. She suddenly felt small and inconsequential among the cast. Whatever confidence boost her magical book had given her faltered with so many famous people around her. There were some big names on this project. For the umpteenth time since she'd arrived in Hollywood, she felt like she was in way over her head.

Even so, many of them smiled at her, introduced themselves, and made small talk with her. Maybe the book's charm worked on movie stars, too.

David strode in, looking harried and annoyed as he accepted a coffee from an assistant. He took a sip and set it down on the table to flip through the notes he held in his hand. He rolled up the sleeves of his dress shirt, ready to get down to business, though everyone wasn't there yet. Kacey caught him glancing at her before she looked back down into her coffee cup. Her cheeks heated. This was one of those instances where she wanted to disappear into the background, and she had to stop herself from going through with it.

Allie came in at that moment, and Kacey gave her a wave. Allie's bright smile reassured her, and Allie sat down beside her in a cloud of expensive floral perfume. Others around them were already murmuring their own predictions about what was happening with production, and Allie said, "I wonder what this is about." Kacey shrugged.

David stood at the head of the long table in the middle of the meeting room. His face looked dour, very different from his usual laid-back attitude. He hadn't shaved. Kacey noticed that the folder in front of each person had the production company's logo on it in gold foil. She traced it with her finger as she waited for the meeting to begin.

A few more people shuffled in and stood along the walls, as there were no seats left. The assistant passed folders to them as David cleared his throat.

"You've all been given the pre-production filming schedule, but we're having to adjust it." David motioned to the folders on the table. "The schedule in front of you is the final production schedule. Thankfully, our timeline hasn't changed." He didn't wait for them to open the folders and read the new schedule before he continued. "While I know that we were anticipating filming at the studio first, we've had to pivot and get everything set up earlier for our trip overseas. Due to scheduling issues with the studio, we're going to have to do our on-location scenes now and come back to film the studio set scenes afterward. We still anticipate being finished within two months."

Murmurs among the cast rose. Kacey's heart thumped as she scanned the new schedule. She'd been rehearsing her lines for the studio scenes, and she'd barely looked at the scenes to be filmed in Wales and Scotland. She'd found that the lines came easily to her, as if her memory had improved along with her looks. Kacey glanced at Allie, whose smile had become a hard line. She was difficult to read at the moment. Was she as uneasy about the switch in schedule as Kacey was, or was this normally how things were done in productions?

David held up a hand. "And honestly, this may be a blessing in disguise, as difficult as it has been over the last twenty-four hours to reschedule everything. Being on-location will get you more into your characters than a green screen would ever be able to accomplish." David gave them a reassuring smile. "This is my fifth film to direct and my third to produce. If this is the only hiccup we have with this production, we'll be doing good."

A few people laughed. Kacey could see the cast visibly relax around her.

David clapped his hands together. "So get your things packed, eat a good lunch, and be ready for departure to LAX. We'll load up here at 1 p.m. and board the charter jet promptly at 3 p.m. We're looking at a twenty-hour flight ahead of us before we reach Cardiff at 6 p.m. tomorrow night, local time."

Kacey sat there wide-eyed with her mouth still agape. She'd barely gotten comfortable with the fact that filming in the studio would start the next day, and now, they were about to fly halfway around the world.

"That's it," Allie said. "I need a drink." She grabbed Kacey's hand and pulled her to her feet. "Let's go to the bar before we pack."

"Before lunch?"

Allie gave her a stare as if such a question were absurd.

"May I join in?" asked a guy with long, dirty-blonde hair and dark blue eyes.

"The more, the merrier," Allie said as she tossed her hair over her shoulder. "This is your King Arthur, by the way. Clint DuPont," she said with a nod at the actor before exiting the conference room, "meet Kacey Wiltson, your Guinevere."

Of course, Kacey already knew who Clint DuPont was. He was a huge star. "Nice to meet you," Kacey said. She leaned in toward Allie as they walked down the hallway. "I need to call Justin."

"They've already told the writers and everyone, I'm sure. We actors are always the last to know everything," Allie said as the three of them slipped into the elevator ahead of the throng of other people coming down the hall. "He probably got a heads-up last night, which is when we should have been notified. David said they'd been working out the details for the past twenty-four hours, which means he knew about it when he took me for an early dinner last night. And that's probably why he was on the phone the entire time we were training yesterday." Allie's eyes narrowed. "I don't like not knowing what's going on."

"He probably just didn't have all the details worked out yet, and he didn't want to stress you out."

Allie frowned. "Are you his PR rep now?"

"Uh..." Kacey said. She glanced at Clint, who gave her a shrug.

Allie's face softened. "I'm sorry. I'm just in a bad mood, which isn't your doing. A martini will help." She rounded the corner and asked the bartender for three martinis before sitting down at a table. Clint went to the bar and grabbed the drinks, then went back to order himself two fingers of scotch. Allie quickly drank the first martini before Kacey could take more than two sips of hers, and then she pulled the second one in front of her. Clint settled in the seat between them and sipped his scotch slowly, and as he did, Kacey noticed him assessing her. He turned his eyes back to Allie.

"So you're going to get smashed before a whole-day flight? You're braver than I am," Clint said.

"I hate flying that long," Allie said. "I get a bit claustrophobic when flights get longer than a few hours. So yeah, I'm hoping I can sleep my way through most of the flight."

"This will be my first time in Wales and Scotland, so I'm excited about it. Not about the flight, though," Clint said.

"Me, too," Kacey said. "I'm surprised you've never been there with all the films you've done over the past few years."

"Yeah, I've just never had the opportunity. London is the closest I've been to where we're going." He sipped from his glass as his blue eyes cut from Allie back to Kacey. "So the rising starlet has never been there either?"

Kacey could feel the heat rise to her cheeks as they flushed. "Nope. In fact, I've never been outside the U.S."

"Wow, that's quite sad," he said. "What did you do before this?"

Kacey's stomach fluttered, and she wasn't sure if it was from the martini or from Clint's mocking tone of voice. "I was a librarian," she said in a quiet voice, sure he'd ridicule that, too.

"Give the woman a break. She's just starting her career. It's not her fault Charlotte got canned."

"Isn't it, though?" Clint didn't look at Kacey.

"No. That's all on David."

Charlotte Beaufort was a French model turned actress who'd scored the Guinevere part before Fiore offered it to Kacey. She only knew about it from the bit of press she'd seen around her name and speculation about Kacey's assumed relationship with the director in the weeks following their initial date. She had no idea what happened before he'd offered Kacey a contract, but Clint obviously thought that Kacey had some hand in the decision, though she hadn't sought out the role. She hadn't even known the movie was being made when she met David. People would rather believe the sordid rumors than reality, so she kept her mouth closed on the subject. She wouldn't waste her time trying to defend herself about things that people had already made up their minds about. In fact, she'd rather be in her room than down here with all the negativity floating around.

"We're better off anyway," Allie said. "I hear she's a total diva. She'd probably be running around the set, not eating, not sleeping, and bossing everyone around."

"Oh, so *you*, but in French," Clint joked.

Allie poked him with the toe of her black Louboutin ankle boot. "Don't mind him," Allie said with a pointed look at Clint. She downed the rest of the second martini and held it up to let the bartender know she wanted another one. "Clint's from Canada and thinks he's superior to us Americans because of it." She rolled her eyes playfully. Even when she made a dig at someone, Allie somehow offered it up lightly, lacing it with a layer of humor so the person wouldn't be too offended.

"We are," he said. "We are."

"See?" Allie smirked. "He's chanting it like a mantra because he's still trying to convince himself."

Clint laughed heartily. "Maybe you'll have to visit someday and see all the wonders we're hiding up there."

"All that maple syrup and ice hockey, huh?" Allie joked.

Clint leaned in toward Allie. "Let me buy you lunch. Lord knows you need something on your stomach with that much gin going down the hatch," he said as the bartender arrived with Allie's third martini.

If Kacey wasn't mistaken, it seemed like the two were flirting. She already felt like she was outside the conversation. *Fine,* she thought, *forget the loser newb.* She'd rather be in her room packing, anyway. She finished her martini and stood. "I have to get my luggage packed. And find my cat. I don't want to leave the country without him."

And what she most wanted to do was talk to Justin and make sure he'd be on their flight.

Allie's eyes were already drooping sleepily as the booze took effect, and Clint was convincing her she needed a steak. They were oblivious to her leaving. And maybe, Kacey realized, that's exactly what she wanted.

CHAPTER 51

KACEY

K acey glanced around her hotel room after closing her door. "Jare—er, Lin? You in here?" She was sweaty from the martini, and she pulled off her fitted blouse and grabbed a thin purple t-shirt with a worn rock band emblem on the front from what little of her old clothes she'd brought with her. It was old and comfy and would probably be better for traveling than her newer clothes. She walked over to the door to the balcony, wondering if Jareth had gotten out there and was stuck.

But no, she thought as she opened the door, *he'd just turn into Lin with his crazy magic hands and use his opposable thumbs to open the freaking door.* She rolled her eyes skyward as she stepped out onto the balcony. She didn't think she'd ever get accustomed to the idea of real magic in the world. It felt like a fairy tale. The sky was a moody gray, and thick clouds hung low in the sky with the threat of rain. Was it rainier than normal for May?

"Might as well get used to this," she said aloud, thinking of what everyone said about the weather in the UK. Still, the city was beautiful.

"There she is!" a shrill female voice rang out from below.

Kacey's brow furrowed, and she looked down. A crowd of about thirty or forty people gathered on the sidewalk in front of the Thompson, and as a din of voices rose, people held up their phones to take pictures and videos of her. A few camera flashes told her the paparazzi were down there, too. Her vision tilted as she looked down, and she gripped the railing.

The voices below grew even louder, almost hysterical. Kacey's stomach turned. Admiration was fine, but if the ordeal with Paul's wife had taught her anything, it was that fans could so easily take it to extremes, and the outcome of that kind of devotion was often scary for the recipient. Who below had a jealous husband or wife? Who had a gun on them this very instant? Was her fear of fans a kind of PTSD from the shooting, even though she hadn't been there?

Kacey shuddered, stepped back from the balcony, and went inside. At least in the Middle-of-Nowhere, Wales, she wouldn't have to deal with people screaming her name every day. She chewed the inside of her lip. Maybe.

After she closed the balcony door and shut out the noise from the street, she realized someone was rapping on her door. Tentatively, she looked out the peephole, expecting to see fans gathered in the hallway. Instead, it was Clint. And he looked upset.

Kacey opened the door. "Clint?" Her first thought was that something was wrong with Allie.

"Oh, good, I hoped you were here," he said as he walked past her into her room without an invitation.

Kacey closed the door and crossed her arms over her chest. "Is everything okay?"

"No," he said as he turned back to her with a scowl. He raked his hands through his blond hair. "I don't know what happened back there. One minute, I couldn't take my eyes off you, practically begging you and Allie to allow me to chase after you like a little puppy to the bar, and the next, it's like you disappeared from my mind. And then, you really were gone."

Kacey's eyes widened. "Wait, I thought you were talking about taking Allie out for lunch."

He batted the notion away with a flick of his hand in the air. "Allie will make herself sick drinking and not eating if I don't force her to get something in her before we leave. But what I really wanted was more time with you." He stepped toward her.

Kacey leaned back instinctively. Sweat beaded her upper lip as her heart raced. She couldn't get away from the crazy anywhere. "Um, I don't think—"

"You're more beautiful than pictures. When I saw you with all that glistening water all over your body yesterday morning in the pool, I knew = I had to talk to you. But you're a hard one to get alone."

Kacey's eyes widened, and she took another step back. She found it hard to swallow. Her heart hammered in her chest, and she wondered briefly if this was how Marilyn felt every time someone got too forward with her.

He raked his hands through his hair. "I haven't stopped thinking about you since." Clint backed her up against the door now, and he put a hand on either side of her head. "I came looking for you last night, but I guess you were out."

Another knock at the door pulled her attention away from Clint.

"I've got it," Clint said in a husky voice before grabbing the handle and pulling open the door. David Fiore stood there, and his face fell when he saw Clint and then Kacey peeking around him from behind. "What do you want?" Clint sounded annoyed.

An afternoon shadow of dark stubble covered his square jaw, and his pupils dilated as he said, "I came to see if Kacey needed anything before we left for the flight."

"She's got all she needs," Clint replied as he shut the door in their producer's face.

Kacey's eyes widened further. "Are you insane? That's our boss. Clint, you need to go." She opened the door, and David still stood there. "I'm sorry, David. Clint just stopped in to see how my packing was going," she lied, "but he's had too much scotch and needs a nap." She grabbed a handful of his shirt and forced him out into the hall.

Clint looked down at her hand on his shirt, and then he looked back up at her with wanton lust in his eyes, which made her drop her hand like she'd been burned. She turned her head and grimaced as if to warn him to keep his mouth shut. Just then, the elevator down the hallway opened, and Justin walked out, looking quizzically at the three of them in the hallway.

"Clint, maybe you should go take a nap while you can." *Forget I'm here,* she thought with as much concentration as she could muster under the scrutiny of David and an approaching

Justin. She gave Clint a fake smile to pacify him, and he turned and headed toward his own room.

"Uh, that was—" David shook his head.

"It's been a weird morning," Kacey said. "Do you need something?"

"If you want off this project..." David didn't finish his thought, but he looked hurt and confused.

"No. What would make you think that?" Kacey asked.

Justin had taken his time getting to them as though he wanted to see what was going on, or maybe to give them space to finish their conversation. Kacey had flashbacks of the last time Justin found David at her door, and she glanced at him nervously as he approached.

David sighed. "I wanted to make sure you're doing okay after the changes in the production schedule. You practically ran from the conference room, and well, I know that such a huge shift in plans on what was supposed to be your first day of filming and on your very first project might throw you for a loop."

"Thank you. It's nice of you to check on me, but I'm fine. I'm excited to see the UK, and I'm excited to get to work on the film." She gave him a smile, which she hoped was reassuring. Justin stopped beside them and gave David a quick nod.

"Also, the photogs and fans are growing outside. We'll be increasing security, especially at departure for the airport. I wanted to give you a little peace of mind about that. They can get out of hand sometimes, and well, it seems like they're already at that point."

Kacey frowned. "Yeah, I noticed. Thanks." When David didn't move from the spot, she said, "See you in a little while." But what she thought was, *Forget I'm here, David*, and he did. He turned and walked away from them.

She was still astounded that she had this kind of power within herself. It seemed to be getting stronger, too, or she was learning how to harness it and use it more effectively.

Kacey huffed out a sigh of relief but gave Justin a wary look. "Good morning," she said.

"Can we talk?" Justin asked in a serious tone with furrowed brows.

Kacey tried to swallow around the lump in her throat. She expected the worst from him—that he wasn't into her enough to get in the middle of some kind of drama triangle, or square, or whatever this was becoming. And would she blame him?

"Of course," she said as she opened her door wider to allow him to come in.

Justin sat down on the couch. He rubbed his palms against his jeans in a nervous gesture. "What was going on there? You looked wild and scared. Is everything okay?"

"Um, yeah," she said. Then, the tension she was holding in her body melted as she let herself fall onto the couch cushion beside him. "No. I think both of them have the wrong impression of me." How could she explain to Justin that both men had the hots for her, and she hadn't encouraged it? Not intentionally, anyway. "Plus, we've got all these schedule changes. And fans were just outside screaming for me, as if I'm some huge star. It's already been an intense day, and it isn't even lunch!"

Would he think she was being a brat about the fame and adoration? How could she explain to him about Sena and Norma Jean and what fame had done to them when he couldn't even read their words in the book? She reached into her bag at the end of the couch and fished out the diary. Her pounding heart returned to normal almost immediately as a calm swept over her. The book was like a drug. She smoothed her hand over the cover.

"Look, I know you'll think I'm crazy, but... it's this book. It's making me irresistible to people." She looked up at him, terrified she would see incredulity, or worse—pity or ridicule, on his face. Instead, she shot her a look of curiosity. "Before I found this book, I was a nobody. I was alone and living a quiet life. It has absolutely changed the trajectory of my career, my personal life, everything."

"May I?" Justin held out his hand.

Kacey sighed and gave it to him, though she felt an ache of separation from the book. He took it into his lap and opened its pages. He flipped through it quickly.

"As I said before, there's nothing on these pages. They're clean, at least to my eyes." He paused on a page. "Well, except for here, at the end." He'd come to the entry she wrote last night.

Kacey cleared her throat. "Yeah, that's where I wrote in it," she said as she took it from him quickly, embarrassed about the things she'd written about him on those pages. So he could see her writing but none from the scores of other women who'd written on its pages throughout history? So strange. Why was she able to see those earlier entries? Because the book had somehow chosen her? Why? How could she make him understand when the pages of the book were blank to his eyes but not to hers? And how could Kacey keep up the mental effort of making people forget or ignore her when more and more people joined in on noticing her every day? She feared it would become exhausting trying to find peace within the chaos of being a celebrity. "People notice me now."

As if on cue, she heard a rise in the volume of screaming fans below her window again. Maybe they had latched onto Allie or someone else from the cast, though, and had forgotten about her up here.

"It's not the book. You were hidden away. You're smart and beautiful and interesting. That's what makes you irresistible to people, Kacey." Justin gave her a little smile as he took one of her hands in his. He looked back up to her eyes, and a smile played at his lips. "That's what makes you irresistible to me. But if it is magic, I'm not complaining."

That's exactly what she'd wanted to hear. Could she dare to believe that, though? Could it just be dumb luck that she'd ended up here? She remembered how much she'd physically changed in that first week of possessing the book. No, she couldn't believe his kind words. She wanted to so badly, but she knew the real power this book gave her—*and* its consequences. Still, her hand felt so good, so right, in his, and she wanted to believe that he was sincere. Yet, she knew the magic was real, so she had to assume it had enchanted him, too.

Kacey squeezed his hand. "Thank you for not telling me I'm delusional. Even if you think so."

"Whatever you think this book is, that's not for me to deny. But what I can say is what I see, and what I see is an amazing person who's been thrust into something new and frightening. You're navigating all of this the best way you know how. Of course, you're going to have people falling at your feet. People always look for others to worship. That's why we have so many extremely wealthy athletes, singers, and actors in modern society, and it was not very different in times past. Fame is an illusion."

"'Fame is a fickle food,'" she quoted from Emily Dickinson.

"'Upon a shifting plate,'" Justin added. "That, it is."

"Impressive! I didn't know a history expert knew American poetry."

"I'm full of surprises. Speaking of plates, I haven't had breakfast, and my stomach is grumbling, so let's get you packed so we can get some real nourishment soon." Justin stood and held out his hand. "I'm thinking we need some good ol' Americanized Italian before we leave California. What do you think?"

Kacey's eyes lit up. "Or street tacos!"

"Or both!

Kacey grinned. "Now, you're talking." Kacey let Justin pull her to her feet.

CHAPTER 52

KACEY

A s the jet rose higher into gold-tinged clouds, Kacey watched her homeland fall away. The studio used a private charter company to fly them into Cardiff, so she'd selected a seat next to Justin as they boarded. She'd successfully avoided both Clint and David all afternoon. Whether it was because she'd willed them away or because they were busy with their own packing, she didn't know.

She'd left a note for Lin at the front desk in case he got back to the hotel to find them all gone. She left him a copy of the production schedule, too, which included their first stop, Llantwit Major, a town on the Bristol Channel coast. They would spend a week there before continuing on to Scotland. She knew he would find her. Lin was much more familiar with the UK than she was.

Kacey texted her friend Amy to update her on the change in filming location so that she wouldn't be worried if she didn't hear from Kacey for a bit. She didn't know what the cell service was like where they were going or how busy she'd be while there. Though she imagined she'd have some downtime, she wasn't sure. She'd also texted Sibyl again before they boarded, but she'd gotten no response before she turned off her phone.

Justin sat beside her, reading a book. She slipped on her headphones and took a nap, the big plate of chicken alfredo she'd eaten before they left L.A., leaving her full and sleepy. Her sleep was going to be screwed up for days, anyway, because of the time change, so she let sleep envelop her while she could get it.

It was the deep kind of sleep that left her groggier than when she'd closed her eyes. She moved in and out of sleep, trying to shake off the weight of it. When her eyes fluttered back open, the sky beyond the windows of the jet was dark. For all she knew, they could be in outer space. It was disconcerting, and she shifted anxiously in her seat.

"Where are we?" she asked Justin. She opened a bottle of water and took a long drink.

He laid down his book and glanced out the dark window. "Somewhere over the Atlantic," he said. "We'll arrive in

Amsterdam in a few more hours to fuel up for the second half of the trip."

"So we have lots of time to get to know each other, huh? Tell me about your family," Kacey said.

"Well, my mom died a few years ago."

"I'm sorry to hear that," she said.

"Yeah, she was such a warm, loving woman." He smiled wistfully. "My parents had me when they were older, so my dad is now almost 71. He's retired and barely making ends meet with social security, so I'm trying to send him what I can to help him out. He worked in factories for fifty-plus years, and he just doesn't have it in him anymore to work. It's too hard on him. He needs a knee replacement as it is.

"Anyway, that's why this job is so important to me. Until I can get a more solid position somewhere, this has been a blessing to me, so I can help him out. Like I said, the social security isn't cutting it, and he used his 401K to pay off the house he'd been paying on for decades. I'm the only family he has left. I don't have any siblings. Well, my mother had another son, but he died in infancy. I never met him."

Kacey pursed her lips, never knowing quite what to say about loss. "I'm an only child, too. It makes for a dull childhood, doesn't it?"

Justin held up his book. "But there was always an escape."

"Exactly. Uncountable worlds and infinite friends in the palms of our hands." She looked out the window at the vast darkness beyond the plane. "My parents weren't the loving, doting type. They were both very busy with their careers, and I took care of myself a lot. I still don't have a strong relationship with them."

Justin opened his palm for her to take, and Kacey laid her hand in his. He gave her hand a gentle squeeze. "That's too bad,"

Justin said as he pushed against her shoulder with his, "because they're missing out."

That made her smile. He always knew what to say.

Kacey was thankful for the long flight. They spent the rest of it getting to know each other's likes and dislikes and all the little things that couples find out about each other in the early days of a relationship.

They'd both grown up watching SpongeBob and vowed to watch the newest SpongeBob movie together for nostalgia's sake. While Kacey was more a horror and fantasy fan, Justin liked thrillers and historical nonfiction books, with a healthy dose of classic fantasy thrown into the mix. He'd gone to a public high school, while she'd attended an academy, but their schools had been close to each other. They'd probably gone to some of the same places to hang out and never ran into each other. They both loved strawberry ice cream, though Kacey loved to mix in pineapple. And they both wanted to get out of California eventually for something new and different, which was why they were both excited for the opportunity to travel overseas with the production company.

Their conversation was normal enough to make her almost forget her new fame. She felt like a normal woman falling for a really great guy.

When they arrived at the airport in Cardiff twenty hours after they departed from LAX, sheets of rain came down in a dark sky, and it was much cooler than it'd been in California.

Kacey pulled her jacket on as David's assistants separated them into two groups, and they boarded buses to head to Llantwit Major. Justin, the writers, and most of the production crew would be going to a caravan park on one side of the town to bunk in trailers during this leg of the production, and the cast would be going to an inn on the other side of town. As he boarded his bus, he promised to call her later. She knew that there probably weren't enough accommodations for all of them at the inn, but she couldn't help wondering if David was intentionally trying to separate her from Justin. It wouldn't surprise her.

When she sat down on the bus with her carry-on bag, she searched for Allie, who'd been scarce during the flight, but before Kacey could motion for her friend to come sit beside her, Clint sauntered down the aisle toward her, a mischievous look on his handsome face. His eyes zeroed in on her, too, though she tried to look away. She braced herself as he plopped down next to her.

"Hello, Kacey. I see you've made yourself comfy here," he said as he wiggled in his seat.

"Yes, I was hoping Allie and I could chat on the way to Llantwit."

"Ah, she's in a sullen mood from flying all day. I'll be better company."

Kacey doubted that. Allie came down the aisle then and gave Kacey a knowing smirk that said, 'It was only a matter of time before he cornered you.' Kacey gave her a 'save me before I die' face, but Allie kept walking.

"I've been patient, Kacey," Clint said quietly as the bus got going. She barely heard him over the din of others talking on the bus. "More than patient."

Kacey frowned. "About what exactly? I only met you a few days ago." She edged closer to the window, wishing she was on the bus with Justin instead.

"Oh, but I've been watching you. Quite a while, in fact. I watched you change when the book finally chose you."

Kacey's eyes snapped to his. How did Clint DuPont know about the Crimson Diary? "You were in San Diego?"

Clint gave her a wicked smile that showed how much he enjoyed surprising her with that information. "I know all about you, Kacey Wiltson. I know that none of this has been earned. It's all been handed to you."

Kacey swallowed the lump in her throat, faced with the accusation that she'd been dreading since she began this new career path—that she wasn't worthy of any of it.

"I wasn't lying when I told you that I was obsessed with you. It's not the book, though."

Kacey looked over her shoulder toward Allie, but she was looking down at her phone a few seats back. Kacey's eyes searched the bus for David. He and an assistant were deep in discussion. Her breaths came too fast, and her lips were going numb. She turned back to Clint, someone she'd seen in the movies and had respected as an actor. It was difficult to reconcile that image with the man who sat beside her now. If Clint hadn't mentioned her book, she'd think this was some kind of practical joke to initiate her into the cast.

"I made sure David gave you the part of Guinevere." When she gave him a look of disbelief, Clint said, "No, really. The book may have won him over for you, but I made sure he showed up at the library that day, and I also gave him the idea to offer you an acting contract, though your friend Sibyl did a fine job of taking that opportunity and running with it."

Kacey shook her head. She had a sick feeling in her stomach, and she wanted to be anywhere but there.

"There's not a lot more I can tell you here," he said, "but you'll want to meet with me tonight after everyone has gone in. Be outside the hotel at 9:30. Don't bring Allie or anyone else—especially that assistant of yours. Where is she anyway?"

CHAPTER 53

SIBYL, NOW

Now

S ibyl arrived at Llantwit Major before the flight from LAX could even get there with the cast and crew, and with her, she'd brought a terrible thunderstorm. Her head hurt, and she was so tired. She checked into a separate inn, where the cast hadn't booked rooms. She needed her own space to think and to plan. But first, she had to recover from the journey. Traveling that great of a distance by magic was exhausting, and giving up Fragarach had done her in emotionally. All she wanted to do was sleep and forget her worrisome future, now that her visions might come true. She had no control over it anymore.

After a cup of hot tea, Sibyl lay on her bed and dreamed of nothing but water: currents, waves, the blues, greens, and grays of it, the glimmering sunlight and cold moonlight filtering down through it, bubbles floating up, the taste of it, the cool and warm waters flowing and mixing, the weightlessness of it, the heaviness of it, the timelessness of it.

When Sibyl's eyes opened, it was nightfall. She felt somewhat rested, though groggy. The others would have arrived by now, and she knew she needed to keep herself scarce until tomorrow, which would be a reasonable time to book a flight and fly in.

In a mist, she swept out her window and into the steady drizzle of rain. The pubs here reminded her of the ones she and Kit had frequented when she'd fallen in love and married. That had been a disaster, though, so she no longer liked to spend much time in places like that.

Instead, she went to the sea. When she was far enough away from people, Sibyl materialized and walked along the street to the cliffs overlooking the Bristol Channel, with England straight ahead and the Celtic Sea beyond the channel to her right. She couldn't see them in the dark, foggy night, but they were there as they had been for as long back as she could remember. And she hadn't needed a map to find the water from the inn. It called to her as clearly as a song. And the sound calmed her.

Sibyl breathed in the heavy ocean air as she walked down a path to the bottom of the cliff, where the beach became rocky underfoot. She took her time, mesmerized by the movement of the water.

Now that she no longer had the sword as insurance, she needed to see for herself again what the waters would show her of her fate. She thought, perhaps, she wouldn't ask the sea to tell her anything this time. But she was a coward, and she relied on her visions to give her courage, or at least caution, about what was to come. She bowed on the beach and asked Poseidon, wherever he might be, to give her access to the visions she was seeking.

Sibyl braced herself for the cold water before plunging herself in. The cold took her breath. Her body adapted to the temperature much easier than a mere mortal's body could, though, and she swam out, allowing the currents to move her. She dived down deep into the black water, and the vision lit up the darkness. She saw horses and men fighting again, as before. Lightning veined the sky like phosphorescent marble as stars fell from the heavens.

Then, she was in the arms of Merlin as he professed his love for her, and that made no sense because visions never showed her the past, only the future. And this inconsistency pulled her from the vision. She kicked and pushed up and flew out of the current that had hugged her down deep into the sea. Sibyl coughed and spat out salt water. She lay on the rocks and trembled.

Where are the stars, she wondered with near hysteria as she looked up at the sky. *Have they truly fallen?*

As the sounds of the waves calmed her, she laughed at herself. Dark clouds covered the stars, and a new moon hid behind them, too.

CHAPTER 54

KACEY

K acey couldn't get off the bus and away from Clint fast
enough. Thankfully, it was a short forty-minute ride from
Cardiff to the town where they'd be filming.

While most of the production crew got settled into their
living arrangements upon arrival to Llantwit Major, Kacey and

most of the other actors and actresses barely dropped off their suitcases at the hotel before driving to a horse-riding school at Dimlands Castle, where they spent three hours being instructed on the basics of riding and becoming more comfortable with the horses.

The break in rain provided them decent weather for riding lessons, though they were all muddy and disheveled by the end of it. Kacey's horse was a gentle gray mare named Dolly, and she was a pleasure to ride. Kacey didn't have a moment's trouble riding Dolly, although thoughts of Clint distressed her.

She'd watched him on his white horse, and she could imagine him as King Arthur, his blonde hair disheveled from the wind and a thin mist that hung in the air. His muscles rippled as he maneuvered the reins.

Before going back to the hotel, they stopped in a pub, no doubt smelling like horses, to grab a drink. The floors were flagstones, and low beams of dark wood gave the bar an even darker appearance. Allie hooked her arm in Kacey's and successfully made herself a shield from both Clint and David, who sat around a table with a few other men in the cast drinking beers, but their eyes kept returning to Kacey and Allie at the bar.

"You sure have cast a spell on the leading man."

Kacey raised her eyebrows but said nothing. If only Allie knew. She sipped at the first shot of whisky, hoping it would warm her. She would have preferred sitting closer to the fire, but that would've meant also sitting closer to the men, and that wasn't the kind of flames she wanted to fan tonight.

"These men are something else," Allie said as she took a shot of whisky and ordered them two more. "I could barely keep Clint from tearing across the aisle at you two on the plane. He was nearly green with envy over Justin holding your attention the entire trip.

What did you do to our young Arthur, hmm? Cast a spell over him like the Guinevere of our story?"

"Nothing, I swear." Her thoughts flitted to the book, and she patted her bag that was slung over her shoulder. She didn't know what he had to say that he couldn't on the bus, but she was nervous as hell to meet with him tonight. What was he capable of when he had her alone? "He's not exactly like I thought he would be." She finished the first shot.

"Actors never are," Allie said dryly. "Well, if nothing else, this is going to be an interesting production."

"At least we get to room together. The Thompson was nice, but it was a bit lonely," Kacey said.

"It'll be like college." Allie grinned at her. "Not that I ever went."

The bartender, a grim-faced man of approximately fifty, with wild brown hair and a chicken pockmark right between his eyebrows, set two more shots out for them without a word. Kacey knocked back the second shot of whisky before her, the liquid burning as it went down. She wanted to drown her anxiety with booze, but she knew she needed to keep her head straight, too. That'd have to be her last drink for the night. She glanced at the clock on the wall behind the bar. Almost 9 p.m. She peeked out the window of the pub and saw that the night was foggy, with a fine mist hanging in the air as if it'd forgotten to fall. Despite the warmth of the whisky, she felt a chill, and goosebumps rose on her arms beneath her jacket.

"Let's make our way back to the hotel, huh? I'd like to get these wet, dirty clothes off and get in a warm shower. I feel like a slug," Kacey said.

Allie nodded and finished her drink. They walked back in silence through the dark, silent streets.

Kacey glanced down at her phone as they neared the inn. "You know what? I'm going to stay down here for a bit and make a few phone calls. Go on up. I'll be a few minutes."

Allie shrugged. "Okay."

Kacey dialed her own home phone number in San Diego, just to look like she was being sincere. When Allie was through the front door, Kacey hit end on the call and looked down the street. She knew Clint would be here any minute. She just hoped David wouldn't show up, too, and make a tense situation worse.

Kacey hugged her arms around herself. A dim street light lit up the sidewalk somewhat, but much of the street was still in shadow. She saw the silhouette of a man turning the corner and striding toward her. When he took a drag from his cigarette, the cherry sparked and lit up his features enough for her to recognize that it was Clint. But that didn't give her much comfort.

Clint stopped just out of the circle of light. He took another drag from a cigarette, which lit up his face a fiery red for a moment. "I don't know what you know of the Mágos," he said as he blew out smoke, "but from the look on your face, I'm guessing you've figured some of it out. I've gone by lots of names—Cacus for the longest time—but I'm loving a bit of the spotlight right now as an actor. When you've lived as long as I have, you find ways to entertain yourself."

"If I'm a Mágos, why am I living the lifespan of a human? Why have you lived such a long life?"

"Lots of human blood in your veins, I guess." He shrugged. "I don't pretend to understand everything." He took another drag of his cigarette. "Anyway, my father is Vulcan. Or you may know him by the name Hephaestus. Or maybe Lugh or Lugus?"

"I remember reading about Hephaestus in school. The legends said he was a blacksmith who married Aphrodite."

"Right. Same one. Of course, the humans who wrote them highly elaborated those stories. Mostly, they wrote what was entertaining or however they could reconcile the magic they witnessed with their small scope of human understanding. Some said he was disfigured. Not true. Some said that Aphrodite made a cuckold of him. Again, not true. Neither of them was particularly monogamous, to be honest.

"What you need to know about my father is that he creates powerful, awful weapons—ones that have killed magical monsters and that can kill the Mágos. He's also the go-between in the realms because he can harness the power of light. He helps the Mágos ascend to the High, and he also sends them to the Below, when necessary. In that respect, he is one of purpose. He has a job to do, and nothing will stop him from what he feels he needs to do."

"Okay, but what does this have to do with me?" Kacey asked.

Clint pursed his lips. "I've got word that he's coming for you."

Kacey's mouth fell open. "Me? Why me?" If he sent the Mágos to their afterlife, was that why he was coming for her? Was her life going to be cut short when she'd just begun getting the things she wanted—or the things she *thought* she'd wanted? It felt like her life had only just begun.

"I haven't ascertained why yet, but you need to be careful. I'll protect you as much as I can, but I'm afraid with his weapons, he's more powerful than I am. If he's coming for you, that means you're Mágos, so I hope you've got a handle on your own powers."

Kacey didn't know what to say. She couldn't wrap her head around the idea of the gods of myths existing in the world, much less why any of them had any business with her, or that she might have to fight one that had survived for many generations. It was useless, really. Completely ridiculous. She had absolutely no chance. And to top it off, tomorrow was the first day of filming. Now, she had to watch her back for a god who had it out for her?

Where was Lin? She needed him to show her how to use her powers. If it would even matter.

When Kacey made it back up to her room, Allie lay across her bed stroking the Maine Coon cat sprawled across the covers, his eyes closed as he enjoyed the petting. Kacey laughed with relief. "Lin," she said as the cat opened one eye to look at her.

How had he gotten here so fast? Then, she remembered the portal he'd opened in her hotel room back in California and wondered if he could use those to go wherever he wanted. She'd have to ask him about that trick later. That could be a very handy talent.

"He's got you wrapped around his finger, too, huh?" she asked Allie.

"He's so sweet! And how good of the production staff to get your kitty to the hotel while we were working," Allie said as she stood up and unwrapped the scarf from her neck. "I thought his name was Jareth, though."

Kacey said, "Yeah, Jareth Lin. I call him by either name."

Allie nodded, accepting her lie, and stepped into the bathroom.

When Kacey heard the water running, she turned to the cat and poked him in the back. "Hey, no morphing around Allie. I'd hate to have to try to explain that." The cat only yawned in return and closed its eyes again, which made her feel foolish. Kacey sighed. "Where'd you go anyway?" she wondered aloud. "Never mind. Don't answer. We'll talk later," she whispered. "I've got some new developments we need to discuss."

Kacey considered grabbing her suitcase and leaving tonight. She could go back to her old life in San Diego and forget about all this craziness. But she knew that they'd find her there. She needed to practice her powers and at least try to outsmart or out-maneuver Clint's father if she couldn't talk sense into him.

When Allie came out in a fluffy robe with her hair covered in a towel, she ushered Kacey into the steamy bathroom. "You're going to feel like a million bucks once you clean up. Don't wake me if I'm sleeping like a baby by the time you get out of there."

"Okay, 'night." Kacey closed the door and leaned against it. She did want to bathe, but the idea of creating a portal to anywhere teased at her mind more than her desire for comfort. Forget her luggage. She could just teleport right out of here.

She turned the water on, but she didn't take off her clothes. Instead, she concentrated on a place close, but familiar. She was afraid she didn't have the mental strength to open a portal to somewhere far away, but she needed to practice the skill in case she needed it eventually. She might not be able to disappear right now, but she might need to at some point.

Kacey brought her hands up and imagined the portal growing between her hands as she pictured the barn where she'd spent the evening with Dolly, the gray mare. She recalled the smells of the hay and the horses. She could almost feel the mare's soft muzzle in her palm. Her whole body vibrated slightly as if she were in a massage chair. It was such an odd sensation that she almost lost her concentration, but Kacey grabbed the barn's image again. Tremors moved in waves across her body. When she dared to peek, the portal was undulating before her, widening, and she took a step inside.

This time, the fall wasn't nearly as long as the first time she'd gone through a portal, and she didn't land as hard. She was kneeling on the road outside the barn. The gentle neigh of a horse greeted her in the darkness. Her breath puffed out in front of her, and she shivered as she realized her coat was back in her room.

Kacey hadn't landed quite where she'd meant to, but it was close enough, considering she didn't know the stables very well. So she could do this. She didn't want to stay gone long. She opened another portal and closed her eyes, hoping she'd end up back in their bathroom. It would be interesting trying to explain why she suddenly appeared in the room before Allie or in the front lobby. She sent all her concentration toward the bathroom. Once the vibration and falling sensation ceased, she was standing in front of the bathroom mirror.

"Better, this time," she congratulated herself.

Kacey was so tired. She peeled off her dirty clothes, showered, and climbed into bed ten minutes later and fell fast asleep to the sound of Allie's light snoring and the gentle purring of the kitty beside her.

CHAPTER 55

KACEY

The next morning, Allie was up before Kacey, flitting around the room with way too much energy for 5 a.m. "Oh, you're awake," Allie said, as if the 4:45 alarm and her movements around the small room weren't enough to rouse the dead.

"Kinda," Kacey said. She glanced around but didn't see the cat anywhere. *Great,* she thought. *He disappears again.* "These hours are crazy. The sun isn't even up yet." She squinted against the glare of the lamp beside Allie's bed.

"Yeah, well, you'll work dark to dark for a few months, but the money you make off a film will last a while if you're not stupid with it, so it's worth it."

Kacey sat up and checked her phone as she rubbed sleep from her eyes. Sibyl had messaged her that she'd arrived safely in Wales and would meet her on location that morning.

Allie pulled at her hand. "C'mon, we have exactly twenty minutes to get moving and grab some coffee and scones before we head to the beach."

The beach Allie referred to wasn't at all what the California-raised Kacey thought of. The beach was rocky and surrounded by grassy cliffs covered in spots of yellow flowers. They were bussed to the top of the cliff, where two trailers and two heated tents were set up. The ocean was dark and agitated behind them as the horse trailers pulled up. Kacey smiled to herself at the prospect of riding Dolly again.

The actors, Clint, along with a few other men in the cast, were ushered into hair and makeup, while the actresses were brought into a large tent where snacks and costuming were housed. A young woman with wire-framed glasses put Kacey in a dark green dress, and she gave a blue dress to Allie. Thankfully, the material was wool-lined with linen and was considerably warm against the chill of the morning. She also handed each woman a cape that matched the dresses they wore. "Be careful. These can get tricky when mounting your horse," she advised.

It didn't appear that the sun would make its appearance today. Sullen gray clouds hung low over the ocean. "Definitely not a vacation," Allie murmured.

They were soon moved to hair and makeup, which took much longer. Both women required hair extensions. Then, the hairdresser plaited Kacey's in an intricate braid down her back. The makeup artist used a heavy hand with creams, powders, and colors, explaining that it was necessary for the cameras. It all went over Kacey's head, but she nodded and let them do what they needed to do while she texted Justin. He was coming to visit at lunch to see how things were coming along. She couldn't wait to see him, and she wondered what he'd think of how they'd transformed her into Guinevere.

David had been right. With all the makeup and costuming and standing with the Bristol Channel before her, Kacey was more in tune with the character she was playing—a fierce, magic-wielding Guinevere torn between two lovers.

They'd made Allie's hair a mass of wild waves, and her makeup was dark and sultry. "Wow," Kacey said and grinned at her friend. Somehow, they'd made Allie more beautiful than ever.

Allie winked. "Let's get the fun started."

The props master, a tall man in his forties with an impressive handlebar mustache named Griffin, handed Kacey her sword. "This one is for looks. It's not the one you'll do your fight scenes with later. See how light it is?"

Kacey took it in her hand. It was considerably lighter than the sword she'd practiced with.

Griffin slid it into the scabbard at her hip. "Many films use a back scabbard, particularly for riding, but it's not historically accurate, as your friend Justin insisted, so we're keeping it at your hip. It may feel unwieldy there while on your horse, but you'll get used to it." Griffin set Allie's sword into her scabbard before they headed toward David.

Sound techs checked their mics to make sure everything was set. David was going over scene specifics for the upcoming shot to a small group gathered around him. He held a clipboard with his production notes, and he hung a pair of headphones around his neck. As Kacey and Allie joined them, he said, "The first scene you're working on is where Morgan le Fay and Guinevere meet on the cliffs to talk. We'll get some action shots of the two of you riding toward the cliff after this, but I want us to work on the confrontation scene initially because it has to be perfect. It's one of the most important scenes of the film." David pointed to his left. "Allie, you will come from that direction on your horse. Kacey, you will come from that direction. I want everyone in place to make sure this take is as safe as possible. No going near the edge, right?"

When the two women nodded, he continued. "So you'll come in and pull back as you near each other, deliver your lines, and Morgan le Fay will be the first to throw magic, which, of course, special effects will add in later. You'll fall from your horse, Kacey, onto the pad placed beneath you. Roll to your right. Your sword is in the way on your left. Remember, you have very different ideas about how magic should be used, and your animosity for each other is coming to a head as the conflict increases. We'll have dual cameras on you for this shot."

Kacey nodded as an assistant guided her toward Dolly and helped her mount the mare. Allie mounted her horse, and David put on his headphones as he positioned himself behind one camera and looked at a small screen. To dispel the jitters that had suddenly hit Kacey, she mentally ran through the tips the riding teacher had given her the evening before as the assistant guided Dolly by the reins to the mark where she'd enter the shot.

You can do this, Kacey thought. *Don't screw up your first day of filming.*

She kicked her heels in when David yelled, "Action!" Dolly bolted forward, and Kacey held on for dear life, the sea a blur to her right beyond the cliff.

"Cut!" David yelled as the women slowed in the middle of the shot. "Let's do it again."

What had gone wrong? she wondered.

David walked toward Kacey and took the reins from an assistant who'd run up to her horse. He looked up at her as he led the horse back to her spot. "You looked scared. Forget the cameras and pay no attention to the onlookers over there. You are Guinevere today. And I need a fierceness from Guinevere. Match energy. She's no secondary character in this tale, and she tries to make the right decisions, though she second-guesses herself, and her heart gets in the way sometimes."

Kacey nodded. "Okay."

"Morgan le Fay hates you. She wants you dead because you have the things she knows she'll never have, and you represent a way of life that she'll never accept."

David strode back to the screen as Kacey gripped her reins. She let a dark mood settle over her as she set her jaw. *She wants you dead,* Kacey thought as she kicked at Dolly to move on David's command. She imagined the woman riding toward her was the villain of the story. With her dark eyes and wild hair, it wasn't difficult.

As the women neared each other, the horses didn't slow as they pulled on their reins. Instead, both horses reared up, and Allie's horse bolted toward the cliff's edge. Kacey's heart dropped, seeing Allie's eyes widen and her mouth spread into an O. She must have screamed, but Kacey heard nothing but the jarring thump as Dolly came down on the ground hard and spun, dirt flying around them.

Kacey let go of the reins with one hand and stuck it out in front of her in a stop gesture. "Allie, no," she screamed as Allie's horse neared the edge.

Allie pulled at her horse's reins fruitlessly as it galloped nearer to the edge. It dug its hooves into the dirt when it realized it was near the edge of the cliff, and in slow motion, Kacey saw Allie pitch forward. Others were running toward her, but they were all too far away to help Allie.

Kacey shut her eyes. She *had* to do something. She tasted ozone, that scent that permeates the air before it rains. *Just stop*, she thought as hard as she could. The world around her went silent. When she opened her eyes, she and Dolly were the only ones moving. Everyone else was completely motionless.

In the silence, she heard someone clapping, and she looked about her wildly.

Lin strode toward her. "Bravo, my dear powerful descendent. Don't falter. Keep concentrating. What can you do to save her life?"

"I don't know. I don't know," she mumbled quickly, trying to think. Dolly let out a huff as if to say, 'C'mon, I thought you were smarter than this.' Kacey held up her hand, and with vibrations running through her body, she opened a portal like she'd done the night before. When all the motion unfroze, Allie fell into it. Kacey immediately opened a second portal that was a few feet from the edge, and Allie tumbled out of it onto solid ground. One horse's front hooves slid off the cliff, but it lay down to keep from tumbling over the side.

All around Kacey, chaos ensued. Kacey glanced back at the camera, knowing it had been filming. Clint stood beside it. He'd obviously moved it off the frame. He grinned mischievously and gave her a wink. Kacey dismounted and turned her attention back to Allie to check on her friend. The crew had gathered around her.

Sitting on the ground, Allie rubbed her ankle and shook her head. "I don't understand what happened. I was headed over the top of the cliff. I could see the rocky beach below, and then the next second, I'm thrown onto the grass."

"The horse must have turned at the last moment," someone offered.

"Are you okay?" Kacey asked.

Allie grimaced. "My ankle hurts pretty bad." Someone was already beside her with an ice pack. "I just can't get over how I'm not dead on those rocks down there." She was trembling.

"We can look at the film," someone else said.

"Nope, no use. It was pushed to the side in the scuffle. It's probably going to have nothing but a skewed shot of grass and feet," the camera-woman said.

As the crew's nurse inspected Allie's ankle and performed concussion protocols, Kacey and Lin backed away from the group. "I knew you had it in you." Lin looked at her with all the pride of a doting father.

Kacey frowned. She looked from Allie back to Lin. "You didn't do this to her to test me, did you?"

"No, of course not. I would never put her life in danger." Lin looked sincere.

"What did I miss?" At the sound of Sibyl's voice, both turned to face her. "Merlin?" Sibyl asked, her eyes as wide as saucers. "What are you doing here?"

Kacey turned to Lin. "Merlin? Like, like... *Merlin*?"

CHAPTER 56

KACEY

B efore Kacey could process this new revelation in her kinship, she heard a commotion coming from where the crew was still gathered. It looked like the nurse and an assistant were moving Allie to a tent, away from the yelling. David had his clipboard in Clint's face, which was beet red with anger. Justin had also appeared and was nearing the confrontation warily.

"Don't tell me how to do my job," David said. "And you," he said, pointing his clipboard toward Justin. "Historical accuracy only gets us so far. That scabbard is what gouged the horse and made it rear up."

"You told me to advise, and that's what I did. I didn't make the call for them to hip-carry their swords. I only said that it was more historically accurate," Justin said with measured intensity.

"I think you're making stuff up to justify your job so you can play footsie with the movie star," David said, glancing toward Kacey, who could only stand there surprised at the juvenile outburst. "And you nearly got another actress killed because of it."

"You are a distraction for her," Clint agreed.

Justin stepped closer to David. "I didn't do anything other than my job, which is advising. You or your props guy or whoever makes those decisions is responsible, if that was even the issue. Horses spook sometimes." Justin turned to Clint. "And you can mind your own business,"

"She *is* my business. She's starring in a film with me." Clint's voice was getting louder, and his face was growing redder by the second. "I want this project to succeed, not turn to shit—or worse, get canceled because someone dies."

"It wasn't my fault," Justin said, his voice matching Clint's volume.

That's all Clint seemed to need. It was as if he was waiting for a chance to rile Justin. Clint strode to him, puffed out his chest, and pushed into Justin with his pecs, who fell back only an inch or two before pushing back.

"Stop it!" Kacey yelled as she stepped forward. "This is ridiculous."

"I want you off the film," David said with vehemence to Justin. "Pack your stuff."

"What?" Kacey asked. "Be reasonable, David. Justin didn't make this accident happen."

"Fine," Justin said. He headed away from the throng of people.

Kacey followed. "Don't go. Look, let him cool off. Let me talk to him. Just give it a little time."

Justin stopped and turned to her. "He's been wanting me off this project since you showed up in L.A. I could sense it. He was looking for an excuse, and he found one." He snarled his lip in hostility as he glanced back at Clint, who'd pulled out a cigarette and watched them through the smoke he exhaled. "And Clint egged him on because-because I don't know. I don't like the way that guy looks at you."

"It's not like that," she said, but she couldn't very well tell Justin that Clint was a Mágos like her and was looking out for her. Despite what he said, Clint's attraction to her, no doubt, was a result of the book. She sighed. "Please, just give it a day. Pack if you want, but don't go yet. Okay? For me?"

Justin's shoulders slumped as he released some of the tension he'd been holding in his body. "I won't go just yet," he said.

"Good," Kacey said and gave him a peck on the cheek and squeezed his hand. "This'll blow over. Surely, this day won't get any worse. After a good day of shooting, David will be in a different frame of mind, and he'll realize that a freak accident wasn't your fault. You'll see."

Her reassurance must have worked because Justin nodded and even smiled at her before he left.

CHAPTER 57

SIBYL, NOW

"Merlin?"

Though he was much younger than the man she remembered, there was no mistaking the mischievous twinkle of those moss-green eyes. He frowned, though. In fact, he looked furious.

Sibyl took a step back. "Wh-what are you doing here?"

Merlin grabbed her by the arm and pulled her away from Kacey, who was focused on the rising voices of the crew. "Ah, you thought I was still locked away in that grotto prison of yours, did ye?" he growled. "Just wasting away down there while you lived lifetime after lifetime, free of me?"

Questions spun in Sibyl's mind. How had he gotten out? *When* had he gotten out? And how had he found her here?

Merlin set his jaw and gave her a steely gaze. "We need to talk." He walked farther down the hillside, away from the film set.

Tears welled up in Sibyl's blue eyes. She saw the anger in his demeanor and in the way his green eyes flashed as they looked back at her to make sure she was following. Suddenly, she remembered her vision at Santa Monica Pier. She'd recognized those green eyes. Her mind hadn't wanted to make the connection. Her heart hammered in her chest at the realization. If that part of the vision was here, then the rest of it was coming soon. Her breath caught, and she whimpered. The latest vision of him holding her must not have been in the past, then. It was to come.

Merlin stopped, and she caught up with him. "I didn't think I'd ever see you again." She placed her fingers against his jaw as if she thought he might not actually be standing before her. "It really is you."

"You mean, you thought I would die in the prison of your making." He looked about as angry as Sibyl could imagine he'd be. The jaw muscles under her fingers twitched and clenched. There was much more anger in Merlin's voice now that they'd moved away from everyone. It dripped with derision and hostility.

And rightfully so, she admitted to herself. It surprised her, though, because she'd never seen him like this up close and personal. Sure, she'd seen him angry in her visions, but never first-hand. He'd always been so reserved, or, at times, passionate. But the anger scared her. She'd heard of his wrath on the battlefield.

Sibyl gulped and took a step back. "I assumed you'd ascended. It's been so long."

"Nope, my curse lives on," Merlin said bitterly. "And thanks to you, years were wasted in that grotto prison."

"I knew there was a chance you'd figure a way out of it." Sibyl felt oddly proud of him for it.

"Aye." His tone was bitter. It was like a poisonous dagger to her chest.

Sibyl gave a slight shrug. "Maybe you could even say I helped you develop your powers. Because... if you got out of that, well..."

"You're incorrigible!"

Sibyl noticed the sky darkening. Though it was midday, it looked like dusk. She sighed. She wanted him to understand why she'd done it. "Your love was intoxicating, but I wasn't sure. I suspected that it was because of the reality manipulation you'd been tinkering with back then. I was afraid my feelings weren't my own."

She fingered the plait beneath her hair. She'd done her own fair share of manipulation throughout the centuries. His own love for her probably wasn't even true, just the magical persuasion she made use of always. Love was a charade. No, worse than that. Love was a synonym for misery.

"And I'd told you before, I've seen the agony that comes from us being together. I didn't want any of that to come to fruition. I just needed time to get away, clear my head, and start a new life," she said, trying to explain.

"A life without *me*, you mean," he said, the tension in his shoulders beginning to melt.

"To clear my head of what I'd given into for so long," she tried to explain. "I suppose I knew you'd get out of it eventually."

His green eyes flashed with anger. "And if I hadn't? My death would be on your head, not that you have any conscience about murder."

Sibyl narrowed her eyes. "What is that supposed to mean?"

"Just as I said," Merlin muttered.

"I don't know what you're talking about," she insisted. Of course, she knew exactly the kinds of things she'd done in her past. And the truth was, she didn't have remorse for the lives of mortals. If she'd caused *his* death, though, it would have weighed on her conscience heavily.

Merlin sighed. "What we had together was real. I didn't manipulate your feelings toward me. You really did love me, and I loved you. I would've stayed by your side until the end of time." His voice thickened with emotion, and he looked away.

It was agonizing to hear that, to witness the devotion he had for her once upon a time, and to face the truth after so long. She'd broken his heart. She'd shattered the great wizard. *See*, she thought, *love is misery, Merlin. We're all better off without it.* Sibyl didn't give her thoughts a voice, though, because Merlin was a romantic at heart. He would never understand.

Despite her fear of his wrath and the guilt over his broken heart, Sibyl moved closer to him again, wanting to smell him and feel his warm skin. She'd missed him so much. She tried to keep her voice as steady as possible, but her heart pounded so hard at the sight of the man she hadn't been able to touch for hundreds of years that she could barely think straight, let alone speak coherently. "I'm not meant to love forever. Only for a time."

With a look of dismay, Merlin said, "We all are. None of us have forever."

Flashes of her visions lit up her mind's eye—images of them destroying each other—but she pushed them away and gave him a weak smile. "Look at you, so young now!" Merlin's face was without wrinkles, and his green eyes were even brighter than they'd been almost a millennium ago. "Besides, at this rate, you'll be a kid before long, and I'll look like a pedophile."

The joke fell flat. He looked deep into her eyes as if he could read the future there. She looked away from his penetrating gaze. She was afraid he'd see how much she'd missed him, how much she still cared for him.

"I don't like what you've become, Sibyl. You're opportunistic, and bad luck follows you wherever you go. It destroys the people around you."

Sibyl wondered how many lives he'd watched her live in the years since he'd broken free. She wondered, too, how he couldn't see that she'd been the author of so much of the misery around her.

Just then, the shouting rose from the set, and they both glanced in that direction as the director yelled. She frowned. Wasn't this part of her one of her visions, too? Her head hurt to remember while being so encumbered by the stress of seeing Merlin again. She shook her head to clear her thoughts.

"The petty worries of men," Merlin said and returned his eyes to Sibyl.

Sibyl asked, "How long have you been following me?" When he didn't answer, she smirked. "I was no different back then. You just chose not to focus on my faults. That's what love does. It makes you weak. It makes you blind. I don't want to be love's fool."

"It wasn't you I came here for." Merlin's jaw clenched. "I have an ulterior motive for revealing myself to you now. I've learned that you've attached yourself to Kacey Wiltson."

Sibyl frowned. "I'm working for her, yes." How did Merlin know Kacey? This was a surprising turn of events.

"Right," he said with an edge of sarcasm. "I want you to leave her alone. If I ever meant anything to you, do me that one favor."

Sibyl leaned against the side of one of the production company vans and crossed her arms. "I'd like nothing more than to do just that, but she has something of mine—something very dear to me—and I intend to get it back."

Feigning ignorance, Merlin asked, "What could she possibly have of yours? Besides, if she does have something that belongs to you, I'm sure she'd be reasonable."

"Oh, no. No one's reasonable with the book." Sibyl gave him a thin-lipped smile.

"The book?" he asked. "What is this book to which you refer?"

Sibyl narrowed her eyes. She ignored his question because another one was gnawing at her. Why did he care about the newest Keeper? "What do you have to do with Kacey?"

"Have you never considered her last name?" He gave her a grin that seemed to challenge her intelligence, and it irked her.

"Wiltson?" Sibyl frowned, and then the memory dawned on her. "Merlin Wyllt.""Wyllt, Wyllt's son, Wiltson." He nodded.

"I'd forgotten that was the name you went by for a time." Sibyl raised an eyebrow. "I mean, I hadn't thought about you at all in a long while."

"Ouch," he said, feigning hurt.

"You know what I mean. When you have near eternity at hand, it's easy to be swept up in the moments and forget the big picture."

"She's my descendant, Sibyl. Whatever your plan is, I won't let you harm her. I know the kinds of things that befall the lives of those you attach yourself to. They suffer, and you come out stronger and happier."

Merlin spoke as if she were a parasite, and she didn't like the implication. She gave him an offended look. "Life is tragic, Merlin. I'm not culpable for the weaknesses of the women around me. We are only truly responsible for ourselves." It was only partly true, of course, but he didn't need to know that.

Merlin had stepped forward, looking out across the channel. The wind tousled their hair, and the folds of her skirt fluttered. Sibyl joined him as he looked toward the ocean and the gray, darkening clouds hanging over the waves.

Suddenly, her eyes widened. "Your descendant? That means you had a child." She felt her throat tightening with... what? Jealousy? Anger? Regret? Why did that realization bother her so much? She'd given him up and locked him away to follow her ambitions. Of course, he'd moved on after her.

"Yes, at a certain point in my life, I fell in love and even married. We had a child before Gwendolen died. Kacey is the last of my line, and I won't let you destroy her."

"The last surviving descendant of Merlin the Great," Sibyl murmured. "How about that?" The book had found a descendant of one of the few men Sibyl had ever loved. It made her wonder how sentient the thing had become. Had the book chosen Kacey as a way to somehow mock Sibyl?

Merlin eyed her suspiciously. "After all these years, I think you should be honest with me. Why do you want the book? What are *you* going to do with it?"

Sibyl clenched her fists at her side. "It's a magical book that I made long ago. It's mine, and I'm getting it back this time." Sibyl wouldn't tell him her plans for it. There's no way he'd stand for it. He never believed that any one man or woman should hold all the power.

"*You* made it?" he asked, with shock in his voice. His eyes mirrored his dismay. Then, Merlin paused, considering his next words. "What makes you think she won't give it back?" Merlin asked.

"The Crimson Diary chooses the next person who will own it," she explained.

"Why doesn't it choose you, then?"

Sibyl screwed up her pretty face with a scowl. "I don't know," she pouted. "I don't know why my book won't come back to me." She felt tears of frustration welling up in her eyes—thousands of years' worth, but she quickly blinked them away. "I suspect that the book isn't fully hers yet—not until she writes on its pages. I have to get it away from her before then, or..."

"Or what?" Sibyl turned away from him, but Merlin grabbed her arm and turned her back to him. "Sibyl?"

"The book won't release itself from her care until she's dead."

Merlin's face fell, and he released her. "I think it's already too late, then."

Sibyl couldn't hold back the tears of frustration any longer. Her vision turned red with anger as her blood rushed into her ears. She wanted to scream and rant and tear the young woman apart, but somehow, she held herself together.

Merlin eyed her with a look of sorrow. "I know all about your book. I've known for some time about it—about what it could become, but I never knew it was *yours*." Merlin shook his head, baffled at this new information.

"What do you mean?" Sibyl asked. "There's no way..."

"The book has been your obsession for millennia, Sybil. Did you really believe that I knew nothing of it? I came to be more than 3,000 years ago, which means I was born right about the time you created the book. I was born of a virgin and a demon, as a cursed creature that was old and would age backward. Orphaned and alone, I understood that I had a specific mission—one that, like my birth, was torn between good and evil. I found myself in Egypt, and my powers were already evident. I was a therianthrope, a shapeshifter. Soon, I took on the cat form and became the revered idol of Ramses II, where I grew in my powers and influence.

"The Effulgent gave me visions of a book that could bring so much darkness over the Earth that the Gloomeer would overtake mankind and create chaos across the Earth once the Crimson Queen took the throne. I have strived through time to prevent that from happening. So yes, I've known of your book. You don't know it, but it protects you, too, even as it denies you the right to hold it and use it. If it hadn't, I would have known that you were its maker."

Sibyl tried to speak, but he held up his hand and continued. "You asked me once why I was still so concerned about Arthur and distraught over his demise. He was supposed to help me save mankind. Instead, the very sword you gave him was the sword that mortally wounded him, and to this day, he wastes away in Avalon with a wound that cannot heal.

"Still, I followed after you," he continued. "None of the Keepers were worthy of the book. None of them had the fortitude to fully harness its power. You aren't entirely to blame for those women because they were never meant to handle the book's power very well. It hopped from one woman to the next when each one died." Merlin looked solemn. "Now it's in the hands of the most dangerous Keeper."

"Kacey?" she asked with incredulity. How could mousy Kacey be the most dangerous? Surely, someone like Cleopatra would have been far more dangerous with the power of the book.

"Yes, because Kacey is *my* descendant. She has *my* blood in her veins. Do you know what that could mean? What it means for a Mágos to hold the power of the book?"

"Kacey is a Mágos?" So, Kacey had inherited some of Merlin's powers. From his expression, Sibyl knew he realized he'd said too much. "What is her power?"

Before he could say any more, a bolt of lightning lit up the sky. Yet, it didn't stop. It streaked farther and farther inland.

"Oh no," Sibyl said. "That isn't lightning."

CHAPTER 58

KACEY

The set nurse iced Allie's ankle to reduce swelling, which ended up only being sprained, and she and Kacey were able to shoot some of their lines, minus the fight scenes, which David said they'd attempt the next day if Allie's ankle felt better.

Next, Kacey would shoot a few scenes with Clint and a few minor characters. She just had to remain professional, though she wanted to give Clint a piece of her mind for throwing Justin under the bus in the argument earlier. She refused to play into the drama they'd created, though. Well, mostly created by David. She had plenty to say to him later, too.

All seemed to go pretty well until lightning streaked the sky during a break in shooting. "Is it going to storm?" Allie asked as she shoved a deli sandwich into her mouth and looked out over the ocean as she chewed. The sky had darkened. Strangely, the lightning didn't stop. It glided across the sky.

Kacey frowned as she watched it, her hand reaching instinctively into the bag on her shoulder that held her book. She felt lightheaded.

"That's not weather," Clint hissed in Kacey's ear. "That's him." Clint had come up behind her, and all three of them watched the sky in fascination.

"Him who?" Allie asked around the sandwich in her mouth.

Clint said, "We need to get the people out of here, or there might be casualties." Toward others on the site, he yelled, "Thunderstorm! Load up the set!" Even as he said it, people were moving and yelling to move props and equipment into tents. When the lightning struck a point on the rocky beach below with a pop, Allie screamed, dropped her half-eaten sandwich, and ran for cover.

Stagehands and assistants came out of the woodwork like ants from an anthill. They made speedy work of grabbing lights, props, sound and camera equipment, and all the other items lying around. They dispersed in a matter of minutes, to Kacey's astonishment.

Assistants tried to move the actors into a large tent, but Clint grabbed Kacey's hand and pulled her away as the wind whipped up, sending debris through the air and stragglers into tents, trailers, and vehicles.

Clint pulled her toward the rocky passage, down the cliff to the beach below. The wind whipped at her costume. She tried to pull free from his grip, but he held her tight. "I thought you wanted to *protect* me from your father!" she yelled into the wind.

Clint looked back at her with a wild, fearful look in his blue eyes. "He won't stop until he finds you. And he's already here. There's no sense in running. You have to stand your ground, see what he wants, and try to reason with him." He grimaced. "Or fight him." He kept moving, pulling her steadily down the path. "I'll be beside you," he said over his shoulder.

Kacey gripped her bag with her other hand and looked up the path behind her, wondering where Lin, or Merlin, and Sibyl had gone. She could use his help right now. If he really was the wizard from the legends, he was much more powerful than her—and maybe even knew what to do in a situation like this.

Kacey turned her attention back to the path before her. She hoped she could trust Clint. Was she being too naïve? Was he leading her right into a trap?

CHAPTER 59

KACEY

C lint and Kacey stopped near the foot of the path. Clint pulled her forward, and as Kacey moved around him, she saw Clint's father standing on the rocky beach. Her breath caught in her throat at the sight of him. His blond hair flew in the wind like a wild halo against the gloom of the approaching evening storm, and his handsome face held an intensity that made her falter. His eyes *glimmered*. He wore a nondescript pair of pants and a shirt, but his torso was covered in shiny scale mail, which was the only thing that seemed to match the shortsword he held in his right hand.

"Word has it that you're looking for Kacey," Clint called out, not moving closer. He kept his body half-blocking her as if he expected his father to attack.

"Aye," he said with a terrible look in his eyes. "There's more to this woman than you know. It's a dreadful business..." The powerful Mágos peered over her shoulder. Kacey turned and saw Sibyl and Merlin making their way down the path. In the ripples of Sibyl's blue and green skirt, it looked as if the two of them flowed down the side of the cliff on a wave of water.

When they reached the base of the path, Sibyl and Merlin moved in front of Clint and Kacey. "Lugh," Sibyl said. "Why are you here? And what are you going to do with Fragarach?" She narrowed her eyes as she looked at the sword with suspicion and apprehension on her face.

"The Effulgent sent me. I am here to mete out justice." Lugh moved forward, and Kacey instinctively took a step back. Lugh was tall and imposing, and his eerie amber eyes were menacing.

"For what?" Sibyl asked.

"I don't like the sound of that," Clint said through gritted teeth.

Kacey didn't like the sound of it at all—and she especially didn't like the look of that blade.

Merlin held up his hand. "Hold on. Let's discuss this."

"I have a job to do, Merlin. Don't stand in my way. The Effulgent sent me. It's beyond you now."

"Now?" Kacey yelled. Was Merlin supposed to have stopped her from doing something? It seemed like everyone was skirting around a subject that she knew nothing about, and it was frustrating. "Someone explain what's going on."

Lugh turned his eyes back to Kacey. "The book. That's what this is about."

Kacey reached her hand into her bag and felt its familiar buttery smooth cover. She shook her head. "Why?"

"They say that the book is too powerful now and that the Crimson Queen will reign unencumbered on Earth if it is not destroyed immediately," Lugh said.

"To destroy the book would be to destroy her," Merlin said.

Kacey's eyes widened. This was news to her. Was she so inextricably bound to this tome?

"It's true. They are one until she dies," Sibyl added. Kacey glanced at Sibyl, who wouldn't look at her.

"And I cannot allow you to do that," Merlin said.

If Lugh was here for the book, then he was going to kill her to get it, and Clint warned her that he would follow through with whatever he was tasked to do. Even with Merlin and Clint on her side, she felt doomed. She was sure she would die on this beach in a foreign country at the hands of this lunatic Mágos.

Lugh frowned as he stepped closer. "You didn't accomplish your mission, Merlin. If you had, we all wouldn't be here right now."

What was that supposed to mean? Kacey chanced looking away from Lugh to glance at Merlin, but his face was stoic and offered no hints. What was it that Merlin was supposed to have done?

Clint had moved between the two as if to mediate. He held up his hands. "Let's not be rash. What are you talking about? What Crimson Queen?"

"The one who harnesses the power of the book and brings an end to life as humans know it on Earth," Lugh said. "The Effulgent have been watching that book—"

While Lugh's attention was on Clint, Merlin threw up his hand, sending a burst of power that knocked Lugh and Clint off their feet.

Sibyl grabbed Kacey's arm and pulled her away from them—and away from Merlin. Kacey wanted his protection. What was Sibyl doing? "Let me go," Kacey hissed. Surely, Sibyl couldn't protect her better than a powerful wizard.

"If what Merlin says is true, you need to get far away from that sword," Sibyl said, still pulling at her arm.

Kacey noticed that Sibyl's eyes were the same moody gray-blue of the dark waters in the Bristol Channel. "He'll just find me. I can't run away." She wrenched her arm from Sibyl's tight grasp.

"Don't be stupid. Of course, you can run," Sibyl hissed at her.

Kacey wanted to reason with him. Perhaps she could even talk with the Effulgent themselves and plead her case. Surely, Lugh and the Effulgent didn't believe that she would abuse the power of the book. She was playing a part in a movie and making some money with its power. It's not like she was trying to control the government or bend the will of nations to her command. Little ol' mousy *her* a threat to the world?

Kacey saw Clint scramble toward the shortsword Sibyl had called Fragarach, which had been knocked out of his father's hand in the blast. The gold on the hilt shone in the weird, hazy orange light of the stormy sky. Lugh grabbed it just as Clint reached for it.

In confusion, Kacey saw cigarette smoke coming out of Clint's mouth. *Why is he smoking,* she wondered, *when my life is in danger?* Then, she realized it wasn't cigarette smoke. With a loud, reverberating belch, fire licked out of his mouth in longer and longer flames like a flamethrower toward Lugh, as if in warning.

Merlin stood immobile, his eyes closed, and Kacey didn't know what he was doing or what his plan was. Was he concentrating, or had Lugh somehow paralyzed him? She didn't know what powers he had at his disposal, which made Lugh a dangerous adversary. Her only solace was that he didn't know what Kacey could do, either.

Sibyl raised her arms, and as if on command, the clouds above the sea moved at double speed toward the land. Lightning, real lightning this time, sliced from the dark clouds above their heads.

Lugh sneered at Clint. "Cacus, what do you think you're doing? You have no right to try to stop me!" he yelled at his son, who backed away as fire roared out of his mouth toward Lugh.

Kacey's mouth fell open. It was all too much at once. Did everyone around her possess some type of magic? Some genetic difference from the humanity that she'd considered the norm all her life? How many Mágos were there?

She couldn't wonder about it long because Lugh swiped the sword toward Clint, who backed further off. Would Lugh kill his own son to get to her? The winds rose to a roar around them, and the sea tossed and crashed into the shore. Kacey backed up as large hail pelted Lugh's head; it flew down in streams of icy white pain within an arc about eight feet wide around him. Lugh covered his head with his arm as the unrelenting hail pelted him.

"Stay out of this, Sibyl, or I'll flay your damned belly with this sword," Lugh warned.

Sibyl dropped her hands, and the hail ceased.

When Lugh moved his arm, he was wholly changed. He looked like a beautiful queen with kohl-lined eyes and sumptuous lips. She wore a royal diadem on her head and gold jewelry on her arms. Rich, dark fabrics were gathered around her slight frame. "You're nothing but a filthy murderer." The intensity of her eyes was almost palpable. If looks could kill.

The queen changed into a man in his thirties with a goatee above a flouncy collared shirt. With wild brown hair, his countenance displayed mischief and mirth. He sneered at Sibyl, who had widened her eyes in dismay and raised a hand to her lips in horror. "Fie upon thee, you lousy beast." He spat the words with such derision that she blinked and seemed to shrink with each utterance.

Then, the image became Marilyn, of all people! Kacey's own mouth fell open in surprise at the naked woman, her platinum blonde curls in disarray and mascara running down her cheeks. "What did you let them do to me?" she wailed so piteously that it would have broken the hardest heart.

Kacey glanced back at Sibyl, who sank to her knees on the rocks. "Please," Sibyl said as she raised a hand skyward, "please stop."

Marilyn morphed back into Lugh, who cackled and dropped his smile for a look of pure hatred. "You make me sick. You've used your gift of the Mágos to become more and more vile over the years. The Effulgent should have ended you long ago. Apollo himself should have come down and squashed you like a roach."

The winds had died down, and the clouds broke apart, revealing a dusky night sky just beginning to twinkle with stars. Kacey realized Sibyl must have brought on the bad weather, as it cleared now that Sibyl was incapacitated. Kacey wondered what else Sibyl was capable of as she looked down at the crying, piteous woman lying on the rocks at Lugh's feet.

"Now, to finish my duty." Lugh gripped the sword and strode toward Kacey with purpose. "The book," he said as she backed up.

Kacey reached into her bag. *I'm holding A Midsummer Night's Dream in my bag*, she thought with fervor. *I know the weight of it and the beautiful details of the cover in blues and gold.* She slowly pulled the book from her bag and smiled with relief to see that it was the copy of the play she'd bought weeks ago in San Diego. *Keep concentrating*, she told herself as she held out the book to Lugh. "Is this what you're looking for?"

"Shakespeare?" Lugh asked with incredulity. "What else is in your bag? Hand it over," he demanded. Lugh grabbed it from her and rifled through it, only to find a notepad, a phone, some gum, and a tube of her favorite lip gloss. "Where's the Crimson Diary? Where've you stashed it?"

"It isn't here. That's all that matters," she said.

Lugh thrust the shortsword toward her neck, but the blade didn't touch her. "Fragarach is also known as The Answerer, for it demands truth. Where is the Crimson Diary?"

"It is here," Kacey said, though she tried to hold it in.

"Where?" Lugh asked.

Try as she might, she couldn't keep the words from tumbling out of her mouth. "In my hand," and as she said it, the book turned crimson in her grasp.

She closed her eyes. Kacey felt sick to her stomach at the thought of Lugh destroying her book. She hugged it to her chest. It had been her friend and confidant for a few months now, but she felt like she'd owned it all her life. How could she part with it now?

Merlin still had his eyes closed as if he'd jumped out of his body and wasn't really there. She saw Clint move out of the corner of her eye, and she screamed, seeing that he was engulfed in flames.

But he wasn't thrashing about as if on fire. She realized he was running toward her and Lugh.

Kacey closed her eyes, tasted the ozone smell again, and felt tremors run through her body as she portaled from the spot on the beach to the path that led to the cliffs. She had to get out of Clint's way, and she'd have to keep her head about her until she could convince Lugh that the book was staying with her. She watched from her new vantage point as Clint crashed into his father, burning Lugh's skin and knocking Fragarach from his hand. Then, they both fell to the rocky beach.

CHAPTER 60

KACEY

M erlin suddenly gave a thunderous clap of his hands, and the stars fell from the sky, but the stars transformed, and as they morphed, the purple sky darkened by what looked like a hundred crows swarming across the sky and then descending on the beach. Kacey screamed and ran. Even Sibyl, in her despairing state, stood and ran after Kacey. Merlin and Lugh both stood still as if expecting something.

"I spent some time with the Effulgent," Merlin said to Lugh.

Kacey stopped and walked back toward Merlin. Her curiosity was stronger than her fear. "How?" she asked.

"Astral projection, my dear Kacey." He gave her a wink. To Lugh, Merlin said, "Apollo says to cease this quest you're on."

Lugh gave a bitter laugh. "Nonsense. You did no such thing. The Effulgent don't speak to anyone down here once they've Ascended."

"You said yourself that the Effulgent sent me to do a job. How do you think they told me of my duties if I could not speak to them at some point?" Merlin eyed him as an old, wise school teacher might look at a boy who wanted to argue about the weather or about the revolution of the Earth. "Don't you think I've had a way to contact them?"

"Or them you," Lugh said. "When they want you."

"No, I can go to them, as well, though I rarely do it. It tires me mentally, and they find it tiresome to be troubled with earthly matters. I haven't spoken to any of them in hundreds of years. But for my descendant, I would, and I *did*. Leave off your assignment. Your job is done for now." His voice was low and dangerous.

Lugh looked at Kacey, still holding the crimson diary in front of her like a shield. "So be it," he said as he turned from Merlin.

Kacey gripped the book tighter as Sybil approached her, a look of wonder in her eyes.

Just then, Clint yelled, "Father, stop!"

Kacey turned and looked back to Lugh as he thrust Fragarach forward. It happened so fast, she didn't have time to prepare a portal. She gripped her book and closed her eyes in anticipation of being stabbed with the blade. Then, she heard Sibyl scream, and Kacey opened her eyes. Sybil had moved to stand directly in front of Kacey, and the blade pierced Sibyl's stomach. Lugh pushed it through her with a growl of effort. Though the blade was short, it somehow went all the way through Sybil and toward the book, which Kacey was still gripping tightly. As the blade touched the book's cover, it was as if a bomb exploded. Kacey, with the book still in her hands, flew back, and everyone else, including Sibyl, was blown forward and to the sides.

Everything seemed to happen in slow motion. When Kacey fell back onto the rocks, the wind was knocked out of her, but the rocks didn't shred her skin as she expected. Or maybe they did, and she was numb from adrenaline. She could no longer hear the ocean. Had the waves themselves ceased?

She lay there, unable to move, looking up at the swarming birds in the sky, which flew down toward them. Were they there to clean the bones of the dead? Was she hallucinating? How many of them were lying dead on the beach?

Kacey lifted her head just enough to see that no one was standing. She lay her head back down and watched in a daze as the birds coalesced into the form of a towering man. He shook himself, and the black of their wings fell away. Then, a golden glow emanated from him and surrounded him, blinding her. It was a glow so pure that tears sprang to her eyes, and a warm comfort flowed through her body.

"Who are you?" she whispered.

"Apollo," he said, and his voice was like an echo or a whisper on the wind from the waters.

Sibyl was kneeling at his feet before Kacey could ask another question. As Kacey sat up, she noticed blood on the back of Sibyl's blouse, and Kacey remembered Lugh thrusting the sword through her. How was she even moving?

"Apollo! I thought I'd never see you again," Sibyl said.

The others slowly rose as Apollo looked down at Sibyl. "I thought if I gave you thousands of years of experience, maybe, just maybe, your heart would grow warm for others. Instead, you are more vile than ever, Sibyl." Though he chided her, his voice was soft and pleasant in contrast to his words, which pained Sibyl by the look on her face. "You wondered why I could never fall in love with you? *That* is the reason."

Sibyl folded her lips inward as if trying to hold back her words. "Have you ever considered that keeping your love from me caused my hard heart?"

Apollo shook his glowing golden curls. "I'm the 'god of justice,' as they say, little Sibyl. You are the very essence of *injustice*. Don't blame your flaws and your dishonor on me."

If what Merlin had told Kacey was true, Sibyl would never stop. She couldn't. It had consumed her every thought for thousands of years—except Sibyl had just stepped between her and a magical sword—one that could even kill the Mágos.

Kacey looked over at Sybil, who fell to the ground, her blouse covered in blood. Kacey knelt beside her and laid Sibyl's head in her lap.

"That's what I've been telling them. I've been sent here to bring a reckoning, and that's what I intend to do," Lugh said as he marched forward with Fragarach raised again. He looked monstrous with his glimmering eyes and burned skin.

Kacey frowned and shrank as he advanced, though she knew she could jump through a portal again if she had to. She was so very tired, though.

"Enough!" Apollo boomed. He turned his golden gaze to Lugh. "The book is protecting her now. It's grown much more powerful than we even knew. There's nothing you can do. Be gone from here. I'll take care of the rest of this. You are dismissed from your duty to destroy the book."

"But—" Lugh began.

Apollo held up his hand. "The Effulgent will deal with this situation." Apollo lowered his voice even more, but Kacey heard him say, "You have someone to assist to The High. And before you go, hand over Fragarach to Cacus."

Lugh stood still, contemplating whether he wanted to argue with Apollo. Then, he strode toward Clint and dropped the shortsword at his son's feet. "Fragarach is a bigger burden than you realize yet." He shot off into the dark night sky.

CHAPTER 61

KACEY

Apollo stepped back as Merlin ran to Sibyl and knelt by her. He took Sibyl from Kacey's lap and held her.

Sibyl looked up lovingly into Merlin's face. "Hi."

"Hello, again," Merlin said with a smile that barely covered the concern creasing his brow. "What have you done, Sibyl?"

"I always thought the Crimson Diary would be mine someday. I thought I was destined to receive it when it was ready for me," Sibyl said. "I don't think it was ever going to be mine."

Merlin smiled. "Sometimes, the things we make are never ours to keep." He looked up at Kacey before he looked back into Sibyl's eyes. "You tried to save her. Despite your desire for the book, you tried to save her life." Emotion overcame Merlin as he pressed his lips into a thin line.

"She's part of you, and I could never allow a part of you to perish. You don't know how many times I refused to search you out over the years." Sibyl grunted against pain. "Our love has been like the push and pull of tides against the shores of our beings. Do you know what the tides do? They clear out the impurities."

Merlin held his hand over her wound, but tears streamed down his cheeks. He shook his head as he lowered his hand. He wasn't able to heal the magical wound.

Kacey glanced at Sibyl. In the darkness, she saw a faint golden aura around her that Kacey couldn't seem to tear her eyes away from. It was the kind of internal light that you'd imagine an angel would possess. It pulled at Kacey and made her want the comfort of it, like looking at the warm glow of the afternoon sun through a window when it's cold.

"Sibyl, why are you glowing?" Kacey asked in a whisper.

Sibyl's breath caught as her eyes widened. She glanced down at her hands. "I am? But how..."

"Yes, it's all around you. And *through* you," Merlin whispered.

A tear rolled down Sibyl's cheek. Her eyes had never looked bluer—the color of the Ionian Sea. They were the clearest, brightest blue, like a cloudless, perfect summer day on a warm beach in Greece.

"This can't happen now. I don't deserve it." Her eyes turned to Merlin. "Apollo promised me so much more time." She had a faraway look in her eyes, as if she were concentrating on that which Kacey could not see. Sibyl whispered, "I can already hear the wails of the banshees coming. It won't be long."

"What would you do with more time?" Merlin asked.

Sibyl pursed her lips. "Love you," she whispered and closed her eyes tight against the tears, but they still escaped and ran rivers down her cheeks.

"I've always known you'd Ascend, Sibyl. I've seen you glowing like the sun. In fact, that day on the battlefield, the day that drove me mad, I couldn't tell you the rest of the prophecy. I couldn't bear to repeat the vision, even in words. It broke my heart to pieces to even witness it. Here, in this place. It was you. And Apollo." He gritted his teeth. "I was in love with you even then. I lose you over and over again, and each time, it hurts even more than the last unbearable goodbye."

Sibyl heaved an agonized cry. "It's not meant to be. You have so many lifetimes left. I have so many lifetimes vowed to me." Her breaths came ragged now. "Why can't I stay?" She made a strangled sound in her throat. "In a cottage by the sea. That's what I want with all my heart."

"And that's why you're finally worthy of Ascension. You understand the meaning of sacrificing your own desires for the happiness of others." Merlin's eyes filled with tears. "Your lifetimes were a promise. Promises can be broken. Mine is a curse, so I am bound to it." He rubbed his fingers over the little plait of hair she always wore at her throat. "Until I see you again, enjoy life in the High. I'll meet you there one day, my little seer." He kissed the tears staining her cheeks.

As the night darkened, Sibyl's glow shone brighter.

"What's happening to her?" Kacey asked.

"Bioluminescence," Merlin said.

"Like in fireflies or jellyfish?"

"Very similar. Technically speaking, when a Mágos ascends, the luciferins in their molecules react to the photoproteins being transmitted by Lugh, or Hermes, or Mercury, whatever you want to call the 'god of light,' as people have described him through the ages, and the ascending Mágos releases light energy as Lugh transfers them to the High. Sometimes, it takes a while, in the case of very powerful Mágos. Sometimes, it's quick. For Sibyl, it will be soon." He paused, his brow furrowing. "Too soon. I cannot bear to see it again. Stay with her? For me?"

Kacey nodded, though she was afraid.

Merlin touched Sibyl's hand, and she looked at him as if she'd forgotten he was still there. "Oh," she muttered. "Merlin?" There was so much questioning in that one simple word, more than she was able to express.

He grasped her hand in his.

"I've always loved you, and I will until I breathe my last," she whispered.

He kissed her parted lips for a brief moment. Then, her gaze returned to the sky above her, but fresh tears streamed down her cheeks.

CHAPTER 62

KACEY

Merlin walked off along the shore while Kacey waited with Sibyl, whose breathing became ragged and shallow. Blood gushed from her wound. "Oh, I'm so sorry, Sibyl." Kacey tucked the Crimson Diary back into her bag so that she could hold Sibyl's hand.

A blazing trail of light shot toward them with two rotating white streamers behind it. As it neared the beach, Kacey heard a shriek like that of a firework screaming through the air.

"Banshees," muttered Sibyl, almost inaudibly. Sibyl pressed something into Kacey's hand. It was a silver and onyx ring with a waterfall engraved on it.

Apollo had returned to Kacey's side. "Move away from her," he advised.

Kacey laid Sibyl's head gently on the rocks as Lugh landed on the beach, followed by two banshees, who gave off a pale blue light of their own. Their wailing never ceased but got louder and shriller as they neared until it was like the disorienting scream of a pair of kettles boiling and whistling at full blast. They looked like eyeless ghosts with gaping mouths and long, dull hair that disappeared into their gray dresses. Gray was the wrong description, though. They were devoid of color. The lack of color was startling, but their terrifying faces were worse. Kacey shut her eyes against the sight and shivered, knowing she'd have nightmares featuring the banshees for years after this.

Lugh picked up Sibyl's body, which glowed so bright now that Kacey could barely see against the glare. She shielded her eyes but tried to look past her arm, blocking the light to see what would happen. The banshees swarmed around Lugh and Sibyl until they were all one blinding light that shot up into the sky into a burst of illumination that left the sky glittering with millions of stars.

Kacey shrank under the gaze that Apollo now turned toward her.

"Now, let us discuss this book," he said. "When Sibyl created it, it was something minor. I didn't even realize it existed for a long while. Merlin knew of its existence even before I did. He was tasked with keeping an eye on it—and destroying it if need be. We underestimated it, but we now see our folly. We allowed the book to grow too powerful, and it is now in the hands of a Mágos, which is something we never anticipated. Your powers combined are too strong to be stopped. So what can be done?" Apollo shrugged.

"What are you so afraid of? It's a book." She pulled it from her bag and held it with both hands.

"You know as well as I do that it's more than just a book," Apollo said.

"But it can't do anything on its own," Kacey pointed out. "Power doesn't equate to doom."

"Doesn't it, though? We've seen that to be the case time and time again amongst humans. The one who wields its power can bring about the end of life on Earth as you know it."

"Good thing I'm not entirely human," she joked. When Apollo only stared at her, Kacey smiled. "You have nothing to fear. I don't have any aspirations to become some apocalyptic queen of the world." When Apollo gave her a look that told her he didn't believe her, she said, "No, seriously, I've spent my whole life making people forget me."

Apollo looked up at the cliffs. The production crew and actors emerged from their shelter now that the storm had ceased. Kacey saw her coworkers spying down on the rocks below them. They peered over the edge of the cliff side at the shining man on the beach, and no doubt wondered what in the world could be happening.

"And all that?" Apollo asked, nodding toward the crew.

"I don't even think the life of a starlet is for me. I was just trying it out." She smiled ruefully. Kacey snapped her fingers. "That's it. I'll make people forget. That'll prove to you that I don't want the fame. I'll make everyone here forget me, and sure, they'll see pictures of me or might remember something about me, but their memories will be foggy, at best. Surely, that will give the Effulgent some solace, right?"

"Perhaps," Apollo conceded, though he didn't seem entirely confident in her plan.

Merlin had turned back around, walking toward them along the water's edge.

When Merlin neared them, Kacey said, "This is what I propose. I'll make people forget me, live out my life in my own quiet way, and keep the book safe. I don't know what will happen to it when I'm gone, but for now, the world will be shielded from this Crimson Queen person. Merlin, wouldn't that work?" She turned to look for him, but he had a portal already open. He suddenly looked younger to her, almost boyish.

"What it is, is a fine plan," Merlin said. "Of course, it'll mean that your new beau will forget you, too. Are you willing to give up love for the good of others? Are you willing to lose him?"

"Justin?" In the chaos of the evening, she'd momentarily forgotten about him. He was probably packed and getting a ride to Cardiff at this very moment. She wanted to say no. She wanted to run to Justin and never look back. But she knew she couldn't. "What choice do I have?"

The loss was already weighing her down, crushing her heart, but she had to be brave and selfless like Sibyl had been. Kacey thought of the regret she'd just witnessed between Merlin and Sibyl. Her relationship with Justin had only just begun, though. Kacey thought of the power of attraction the book had given her, and she decided that she probably never truly had him to begin with.

Kacey shrugged. "It's for the best."

"Then you'll have to use all that is within you to cast that level of influence over all those here."

Kacey knew what she'd do. She would stop time, as she had on top of the cliff earlier, and with everyone immobilized and susceptible to her influence, she'd make them forget her. It was a solid plan, and she was certain it would work.

Merlin leaned in and gave her a hug. "I've no doubt you'll do just fine, *dwt*." Though he smiled, Merlin looked sad. Sibyl's ascension had affected him so much more than Kacey even realized. "*Hwyl fawr*."

She'd heard the bartender bid them farewell the night before with that phrase, but even without knowing exactly what it meant, Kacey felt the sense of it, the finality.

"Goodbye," Kacey said as Merlin stepped through, and the portal closed after him.

Kacey sighed, She was drowning from the goodbyes tonight, and the biggest one that was yet to come. Apollo stood still and allowed her to grieve for a moment. Time was running out, though, because some of the production crew were making their way down the side of the cliff toward them.

Kacey turned to Apollo. "Maybe... maybe the book chose me for a reason. If the book itself isn't evil, then who it chooses is pretty important. I'm different from any other Keeper, right? I have Merlin's blood in my veins. Maybe that's why it chose me. I'm not ruled by the whims of earthly fame and fortune. I have something greater in my very essence than the worldly gifts that it bestows." She looked down at the book in her hand. "Being a Mágos gives me an advantage over the other Keepers. Just maybe the book came to me for its own respite from the troubles of this world. To be protected."

"It could have gone much differently if it'd ever gotten into Sibyl's hands," Apollo said. "With its power, I don't think she would ever have become as selfless as she was this night."

"I think you might be right. Merlin certainly believed she would become the villain, even as he loved her. It must have been very difficult for him to love her— or to try to *not* love her."

Apollo looked toward the heavens as though he heard a sound that she could not hear. "I have your word?"

"You do. Clint is here with Fragarach if I go back on my decision. But I won't."

"Goodbye, Kacey Wiltson, the Crimson Keeper. I wish you well." With that, Apollo morphed into a giant golden wolf that ran so fast across the beach that he became a shimmery blur before leaping into the sky and disappearing from sight.

"Thank you for standing by me tonight, Clint," Kacey said. "Will you be affected by what I'm about to do?"

"Nah, I could never forget you, Kacey. Not if I had a million years," he said with a wistful smile.

"Then, you'll have to keep my secret," Kacey said.

He nodded and headed toward David and the others coming toward them across the beach.

Kacey closed her eyes and tasted ozone. A tear escaped as even the sea behind her stilled and went silent.

EPILOGUE

Kacey left her apartment just after sunrise. When she'd moved to Wales, she'd planned on finding a little country cottage outside of town, but she'd been so busy building up her new business that she hadn't put in the legwork yet. It was nice being only a short walking distance from her shop, though. A fine mist hung in the air, and clouds covered the sun. She pulled the cardigan closer against the chill of the late April morning air. She was finally getting accustomed to the cooler climate, but she still dressed like a tourist. People who passed her on the street were wearing t-shirts and spring dresses.

At first, she'd found it weird walking down the street without people stopping her or taking pictures, but she didn't mind it. She liked the anonymity. Fame never made her happy as she thought it would. It'd somehow made her feel lonelier because all the people that surrounded her weren't there for her, but for her celebrity status and the attraction they felt because of the book's influence. None of them had known her, only an image they saw. It was as false as the impression of a footprint in the sand, only a hint of what made it. None of the stardom was really her. It all had felt inauthentic.

The village of Hay-on-Wye, famous for second-hand bookshops and the Hay Festival, the area's best literary festival each May, was her home now. It was a booklover's dream town with its small-town coziness, the idyllic grassy hills and pastures surrounding it, the beautiful Hay Castle, with its tumbling, ancient walls overlooking the village, and a bookstore on every other corner. It was hard to believe that only a year ago, she was walking the sunny streets of San Diego.

Kacey used the money she'd made from what David Fiore had paid her, plus what she'd made from selling her place in California, to relocate and buy the shop. But in truth, it wasn't the beauty of the land or the books that had brought her back to Wales. Though she'd been a Cali girl her whole life, she'd never felt like one. And now that she knew her ancestors had lived on this soil, she was at home here, too. She belonged here, if ever she belonged anywhere. She felt that in her bones when she smelled the fresh air and peered across the rolling green hills. She felt it in the singsong voices of the local people. She even felt it in the calm that came over her when hearing the twittering of birds and the rustle of leaves in the wind.

Despite finding what felt to her like the perfect place to live, she still felt wistful sometimes. After all, sometimes sadness lingered even after making the right decision.

It was early to open the bookshop, but Kacey wanted to get a jumpstart on shelving a new shipment of books that'd come in yesterday, and she needed to figure out how she was going to rework some displays to showcase the indie books she'd also ordered.

The store she'd purchased had been an antique store previously, and the large front picture windows were her favorite part of the store. The building had lots of character. The front counter was made from wood that was once the bar inside a pub, and the woodgrain was beautiful after she'd sanded it, stained it, and sealed it. Now, it shone like glass. The wall behind the front counter was still an original stone wall, though much of the rest of the store had been sheetrocked over. She suspected more of this beautiful stone wall was behind it, though, and maybe someday, she would find out. The store was complete with a small room on the second floor, not big enough for an apartment, but she'd converted it into a cozy office space for herself. Sometimes, when Freya, a young single mother she'd recently hired to help out at Wiltson Book Shop, tended the store for her, Kacey would go up there to write.

Not in her Crimson Diary anymore.

Words themselves were a special kind of magic, though, and she liked to see them transform on the page. Maybe she'd publish her own novel one day.

The book had been like an old friend. Just the thought of its worn pages and buttery soft cover made her ache for it. She knew that if it was always present, she'd *have* to write in it. And to write in it was to give it power. That was something she'd promised Apollo she wouldn't do. So, she put it away in an effort to keep the temptation away from her. It was locked away in a place only she and Merlin could reach. Witheryn was the safest place she could think of to stow it where she couldn't easily get to it in a weak moment. It took enough mental effort to get there that if she *did* try, she'd talk herself out of it before getting there and opening it.

Kacey often wondered why the Crimson Diary was destined to be the downfall of mankind. Had the way it had been forged created in it some kind of darkness? Kacey had so many questions, but Apollo wouldn't answer them that night on the beach, and she had no way to ask any of the Effulgent. They hadn't contacted her since that night. And Sibyl had died before she had a chance to even know what kinds of questions she needed to ask. And Merlin, well, he was gone, too.

Just as she missed her book, she missed the life she lived for a little while—and the relationships she forged. It was a special kind of hell to choose to be forgotten by everyone important to you.

Kacey turned a corner and saw the outline of a Maine Coon cat. She stopped. At least, that's what it appeared to be in the early dawn light. It disappeared and reappeared in the moving mist swirling in the sunlight. Her heart skipped a beat as she thought of Merlin. She hurried toward it as it slipped into an alleyway. When she stopped at the entrance to the alley, she spied no felines.

"Jareth? Lin?" She shook her head. "That's silly, Kacey." She made her way to her shop, unlocked the door, and went inside.

Kacey got busy pulling open boxes, moving books off the old display, and creating piles for the new display. She stood back and admired her handiwork. The books were beautiful, and she smiled at her work.

After Freya arrived, Kacey wandered to the back to unpack the rest of the shipment. It took her almost an hour to shelve the titles. She swiped at a strand of hair that had fallen over her face, tucked it behind her ear, and straightened her cardigan as she wandered back to the front of the bookshop.

"Has it been a good morning?" she asked Freya.

Freya nodded. "We've had a few customers, and I had an order phoned in from Mrs. Clarke. She's absolutely out of reading material, she says, and must have something new soon." Freya smiled.

Mrs. Clarke was nearing ninety and was still a voracious reader. She read a book a day and was probably their best customer. She loved true crime and steamy romances.

"I have a new fantasy romance series that just came in. I'll call her about it later if she's too antsy to wait for her order to come in," Kacey said. "If you're ready for a break, I'll man the register for a bit."

"Great, I do need to make a phone call." Freya rounded the counter and exited the front door.

Kacey straightened a display of bookmarks. Then, she pulled out a feather duster from beneath the counter and dusted the display of mugs and tins of tea to the left of the counter. One thing about an old building was that everything was forever getting dusty. She didn't know where all the dust came from. She heard someone enter but only gave a glance at the figure as he walked by. "Good morning. Let me know if you need help."

Kacey sat down on the stool at the counter, put the feather duster away, and pulled out a notepad to create a to-do list for herself. It helped her focus her day. As she wrote, she felt before she saw that someone had appeared at the counter. A thriller book was placed on the counter near her notepad, its striking image beneath the bold title font familiar to her.

"Oh, this is a good one." Kacey looked up as she reached for the book, and she peered into familiar eyes. A smile spread across Justin's face as recognition hit her like a tidal wave. As she blinked, her mouth fell open, and she made an unintelligible sound of surprise.

"Good morning," he said.

What was he doing in Hay? Or in Wales in general? And in her bookstore, of all places! Her heart pounded so fiercely, she thought it might jump out of her chest. Did he remember her? How could he? No one else did. She swallowed hard as her heart sank. He wouldn't remember her.

"Um, good morning. Did you find everything okay?" Kacey picked up the book with trembling hands. She felt tears coming, and she blinked them away, willing them to disappear.

Justin's eyes didn't move from her face. "Yes."

Kacey rang up his book and put it into a bag. She couldn't force herself to look at him, so she was glad to have her trembling hands busy doing something. He didn't move to pull out his wallet.

"That'll be £9.49." Finally, she glanced up at him.

Justin blinked. He acted as though he suddenly needed to reach for his money, and he scrambled to get a note from his wallet. He looked back up at her before he placed it on the counter beside the bag.

Kacey faltered. If she gave him his change, he would turn and walk away from her again, possibly forever. She wanted this moment to last longer. "Staying in Wales? Or just on vacation?" As she handed him the coins, their fingers touched.

"Would you like to go get a chai tea latte?" Justin asked abruptly. He raked his hand through his hair. "I mean, we have things to discuss. For starters, where the hell have you been?"

"What?" Kacey's heart skipped a beat. Her mouth hung open, but she didn't think she was breathing.

Justin frowned. "I mean, here, I guess." He made a gesture with his hand. "Kacey, you disappeared. Like no one would even speak to me about you. It was like you dropped off the face of the Earth. Like you never existed. But there were still photos of us, like the one in front of the Hollywood si—"

"You remember me?" she interrupted.

"Of course, I remember you. I could never forget you. Not since the first moment I laid eyes on you in that library in San Diego. I followed you halfway across the—"

Kacey rounded the counter, grabbed his shirt, pulled him to her, and smashed the rest of his words with her lips. That's all she'd wanted and needed to hear. He wrapped his arms around her as if hanging on for dear life.

"So you still think I'm interesting?" she asked when she pulled herself away from his lips.

"And beautiful and smart—Oh!" he said as she wrapped him in a tight embrace. He gave a laugh and hugged her back as she clung to him.

"I can't believe you're here. Why are you in Wales?"

"I got on with an archaeological dig near here. Well, it's in England, some kilometers west of here, but I'd heard of this town, with its fame for books, and had the day off, so I thought I'd drive over and walk around a bit. The strangest thing was, I thought I saw your Maine Coon cat."

Kacey's eyes widened. "But I lost him."

Justin shook his head. "I know. What was the probability of it being Jareth? Anyway, I followed him down the street, and he was sitting right outside this door. When I looked up and saw the name of the shop, I knew it couldn't be a coincidence that I was standing in front of Wiltson Book Shop. Then, I saw you in the window. Your beautiful face. It was like someone threw cold water on me and woke me up. After wondering about you for so long, I couldn't even bring myself to speak to you. Not unlike when I first saw you in the library. It took me weeks to get up the nerve to ask you out for coffee back then."

Kacey smiled. "I'd thought you'd only been interested in me that first time we actually talked."

"No, I'd grown fond of you well before that," Justin said.

Had the book really not affected him? And how had he not forgotten her like the rest? Was it all because of his feelings for her, a true, deep affection for her not affected by the book's persuasion? Or was there something more magical at play here? Could it have been because he was long gone from Llantwit Major before she made everyone there forget? Or was he perhaps unknowingly a Mágos, too? Kacey's mind spun in so many different directions.

"Anyway, what happened with the movie? You disappeared, and the production carried on like it was no big deal. David fired me after the horse thing, so I left, but when I tried to get in touch with you, no one could tell me anything. They found some Scottish actress to play Guinevere, I heard."

Kacey shrugged. She didn't think she'd ever be able to tell him the whole truth. "Fame is a fickle food," she quoted.

A smile spread across Justin's handsome face. "Upon a shifting plate."

He remembered. Kacey grinned and recited the rest: "'Whose table once a guest but not the second time is set. Whose crumbs the crows inspect and with ironic caw flap past it to the farmer's corn— Men eat of it and die.'"

"Aptly said," Justin said with a grin.

"Yep. It's like cake. It looks, smells, and tastes good for a bit, but ultimately, it isn't good for you." Kacey gave a little shrug. "You could say I had my fill of celebrity. The cake didn't nourish me. And celebrities are easily forgotten. Sometimes, the forgetting is better. I came here to live a different kind of life, one that isn't fulfilled by what others think of me. I'm enough just as I am."

Justin nodded he understood as he looked down at her lovingly. Kacey missed the warmth that filled her with that kind of look from him.

Just then, Freya came back into the bookshop, and she stopped when she saw Kacey and Justin in half-embrace and half-serious discussion. "Um, morning," she said as she took her place behind the register and put her phone away, a smile teasing her lips.

"Freya, I'm going out. I'll check back in later." Kacey grabbed her purse and exited the shop, holding Justin's hand.

She'd gotten another chance without the book's influence, and there was no way she was letting him go this time.

ABOUT THE AUTHOR

C S C Shows is a Mississippi author who writes poetry, thrillers, horror, urban fantasy, short stories, children's books, and more.

Find the Spotify playlist for *The Crimson Diary* here: https://open.spotify.com/playlist/1rWH9DIAlJ8Kq6hMrIXx2 cor scan this QR code to go straight to the playlist.

Want more from C S C Shows? Check out her website at http://www.CSCShows.com or find her on social media. Don't forget to leave a rating or review! Thanks for reading.

Acknowledgements

Thank you to:

My husband, who was so supportive and helpful when bouncing ideas around about magic, characterization, and motivations. I enjoyed our discussions about the plot more than you know.

My editor Kimberly Coghlan, who is a rockstar at making my manuscripts as solid and mistake-free as possible. You give me the confidence to put my book out in the world knowing that we did our best to make it professional and enjoyable for readers.

My ARC team, who cheered me on as I finished this manuscript and was as excited about the story as I was.